DON'T
YOU
DARE

ALSO AVAILABLE BY JESSICA HAMILTON

What You Never Knew

DON'T YOU DARE

A Thriller

JESSICA HAMILTON

CROOKED
LANE

NEW YORK

Copyright © 2023 by Jessica Hamilton

Published in the United States by Crooked Lane Books, an imprint of The Quick Brown Fox & Company LLC.

Crooked Lane Books and its logo are trademarks of The Quick Brown Fox & Company LLC.

Library of Congress Catalog-in-Publication data available upon request.

ISBN (hardcover): 978-1-63910-305-8
ISBN (ebook): 978-1-63910-309-6

Cover design by Nicole Lecht

Printed in the United States.

www.crookedlanebooks.com

Crooked Lane Books
34 West 27th St., 10th Floor
New York, NY 10001

First Edition: May 2023

10 9 8 7 6 5 4 3 2 1

To Josh—for all the times you've dared me to live bigger
and the adventures that always follow.

SEPTEMBER 27, 2018

I wake with a start, my dream having kicked me from sleep. The girls were standing in the middle of a field at a park when the ground started to slowly sink at the edges. I started running toward them, knowing the whole time I'd never make it before they were swallowed into the earth. I woke just as they began to disappear from sight.

I lie there waiting for the terror of the dream to subside, working hard to push away the fatalistic sense of warning that dreams about my children always produce. There's an unusual stillness to the house, the kind that's more of a presence than an absence. I don't know if it's the dream lingering or true emptiness.

My head throbs with a dull pain behind my eyes, and as I roll over, a wave of nausea moves through me. I reach for the glass of water on my bedside table to relieve the itch of dryness in my throat and the sickly-sweet taste in my mouth that only wine before bed can create. The easy pull of the covers alerts me to the emptiness of the bed. Looking over my shoulder, I see that Evan isn't there and the clock on his side of the bed reads 9:30 AM.

It's Thursday. I should have been up two hours ago to get the girls to school. Throwing back the covers, I swing my legs out of bed and reach for my phone, which isn't there, but a note from Evan is. *Hannah, your alarm didn't go off. Got the girls to school. We need to talk.* Why wouldn't Evan just wake me up? Irritation with him is only a brief respite from irritation with myself.

1

Sitting on the edge of the bed, staring down at my pale feet, stark against the burgundies and blues of the Persian carpet, I wait for the self-loathing to pass. I want to flop back into bed but am afraid I won't get back up again and my whole family will return to find me exactly where they left me.

Looking for something to tether me to the day, I wander into Rose's room. Evidence of her morning litters the floor—discarded pajamas, three different attempts at the perfect outfit. At fourteen she oscillates between a needy, emotional mess and a remote island unto herself. I don't deal with either very well.

I pull the covers up on her unmade bed but can't face bending down to pick the clothes up off the floor. She can do it when she gets home. I convince myself it's the lesson, not the hangover, and then shut the door on the mess.

Peeking into Gracie's room, I'm not surprised to see the bed made, no clothes on the floor, papers stacked neatly on her desk. The sight settles me; at least something is going right in the world. At eleven, Gracie is more organized than her mother and older sister combined.

Children are mirrors, showing us bits and pieces of ourselves refracted, splintered, mixed in with their own bits and pieces like a Picasso masterpiece. Rose is a dreamer, moody, drifts from one thing to the next, would rather be reading than in the real world—just like me. She can be socially awkward, often says the wrong thing at the wrong time—just like me.

Gracie, on the other hand, is sociable, driven, meticulous, just like her dad. She's judgmental and intolerant, just like her dad. I worry about Rose. About the bits that are mine. And I worry about Gracie, the bits that are his. Mostly I just worry.

Starting the day without my girls makes everything feel out of whack. I usually stand at the front window, still in my pajamas, waving good-bye as they get on the school bus, feeling an awkward combination of relief and emptiness as their bus pulls away. Our routines are the yardstick that measures my day, its productiveness, its purpose. Sleeping in means I've already failed.

I leave Gracie's room and go downstairs to the kitchen. Toast crumbs litter the counter; cereal boxes sit out beside bowls of warm milk with flaky bits floating in them. A cutting board shows evidence of the cheese-and-tomato sandwiches Evan made for the girls' lunches—sandwiches that will go uneaten. Doesn't he know that tomato makes the bread soggy by lunchtime?

An empty wine bottle sits out on the counter, Evan's silent reminder of how much I had to drink last night. I chuck it in the recycling bin, wipe the crumbs from the counter, put away the cereal boxes, and cram the breakfast dishes into a too-full dishwasher.

Did I really drink the entire bottle? I opened it with dinner; Evan said he didn't want any. I had two glasses while we ate, then a long, drawn-out glass while helping the kids with homework and getting them to bed. Then I poured one last glass to sip while reading. Did I pour another after that?

I turn to see a half-full bottle of red wine tucked over in the corner with the cookbooks. A bottle and a half. That's a lot on a weeknight, even for me.

Dark rings color the bottom of the coffeepot. Evan could have at least left me a cup. It's all my tenuous stomach feels up for. I rinse the pot and start a new one, then stand against the counter, listening to the machine gurgle and spurt. The sound and smell make the day start to feel just a little bit more normal.

Taking my coffee mug into the living room, I turn the radio on to NPR, my direct link to the outside world, and sit down on the couch, pulling a blanket from the back to wrap around me. The picture window across from me displays a gray sky, the dependable kind; no way any blue is going to penetrate its steadfastness. Rain is supposed to fall from it later, which will chill the air as we move deeper into fall, warning us of what's coming. Leaves are just starting to turn color, the kind upstate New York is known for. Soon they'll drift casually down from the mature, thick-trunked trees that watch over the backyard—another warning.

I put my mug on the coffee table, grab the book I was reading last night, and slide down on the couch. I tell myself I'll read just a few pages, until my coffee is done.

* * *

3

It's the ding of my phone that pulls me back into the real world. I glance up from my book and realize I've been reading for almost two hours. I'm shocked, but shouldn't be. It's becoming my habit, losing large chunks of time to books, addicted to the escape. I search for my phone. Try to recall the last place I used it. Finally find it between the couch cushions. The ding was a text from Evan. *If you're awake, please check the mail. I'm expecting mortgage renewal information. If it's there, get the bank what they need for it.* I resist the urge to send an aggressive response to the dig about being awake and send a thumbs-up emoji instead.

I take a quick peek to make sure no one is around to see me still in my pajamas before stepping out on the front porch for the mail. I'm almost safely back inside when I hear two sets of footsteps pounding the pavement and the singsong voice of my neighbor Libby calling out, "Good morning, Hannah."

I glance over my shoulder to see her and her husband, Rob, jogging past the house, both in top-of-the-line running gear, both looking ready for a photo shoot in *Runner's World*. I give a limp wave in return and scurry through the front door. Libby is the neighborhood busybody and self-proclaimed social convener. Her short black bob is never out of place, her makeup is always present and perfect, and her ass is as tight as her personality.

I don't know her husband very well; he's aloof and only seems to talk to people with networking potential. He's at every neighborhood event, looking bored and vacant behind the eyes. I think of him as Libby's trophy husband—tall, dark, good-looking, makes lots of money, doesn't say much. Together they're the neighborhood power couple and the last two people I would have wanted to see me in my pajamas after eleven o'clock on a Thursday.

In the pile of mail is the letter from the bank that Evan was referring to, some bills, a flyer for a sports store, and a plain white envelope, no address, my name handwritten on it: *Hannah Warren*. Someone must have dropped it off personally, and whoever did used my maiden name.

Dropping the other mail on the hall table, I rip open the white envelope. Inside is a piece of white paper folded once. Opening it, I find a simple message: *Daring Tree tomorrow at 12pm—if you dare.* Signed *Thomas.*

The name snatches my breath away. Straightening my pajama top, then pulling my greasy hair out of its elastic, I give it a fluff as though he might suddenly appear. Thomas. My Thomas? He was here, at my door, and I had no idea. A wave of butterflies sweeps through my sensitive stomach.

I picture him, still young like the last time I saw him roughly sixteen years ago, in 2002. Wearing worn ripped jeans and a black T-shirt with some band name on it—*Pearl Jam*, *Misfits*, or maybe *The Ramones*. His thick brown hair sticking up in every direction from the constant tug-of-war he had with it, the storm that was always brewing in his dark eyes, his black Converse shoe tapping a quiet morse code on the speckled linoleum floor of the classroom. Nostalgia tugs at the loose flesh of my heart and then blossoms into an uncomfortable longing for my youth—for Thomas. The two are synonymous.

His message has shifted me into a no-man's-land between the past and present. I wander aimlessly around the house for a bit and find myself back upstairs in my bedroom. I stand staring out the window at the street below. The possibility that Thomas is in the city makes it look and feel different—brighter, more alive.

I used to stand at the very same spot when I was going to college, watching for him. When it was still my father's house, my father's room. Standing here now, I could be nineteen again, if not for the image reflected back to me in the windowpane. I'm thirty-six. My blond hair comes from a bottle, accented with dark roots and stray grays. My eyes are feathered with wrinkles and moated with dark circles of fatigue, the blue dulled by time. My body is different—boobs bigger, stomach softer and etched with stretch marks, thighs rounder.

I'm a mother; my body tells that story. What would Thomas think of that? The last time I saw him, I was twenty, untouched by two pregnancies and sixteen years. I wonder what time has done to him. He isn't on any social media, so I really have no idea what he's been up to or how he might have changed.

I signed up to Facebook a few years back, mostly to look for him, but I also appreciate the voyeuristic element of it, peering into other people's lives. I've never even added a profile photo, preferring the featureless blue silhouette, and I've never posted anything. Mostly out of embarrassment—I live in the same house I grew up in, we never take vacations to idyllic locales with white sand beaches, and my meals are anything but picture worthy. It's just another place for me to fall short.

The clock on the wall reads 11:50. Since I left my job at the library over a year ago, the days have slipped through my fingers like chalky sand in a playground sandbox. No matter what I do or don't do, it always ends up feeling like I've done nothing.

A shower seems like a good idea. I smell sour from last night's wine finding its way out through my pores and ripe from sweating in flannel pajamas too long into the day.

* * *

My reflection is there to greet me in the bathroom mirror when I step out of the shower. For the first time in a long time, I stop and look. I don't like what I see, but I don't not like it either. If I arch my back slightly, my boobs still look pretty good—round and full, my nipples pink and hard. If I put my hands at my hips and spread my fingers across the fleshy bit of my belly, it doesn't look as loose and most of the stretch marks are covered up. Turning slightly, I see small pockets of bumpy, soft skin, cellulite, resting uninvited on the back of my thighs. I turn so they aren't visible anymore. If I can't see them, they're not there.

Crossing my arms over my boobs and lifting them higher to create cleavage, twisting slightly to elongate my waist, letting my hair fall forward—for a split second I stop feeling like me. Then the self-consciousness returns. Grabbing a towel, I cover myself.

Back in my room, the unmade bed calls to me and I flop into it—naked, relishing the feel of the soft sheets on my skin. It rarely happens these days; Evan and I stay mostly clothed around each other. Restless, agitated, with a charge running through me that needs somewhere to go, I slide a hand between my legs and close my eyes. The cool air of the room on my bare nipples and the well-rehearsed movement of my fingers make me come quickly. It's Thomas's face I see.

Warmth hums across my skin and the agitation is gone, as though a pressure valve has been released, but then the shame quickly finds its way in, leaking through the edges of my pleasure to eclipse it. I think about the parent council moms, the dance moms, the park moms. I can't imagine them naked, hungover on a Thursday, masturbating in bed to thoughts of college obsessions.

Forcing myself out of bed, I throw some clothes on, determined to milk some productivity out of the day. Downstairs I get out some crackers and hummus to eat while I unload the dishwasher. Then I make myself fold the clothes in the dryer, put them away, and start a new load. I roam from the kitchen to the dining room to the living room to the front hall, looking for something to tidy, but somehow, today, things are more or less in their right spot.

Lots of times Evan walks through the front door and frowns disapprovingly at the pile of coats and shoes and backpacks waiting to be put away. A frown that says, *What the hell does she do all day?* I always give him some lame excuse about appointments, having a headache, whatever I can think of in the moment, and he pretends he isn't judging me. It's one of our many tiresome domestic dances.

In the kitchen I check my phone and find an email from a former work friend, Lucy, asking if I want to go for coffee to catch up. When I first left my job at the library, I stayed in touch with people, going for drinks, dropping by to say hi, thinking I'd be back one day and should keep up the connections. The longer I've been away, though, the more out of the loop I've gotten and the harder it is to pretend I can just jump back into my old life as though nothing's happened. Without even meaning to, I seem to be slowly shedding an old skin, and work life is a part of it. Lucy is the only one still trying to stay connected, which is sweet, but the truth is, her attempts just remind me of why I left work in the first place and my mind never likes going there.

Out of boredom, I pull the fridge open. It has plenty of food, but I don't have the appetite for a single thing in it. I slide a piece of salami out of a deli bag and eat it whole, followed by a few grapes. There's a half-finished bottle of white wine in the door of the fridge. I glance behind me at the clock on the wall—two PM. A respectable time to enjoy a glass of wine, and it might help with the hangover. I'll just put lots of ice in with it.

Carrying the wine back into the living room, I once again settle myself on the couch. Outside, the gray of the sky has deepened and the wind has picked up, sending leaves rolling along the ground and freeing them from their branches in the trees. As I stare, trancelike, out the window, I try to imagine what it would be like to see Thomas after all these years.

I'm lifetimes away from the girl he saw last. Time is no longer laid out in front of me like a feast. I'm on the other side of endless possibilities and firmly rooted in the life I've created. It's sad and comforting and I can't tell which is worse. What will he think of this new version of me? What will this new version of me think of him?

I take a sip of my wine, swirl the ice cubes around in the glass, and then take another, enjoying how it spreads through my body, loosening my muscles, making everything less sharp.

Reaching for my phone, I tap on the Facebook app and scroll through until I find her, which I inevitably do; she posts almost every day and has good reason to. This time she's posing with a plate of pasta and jumbo shrimp in a modern restaurant setting, the blue of the ocean visible through the large windows behind her. As she holds up a glass of wine, her white teeth gleam against the deep tan of her skin, her short, stylish, white-blond hair looking casually tousled, as though she's just come in from a walk on the beach. *Fresh seafood at my local joint* is the caption, followed by a million hashtags about being grateful and the Australian flag emoji that accompanies every single post.

After staring at the photo for way too long, jealously soaking in every detail, I open my messages to her and type—*You'll never guess who's back in town . . . Thomas!!! And he's called me to the Daring Tree. Do I go???* I add a mix of laughing and scared-looking emojis. Trying to keep it light, not let her know how much emotion is under the surface of that message.

I stare at her photo even longer, let myself daydream that it's me in her place, tanned and windblown, sitting in a posh restaurant in Australia with a plate of fresh seafood instead of on the couch in my childhood home, skin already losing its summer color, gray chilly weather outside, bored out of my mind.

Even after all these years, it's strange to be so far away from her. Scarlett and I spent so many years living like conjoined twins, doing everything together, that it still seems unfathomable that we ever found a way to live separate lives.

THEN

Scarlett and I became friends in grade five when her family moved into the neighborhood. My mother had died earlier that year and I was the lonely, sad one in the back of the class. Despite this, she picked me.

It was only in my twenties that I realized why—my pliability. Scarlett was a force, and she needed friends who would bend in her wind, not snap. She saw that in me even back then. Both of us were also only children, and that simple lack of a sibling made us fit together better and, for some reason neither of us could fully understand, never quite fit with the rest of the kids.

We were opposites in almost every way, especially once the teen years hit. She was tall, thin, flat chested, and athletic, with a square jawline and broad shoulders, white-blond hair that fell in a sheet down her back. I was on the shorter side with boobs that looked good even in bulky sweaters, full lips and hips, long eyelashes and dark-blond hair that rolled in messy waves over my shoulders. She was bossy, outgoing, manipulative, and hilarious. I was a follower, a blender, easily manipulated.

We were inseparable all through public school, picking up some other friends along the way, but they lasted only as long as houseflies and it always ended up just the two of us again. Even through high school, we only dated boys who were friends so we could double-date. Scarlett came up with the idea; she was also the one to determine when we were ready to move on to the next set of boyfriends, which always seemed to happen just when I was starting to get attached.

When it came time to go to college, we were determined to go together. My father was a philosophy professor at the local college, so it was expected that I would go there; it was all we could afford. Scarlett could have gone anywhere—she had the marks, and her parents had the money—but she insisted on going to college with me.

The first year, we both lived at home and were disappointed when college didn't feel much different than high school. We were still under our parents' roofs, making very few new friends and only going to the odd party, but not old enough to drink. So the second year Scarlett convinced her parents to pay for her to live on campus. She said it wasn't hard to do; her stepfather had started looking at her in a strange way whenever he'd had too many Scotches, so her mother was happy to get her out of the house.

We had big plans for our second year. I hung around Scarlett's room for entire weekends at a time, pretending I could afford to be her roommate. Even surrounded by dozens of other girls on the floor, we spent most of our time snuggled up together alone, watching horror movies. Making friends just seemed out of our reach, as though nobody was brave enough to step into the circle of closeness that Scarlett and I had created over the years.

Boys, on the other hand, were a bit easier to pull into our orbit. We managed to go on the odd double date, some nights ending in a dorm room with Scarlett and her guy in the top bunk, me and my guy in the one below, the creaking, sighs, and grunts combining as though it were only one couple in the room. The whole thing feeling slightly incestuous.

I didn't know any other way of being. Scarlett and I had clung to each other from such a young age that we'd forgotten how to live lives that weren't entwined.

By the end of October, our second year of college was already seeming more boring than the first, and we had no idea how to change that. And then we met Thomas.

SEPTEMBER 27, 2018

The girls are doing their homework at the kitchen table, taking turns regaling me with every single second of their school day, while I cook dinner. My attention swims back and forth between their stories and my own private thoughts about the mail I received earlier today. Already I've been accused twice of not listening, but I manage a clever recovery and no feelings are hurt.

When Evan gets home, he comes over and kisses me on the cheek. He does it every day. No matter what state we're in. As predictable as the cotton button-downs he wears each day with his durable khaki pants and his soft, dark blond hair that falls in the very same place no matter how you cut or comb it.

He eyes my wineglass. "Starting early, are we?"

I point at the pot in front of me. "I needed some for the sauce."

"Will we get drunk if we eat it?" Gracie asks. I shake my head and laugh.

Evan gives me a tight, forced smile before walking away. The kind of smile that has the opposite effect of an actual smile.

At dinner I wait for Evan to finish telling us about his day at work—the secretary that kept mucking things up, the shifting of people in HR, some stupid joke a colleague told him—before telling him about Thomas.

"I got an interesting letter this morning," I say when there's finally a lull in the conversation.

"I saw the mortgage papers from the bank on the hall table. Unopened. I'm assuming you didn't get in touch with them?" Evan's

12

words roll right over my news. I'd completely forgotten about the mail from the bank.

"Um . . ." I pretend that the day was so busy I need a second to recall. "No. Sorry. I didn't quite get around to it."

"Hannah, we really need to get going on that if we want to—"

Gracie suddenly knocks her glass over, turning the bowl of peas into milky green soup. I swear under my breath but am relieved she's interrupted Evan's lecture. He jumps up for some paper towels.

I give her a smile and pat her hand. "It's fine, Gracie."

Evan returns to mop up the milk. "No problem, sweetie. I hate peas anyway. I'll get you some more milk." He takes the bowl away, and Gracie visibly relaxes. I'm torn between annoyance at him for criticizing dinner and gratitude for how patient he always is with the girls.

"Are we out of milk, Hannah?" He calls from the kitchen.

"If you don't see any, then yes." I don't know why he insists on asking me when he's the one with his head in the fridge. I don't hide milk in secret places around the house.

He returns and sits back down at the table with a dramatic sigh. "Sorry, Gracie. No more milk."

"I'll get some tomorrow," I say to no one in particular.

"Did you go out at all today?" Evan tries to make the question sound simply inquisitive, but disapproval is laced all through it.

"No." I reach for the bottle of wine and top up my glass—an instinctive action in moments like these.

"It's Thursday, Hannah."

I lift my glass to him. "Cheers to that, Evan."

He sighs yet again and gets up with his plate. Grabbing at the wet paper towels, he scrunches them into a ball and walks away from the table.

I sit back and sip my wine slowly, waiting for it to numb my insides against his disapproval. We've been in this place for a while now, him acting like a boss who isn't happy with his employee's work performance but is too nice to fire them and instead tries to shame them into improving.

* * *

13

I've only just gotten into bed and opened my book when Evan comes into the room. We avoided each other through the evening, him watching TV while I cleaned up the kitchen after dinner and then fought with the girls to hand over their devices for bed. He's carrying a full glass of water with him, which he places, with extra care, on my bedside table.

"Thank you?" I say, even though I'm suspicious of the gesture. I've come to realize that every time Evan does something kind or thoughtful, it has some underlying meaning to it. Just like letting me sleep in this morning meant *You were too hungover to disturb*, this glass of water says, *You should drink it instead of the wine.*

Evan sits down on the end of the bed and lays a hand on my ankle. It feels heavy, as though it's trapping me there.

"I'm worried about your drinking." He comes right out with it this time.

"Don't be." I hold up my book. "I'm not drinking now. Just trying to read."

"I'm worried about that too. I feel like you spend more time reading than engaging with the world."

I shift my leg out from under his hold. "That's a grave exaggeration."

"Hannah, I know you're still grieving, and I understand that, but drinking and hiding behind books is not the way to cope."

"Are you going to have me committed again?" The barb is out before I even give it a thought.

"Do I need to?"

I point to the pile of books on my bedside table. "If reading is a sign of insanity, then yes, you might."

He gives his head a shake. "Jesus Christ, Hannah, why do you make it so hard to talk to you? I'm not being an alarmist here. Your mother suffered from depression and drank herself to death by the time you were ten. Does that not worry you?"

"My mother kept a bottle of vodka under the bed, Evan, and started drinking the moment she woke up, rarely getting out of bed to do so. I have a few glasses of wine now and again, so no, I don't see the need to worry."

He holds up both hands as though he's going to surrender, but I know better than that. "I understand there are differences between you and your mother, Hannah—I mean obviously. It's just . . ." He pauses, searching for the right words. "It's a slippery slope, you know, and you're still fragile, which is understandable, which is also why I think you should consider going to see someone again?"

The word *fragile* makes me want to scream in his face. I take a deep breath instead and clutch my book so tightly that the corner of it digs into my palm. "It was eighteen months ago, Evan, and I did see some-body for the entire year afterward. Remember, you made sure of that."

"And how long are you going to resent me for it? I was grieving too, remember? And trying to make sure the girls were taken care of. And worried about you. I only had so many options."

My chest constricts as he heads into history that I do not want to explore with him. "Fine, I'll watch the drinking." I slide down under the covers and turn my back to him.

"Thank you." There's a hint of smugness in his voice for the win.

"Leave me alone about the reading," I quickly add, once I feel the weight of him lift off the bed. He doesn't say anything before leaving the room.

* * *

I met Evan in college. Nothing about him was my type, which is why I chose him. I was in recovery mode from Thomas, who had been exactly my type, but who had also caused my world to implode. Evan was a fixer, still is, and I believed that fixing was what I needed. Before I could realize how ridiculous and dangerous that mind-set was, my dad started dying and my entire life was put on hold, including ending things with Evan. Then I got pregnant and the idea of another soul dying in my vicinity was too much to bear, so I kept it, and I kept Evan, and Rose was born. A few years later we had Gracie, and we were a family—whether he and I liked it or not.

Time gives marriages a beating. Just over two years ago my mar-riage was feeling the wounds. Evan and I were good at going through the motions, but distance was growing between us as a couple. He seemed to be getting more and more conservative, suddenly caring so much about what the neighbors thought, strategizing for promotion at work, becoming more and more consumed by money and material things. He kept pushing me to do more with the house, get outside and garden, be more driven in my own career.

He wanted us to fit in with the other young families who'd infiltrated the neighborhood. They drove nice cars, used block parties as an opportunity to parade their children around like human trophies, talked way too much about the best grass seed and watering times, and didn't read books that were too dark, because *there's already enough darkness in the world.*

All of a sudden, he didn't like that I used a messy bun to hide the fact that I hadn't washed my hair in days, that I spent more time reading in the hammock than weeding the flower beds, that my sweaters had tea stains down the front and reading glasses were my only accessory. Things that at one time were endearing quirks had grown into thorns in the side of his affection for me.

I did my best to compromise—washed my hair more often, planted some more flowers hoping they would outnumber the weeds, spent more time on stain removal. It didn't seem to make a difference.

Then I got pregnant. It was a surprise, but a welcome one, and it seemed to turn things around for us. Evan was excited at the idea of a new baby, hoping it might be a boy this time around. The girls were ecstatic about it, and I was too, happy that the baby years weren't over just yet.

At sixteen weeks I had a miscarriage. It was my faulty uterus. I had to have an emergency hysterectomy because of bleeding that couldn't be stopped. I lost a baby and the chance to ever have one again in one swift, devastating motion.

It was a boy. The boy that was never meant to be, but I just couldn't quite accept that fact. I wasn't able to shake the feeling that someone had made a terrible mistake. That if I could just surface from the fog of grief for half an hour, I'd be able to correct it, be able to go and get him back from wherever he'd mistakenly ended up. My brain stayed snagged on that possibility for months.

The only thing that helped were the painkillers that had been prescribed for my hysterectomy. In that quiet, peaceful, drugged place, I no longer had the sense I'd lost something that desperately needed to be found. My brain emptied, my body slept, and I escaped it all. I had to go to multiple doctors for prescription refills with claims of continued pain. I wasn't lying, though—everything in me hurt.

One day, I forgot I'd already taken a pill and took two more. When the girls got home from school, they couldn't wake me up and Rose called Evan, who called an ambulance.

No matter what I said, nobody would believe I hadn't tried to kill myself. I was too tired to fight it, so I agreed to a one-month stay at a psychiatric facility. It was nice enough, kind of like a bare-bones hotel but with lots of locking doors. During one of my counseling sessions, it came out that Evan had told the doctors at the hospital I'd talked of killing myself before the day I took too many pills. He said he believed I was suicidal with grief over the miscarriage and should not be sent home, for my own safety.

Evan lied. It was for his safety, not mine.

I could understand his motivation. He wanted me out of the house. He wanted someone else to deal with me and my grief. He wanted the mess of me cleaned up, but not by him.

Understanding all of this didn't make it feel like any less of a betrayal.

I came home free of painkillers. The hold of my grief loosened enough to let me breathe again and stop looking for that lost thing, but with a new mistrust of my husband that hadn't been there before.

He had his own mistrust of me. He was sure I was going to break again at any moment, look for escape in drugs or drinking. After becoming more clearheaded, I also noticed a new resentment in him. It was my fault that I had lost his boy—my defective uterus. He thought he hid it well, but it was there in his eyes every time I fell short on something. I could almost hear him tack it on: *and your body killed my boy.*

We both knew we were existing on separate islands populated by bad feelings, mistrust, resentment, and regrets. Just trying to keep it together for the kids and because, truth be told, we didn't know what else to do with ourselves.

* * *

I lie there after Evan leaves the room, attempting to deep-breathe my way through the bad feeling like I was taught in therapy, at the same time pushing thoughts of my depressed, alcoholic mother from my mind and trying to keep the sorrow of a lost baby and a crumbling marriage away from my heart. I'm thinking it all might bury me alive when a ding from my phone interrupts the noise in my brain—as they're trained so well to do.

I scramble for it, grateful for a means of escape. It's a Facebook message from Scarlett. *What the hell is Thomas doing back in town? To be honest, I don't know if you should go. After all you've been through, Thomas seems like the last thing you need in your life. I just worry about you. xoxo*

Coming on the heels of Evan's lecture, Scarlett's message is like gas on a low flame. Another person treating me like I could break at any moment, like I need to be contained and controlled. Rebellious anger burns in the pit of my stomach, and the only thing that calms it is the thought of meeting Thomas at the Daring Tree. The decision has been made. I close Scarlett's message without replying and toss my phone onto the bedside table.

THEN

It was Halloween night 2001. Scarlett and I were sitting on the curb outside a convenience store, plotting a way to get some booze for a party that was already under way a few blocks down the road in what was known as the student slum. I was dressed as a devil, Scarlett as an angel. Ironic, really, considering that any sin I'd ever committed was Scarlett's idea.

I was adjusting Scarlett's halo, which kept slipping, and she was working hard to convince me to show the store clerk my boobs in exchange for letting us buy a six-pack of beer.

"A devil and an angel. How original." The words stopped us short.

I let go of the halo, and it slipped back to one side. Scarlett stopped talking. It was a boy I recognized from my art history class. His name was Thomas Sutton. I'd memorized it from roll call. He gave off that cool alternative vibe that made me imagine him having an older fine-arts girlfriend who worked in a coffee house to save money for the trip to Europe they were planning to take as soon as they were done with school. I'd admired him from afar, never thinking there would ever be reason for him to talk to me.

That night he wore faded black jeans, a Sex Pistols T-shirt, and black Converse. I sat on the curb looking up at him speechless, wondering where his fine-arts girlfriend was.

"And you're dressed up as what?" Scarlett said, disdain dripping from her tongue. "A lame Gen Xer who thinks liking punk still makes him cool?" I elbowed her softly in the side, hating her rudeness while at the same time admiring her confidence.

He frowned, his eyes darkening, his full pink lips scrunching in such a way I could clearly imagine how they'd feel against mine. I thought for sure he was going to call Scarlett a bitch and walk past us into the convenience store, ending the interaction. Instead, he ran a hand through his thick, messy, dark-brown hair and laughed. I thought it might be the most wonderful sound I'd ever heard.

"I'm actually not in costume," he said, still smiling. "And for the record, liking punk rock IS still cool. Don't think it ever won't be. You girls need someone to buy you some booze?"

"We do," Scarlett was quick to say. "But not if you're going to make us blow you behind the dumpster for it."

He laughed again and shook his head, then looked directly at me. "It's Hannah, right?" he asked, and my stomach plummeted. "We're in art history together?"

All I could do was nod.

He thumbed in Scarlett's direction. "Is this girl really your friend? I took you for the nice type."

"Don't let her fool you," Scarlett was quick to chime in. "She's literally the devil. We're not in costume either."

Thomas laughed again. "I didn't know that angels went around accusing people of wanting blow jobs in return for some beer."

"She's a fallen angel, actually." I forced myself in on the joke, afraid that if it went too far with only Scarlett, she would end up behind the dumpster with him. "She goes around looking for opportunities to give blow jobs. That's why I'm here, to save her. And yes, it's Hannah. Good to meet you."

I could feel Scarlett give me a sideways glance, surprised at my boldness. I didn't usually warm up to people so quickly. But he wasn't just anyone and I knew that even then, right up to the sparkly red horns on my head.

"And this is Scarlett," I added. "My best friend."

"I think I'll just call you Scary, if that's okay," he said with a smirk.

"As in the spice girl?" she asked.

"No, as in you're kind of scary, and it includes the first four letters of your name, so it seems fitting." He had no idea how accurate the nickname would come to be.

"And my name, in case you're interested . . ." Then he looked right at me. "Or in case you never noticed, is Thomas."

I nodded slowly, as though the fact were only just dawning on me, as though I hadn't memorized his name on day one. "That's right." I snapped my fingers. "Thomas." He reached down to shake my hand, and I used it to pull myself up. "Good to officially meet you, Thomas. Now how about that booze?"

"I like a girl with goals," he said, a mischievous smile spreading across his face, causing me to fall fast in love.

Thomas had fake ID, and he bought a case of beer. He didn't want a blow job behind the dumpster, just someone to drink it with. To my great surprise, there was no older girlfriend; he didn't even have that many friends yet. He rented a basement apartment in the student slum and detested the idea of fraternities, playing sports, or living in a dorm that came with a litany of rules, so his friend-making options were limited. He also had that only-kid, tragic-childhood thing going on. Both of his parents had been killed in a car accident when he was eight, leaving him to be raised by his standoffish, career-driven, bachelor uncle.

That Halloween night, Scarlett and I didn't even make it to the party. We went back to Thomas's damp, musty-smelling basement apartment and listened to records, drank beer, and tossed around stories and jokes like we'd been friends for years. There was a special kind of chemistry between us, not just me and Thomas or Scarlett and Thomas, but all three of us. I'd wanted him to myself, but it all happened too quickly for that.

It felt as though the three of us had found each other for a reason. We had matching wounds from family dysfunction, tragedy, and being lonely only children. That meant Thomas was able to accomplish something nobody else had before, sliding between me and Scarlett without disrupting the fold, and we let him, naïve to the dangers of a boy nestling in between two girls.

SEPTEMBER 28, 2018

The cobblestone square is busy with people cutting across it on their way downtown or sitting on benches having their morning coffee. A child is chasing pigeons, forcing them into the air for short flights only to have them land back down again looking for food, bringing flurried chaos into the space.

I study the small crowd of people, thinking Thomas might be one of them, looking for the young version before realizing he could have changed so much, become almost unrecognizable, as some people do with age.

I pull my black cardigan around me tighter. There's a bite to the air that I didn't prepare for. It took me an hour and a half just to put together an ensemble of jeans, cardigan, and a gray wool scarf. It wasn't easy finding that delicate balance of looking good but not like you'd tried too hard.

Our meeting spot, The Daring Tree, sits in the back corner of the cemetery, which borders the square. I take one last look around for Thomas and then head into the landscape of tombstones.

Nothing about the tree stands out from the any of the other ancient trees in there with their branches spreading up and out, reaching high into the sky, their roots growing down and deep into the occupied earth. It's what took place at our tree that makes it different. Secret meetings where we exchanged dares like black-market items, always trying to one-up one another, to push the boundaries.

Thomas isn't there yet, so I walk around the entire circumference of the tree, taking in its familiarity, its steadfastness. I haven't been back since our last dare. Stepping up onto the tree roots, I reach into a hollowed-out part of the tree. The hiding spot where we kept the notebook of dares. I come up empty-handed, wondering what happened to the last record of our game.

Trying not to stare at the horizon in anticipation of him, I pick at the rough bark and force myself to be patient. Part of me wants to flee before he even gets here. Part of me feels like I can't stand one more second of waiting for him. Even after sixteen years of absence, Thomas acts like a bright sun in my life—the warmth and splendor drawing me to him, the heat and intensity warning me away.

I look down at my watch. He's five minutes late. I'll give him five more minutes, I decide, foolishly believing I can make myself just walk away when the time's up.

I study the gravestones around the tree, finding one tombstone that's for both a husband and wife. It reads, *Husband and Wife for sixty-five years / Beloved and dear in life / In death they are not divided.* Instead of making me feel sentimental for my own husband, the idea of being buried next to Evan after sixty-five years of marriage makes me feel suffocated, like I'd want to claw my way through the dirt to escape. Feeling guilty for it, I look away, and there he is, zigzagging through the tombstones toward me.

Why had I thought I might not recognize him? It's Thomas, my Thomas, his energy reaching me before he does. His approach hollows out my chest cavity so that my heart thumps around in clumsy, heavy beats. My feet stay firmly planted to the ground, but my emotions swarm me like hysterical swallows.

"I knew you couldn't resist a dare," he says as soon as he reaches me. I laugh, not at the humor, but out of sheer delight in seeing him again.

It's Thomas, but different. Still slim, but he's filled out. His shoulders are broader, his arms thicker. His round, boyish face has become squarer, chiseled; his hair is still thick and unruly, but there's a hint of gray at the temples.

He leans down for a hug, and I reach up to wrap my arms around him. The wool of his blue pea coat scratches against my cheek and smells strongly of cologne. It's sweet and musky, but I can still smell his original scent just below it.

"It's so good to see you," he says into my ear, holding me tightly.

"It's good to see you too, Thomas." I take a step out of the embrace and look at him up close. He has some wrinkles around his eyes. His skin's slightly weathered, and there's a reserve in his expression that only comes from years of living. He's dressed stylishly, with clothes that fit well and were obviously expensive. No more music T-shirts, ripped jeans, or black Converse.

"My god, you're an adult," I say without thinking.

"Actually, we both are."

I put a hand to my face, as though I can hide that truth. "No, I know. I just meant . . . I just haven't seen you for so long. And god, I mean, look how much I've aged." I'm already flustered and hate myself for it.

"You've barely changed," he says. "You look just like you did the last time I saw you."

I think of the dark circles under my eyes and the crow's-feet and every other bit of aging that's eaten away at my body and can't help but scoff.

Thomas shakes his head. "Seriously, Hannah, you look great. I'm not just saying that."

I glance away, uncomfortable under his scrutinizing gaze. "Well, thanks. You do too, Thomas. Really." Crossing my arms and taking a deep breath to center myself, I turn back to him. "So. How've you been? Are you married? Kids?" I ask with forced enthusiasm.

The shake of his head floods me with relief. "No, I haven't been down that road yet. I traveled for a long time, moving from place to place, which made it hard to have any kind of long-term relationship. Then I got caught up in my career. I work in commercial real estate, so it's pretty all-consuming, not the best for starting a family or . . ." He trails off, and I can't tell if I hear regret in his voice or not. "How about you? Did you end up marrying that guy Ethan?"

"Evan," I correct him. He gives a sideways nod of his head, as though the information is incidental. "We have two girls, Rose, who's fourteen, and Gracie, who's eleven."

"That's wonderful." He smiles wide, but it feels forced. "So, it all did end up happening for you, then?"

I nod but don't say anything. We're both working to avoid the uncomfortable topic of our last phone call. When Thomas found out that my father had passed away, he called me at home. I hadn't heard from him in over two years, so he got nothing but coldness from me. I told him about Evan, that we were engaged, that I was pregnant. There was so much I wanted him to say in that phone call that he didn't, so much that I needed to hear that was left unsaid. He just wished me luck, hung up, and I didn't hear from him again, until yesterday when he called me here to the Daring Tree.

"So, what brings you back?" I ask, hoping to steer things away from those painful waters.

He shoves his hands in his pockets and perches on the top of a tombstone. "My company had an opening here, and I thought it might be nice to live somewhere familiar. See if I might like to stay."

"You mean settle down somewhere? That's very mainstream of you." I play at mocking, but the thought of Thomas being back for good makes the future suddenly seem brighter.

He chuckles, the sound of it low and rumbling—an octave that makes my insides twitch. "Your midthirties will do that to you, I guess. And I'm pretty late to that party anyway, so I thought I should at least give it a try."

There's something different about him. He's settled into himself, tamed the raw energy, making it controlled, sexy, magnetic. And my blood is suddenly thick with metal shavings standing on end, pulling to get close to that magnetic force. Clamping my hands behind my back, I lean against the tree to trap them there.

He leaves the perch of the tombstone and moves closer. "I think I've been looking for something for years to make me settle down, make me want to stay in one place, but I just haven't found it yet."

I move over to the tombstone where he's just been, trading positions because being too close feels dangerous. "Then you have me, who's literally never left her own backyard."

"Are you glad, though, that you ended up staying?"

"I have mixed feelings around it, to be honest. It wasn't really what I'd planned to do, but I made a family and a life here, and I'm grateful for that."

He moves right up to the tree and puts his hand on it, spreading his fingers wide across the bumpy bark as though searching for a heartbeat.

"But you're happy?"

For a split second I think about saying no. Telling Thomas that I love my children and my husband but most days I feel empty inside, as though everything in the world has dulled to a bleak gray color. That life at thirty-six feels like a ride going around and around and you can never get off.

"Well, sure," I say, sounding more tentative than I want to. "I mean. There are good days and bad days. Kids aren't always easy, and god knows neither is marriage."

"What about Scarlett?" he asks. "Have you kept in touch with her over the years?"

"We've more or less kept in contact. Mostly through Facebook messages, the odd phone call." He frowns and gives his head a little shake. "What?" I ask, trying not to sound defensive.

"She's trouble, Henny. Always has been."

"I could have said the same about you."

He laughs, but it has a heaviness to it. "Not in the same way. Scarlett was in a league of her own."

"We were all a part of it, Thomas. The game, the friendship, the lies."

"Sure, but she was the puppet master. You must see that now?" He looks at me hopefully, needing me to be on his side.

"Do we really want to rehash all of that?" I give him a pleading look. "It was so long ago, Thomas."

He shakes his head and holds up a hand. "You're right. I'm sorry." Coming closer, he searches my face for a few seconds without saying anything, studying me with his dark eyes until I have to look away. "I hope we can be friends. Despite everything that happened in the past."

I nod and look back at him. "Of course we can. I've missed you. But don't get too excited; I have zero social scene and spend most of my time at home reading."

He shrugs and gives me a mischievous smile. "I'm sure we can find some way to get into trouble. We always have."

"I know we can. That's what I'm afraid of." I'm not really afraid, but I should be. I'm excited. The dull gray of my life is suddenly surging into Technicolor.

Thomas's phone buzzes with a text. He takes a few seconds to read it and respond, then slides it back into his pocket. "I'd better get back to work."

"You didn't book off much time for our reunion." I'm joking, but also a bit hurt that he just fit me in around a break at work.

He gently bumps me with his shoulder. "I honestly didn't know you'd come. I thought maybe you'd think it was better to keep your distance. Or you could have been busy with work. I really had no idea. I wasn't even sure you still lived there when I dropped that note off."

I bump him back. "Have I ever been able to keep my distance from you, Thomas?" As soon as the words are out, I regret them; they reveal way too much truth. "But in terms of work," I quickly add, "I *am* very busy but decided the laundry and grocery shopping could wait until after our visit." He gives me a confused look. "I'm a stay-at-home mom," I explain.

"I thought you wanted to work in a library."

"I did—for quite a while, actually." I shrug. "But I quit a year or so ago."

"Why?"

I could tell him about the miscarriage, about how I took a leave and then just never went back, about how they eventually replaced me. How I just haven't had the heart to find anything else since. How before the miscarriage I was practically running that library, having started there as soon as I finished the librarian program at college. How I'd worked my way up and then watched it all fall apart when I did.

Instead, I slap on a nonchalant smile. "Life just kind of got in the way, I guess you could say. It's hard juggling a career and kids at the same time."

"Well, I have a lot of admiration for women who sacrifice careers to be at home with their children. To make sure everyone else is taken care of. Not everyone would do that."

"Thank you. That's a very noble description of it, which is rare."

"I'm sure Evan appreciates it."

"You'd think." My sarcastic reply comes too quickly, but he doesn't seem to notice.

We reach the entrance to the cemetery, and he turns to face me. "I'm really glad you came, Henny."

All I want to do is lean forward and breathe him in, to be transported right back to youth before the world had its way with us. I cross my arms to contain it and rock on the balls of my feet. "Me too, Thomas."

"Maybe you, Evan, and I could all have dinner together? We still have so much catching up to do."

I'm surprised and a little bit disappointed that he includes Evan in the suggestion of dinner, but I figure it's probably for the best.

"How about next weekend?" I offer. "Saturday should work. But I'll have to check with Evan."

"Great," he says, sounding honestly excited. "I know a new place that's apparently good. The entire basement is a cellar for local wines."

"Sounds great. I love wine." *A little too much*, I think, but keep it to myself.

"Oh, I remember your love of wine," he says with a smirk.

I put his number into my phone, compelled for some yet unknown reason to save it under the name of my former work friend, Lucy. Is it because I want to keep him a secret for a little while longer or because I have some sense of what's to come?

When he leans down to give me a good-bye hug, my stomach dips low and then rights itself. I inhale his scent, not knowing in that moment that I will forever linger a bit too closely to any stranger who emits even a whiff of the same cologne.

OCTOBER 6, 2018

I brought a bottle upstairs with me. I'm sipping it not so slowly as I get ready. Black pants, a black sweater, and black flats—as dressy as I can manage. I did blow-dry my hair. Put on some eyeliner and mascara, even a bit of lipstick. Surveying myself in the mirror, I wish I didn't feel like stripping out of the clothes, washing my face, and getting under the covers in bed.

I turn the lights off and watch Thomas arrive from the bedroom window, just like I used to years ago. Evan has never met Thomas. When I proposed the dinner to him, I packaged Thomas as an old college friend, because he was, but also so much more.

Bringing Evan and Thomas together does not feel comfortable. The person I was with Thomas is very different from the person I am with Evan, or ever have been. If Evan met Thomas's version of me, I doubt he'd like her.

I let Evan welcome Thomas into the house. I stay up in my room, drinking wine in the dark, trying to numb my nerves, get my feelings in check, and convince myself that bringing Thomas into my family fold is not as risky as it feels.

The bedroom door slowly creaks open, and then the lights go on to expose me.

"Why are all the lights off?" Gracie asks, frowning. "Your friend from a long time ago is here." She walks across the room and comes to stand in front of me. "He's very handsome." Her eyes widen on the last word.

"You think so?" I ask, wondering if my eleven-year-old buys my act of nonchalance.

She tilts her head and gives me a scrutinizing look. I'm used to it. She's a scrutinizing kind of kid. It's the kind of look that would make me squirm if it were coming from anyone else, but not from Gracie. At this point there's no risk of her uncovering some hidden flaw that she hasn't already accepted about me.

"You look really pretty, Mom."

Her words get me to my feet. "Thank you, sweet pea. I needed that."

She takes my hand in hers and gives it a little tug. "You should go downstairs and say hi." Something her father would say. Warmth from her skin pulses against mine.

I give her hand a squeeze, our secret signal of love, and then let it go, ready to face Thomas and my husband.

Once downstairs, I act surprised. "Evan, why didn't you tell me Thomas was here?" He ignores the question, knowing I was up in my room hiding and would have heard him arrive.

"Henny," Thomas says enthusiastically, bending down to give me a peck on the cheek. "You look lovely."

"Henny?" Evan asks, passing Thomas a glass of wine.

"Yes?" I answer, before realizing it was a question.

Evan laughs. "No, Hannah. I'm asking what's a Henny?"

Thomas puts an arm around me and pulls me in close. "This is a Henny." A frown clouds Evan's face for just a second, then disappears as he takes a sip of his drink.

I step out of Thomas's embrace. "Thomas and Scarlett called me Henny because I was the worrier of the group. You know the storybook *Henny Penny*, about the chicken who thinks the sky is falling?"

Thomas and I both laugh at the memory, but Evan stares back at us as though still waiting for the punch line. The room tenses with awkward silence. I wonder if it's going to be like this all night.

"All right if I use your bathroom?" Thomas asks, and I'm not sure if it's to escape or if he really needs to go.

Evan points to the kitchen door. "There's one just back down the hall—"

Thomas holds up a hand to stop him. "Don't worry, I know."

"That's right," Evan replies with a tight smile. "It's not your first time here."

"That's for sure," Thomas shoots back on his way out of the kitchen. Evan frowns again, and this time it lingers.

"Why don't you go put on some music in the living room?" I suggest. "I'm just going to open another bottle of wine."

Evan's frown intensifies. I ignore him and bend down to get another bottle out of the cupboard, coming up only when I know he's left the room. The pop of a cork has never sounded so good to me. I pour myself a full glass and take a few gulps.

Thomas is taking a while, so I go looking and find him in the hallway outside the bathroom, looking at the wall that's lined with family photos. He's studying the one of me in a bathing suit when I was pregnant with Rose, lying on a blanket on the beach, smiling up at the camera.

"I was pregnant with Rose in that one." My voice causes him to jump. "Sorry. I didn't mean to sneak up on you."

He gives a self-conscious laugh. "I was just getting caught up on all the things I missed."

"So this is Gracie?" He points at her first-grade school photo.

"That's right."

"And this is obviously a young version of Rose." He taps a photo of Rose as a toddler. "I can't believe how much she looks like you." He moves on to a more recent picture of my entire family. "And where was this photo taken?"

"That was at Evan's parents' farm three Christmases ago. They live an hour from here."

In the photo, Evan has his arm around my shoulders and one hand on Gracie's arm. I'm leaning into Evan's body and have one arm wrapped across Rose's chest, and the girls have their arms looped together. We're all connected by touch, the current of family flowing from one member to the next. If someone were to step away, everyone would become disconnected.

"You all look so happy." Thomas turns to look at me. "Like you belong together."

I shrug, sending the wine in my glass sloshing from one side to the next. "Looks can be deceiving."

He raises an eyebrow at the comment, and I'm sure he's going to question it, but instead he gestures at the house around us. "A lot of changes have been made around here. Doesn't seem like the same house aside from the outside."

Thomas would remember the wood paneling that lined most of the walls, the yellow plush carpet that ran through almost every room, the brick-pattern linoleum on the kitchen floor and the pine cabinets with the rust-colored Formica countertop.

"It was a seventies time capsule the last time you saw it, Thomas. Of course it's changed."

He gets a pained look on his face. "I know, but it always seemed so warm and homey. I liked it."

I pat him on the arm. "I'm sorry we didn't preserve it on the chance that one day you might return."

Evan had insisted on all the changes, ripping out the carpet to lay hardwood, painting the paneling white with a light gray on the walls, putting in granite countertops and custom white cabinets in the kitchen. If it had been up to me, I probably would have just left it, preserving the smell of my father's pipe in the carpet, the dining room light made of amber glass that gave everything a warm glow, the heavy wooden bookcases in my father's office that had once held every book he owned, the strong scent of garlic that had permeated the wood of the kitchen cabinets.

The original scent of the house was still there, buried under everything new. I caught whiffs of it after we'd been away for a few days and the place had been shut up. It made me wish I could go home again even though I'd just walked through the front door.

"I'm only joking," Thomas said. "I think what you've done with the place is great. Just being back here is making me kind of nostalgic for, well . . ." He shrugs. "Us."

A prickling warmth spreads across the back of my neck. The idea of *us* with my family crowded around makes me self-conscious. "Evan's in the living room, if you want to join him while I check on the girls," I offer, moving the exchange to safer territory.

Rose and Gracie are watching a movie in the TV room. They've both showered and are in their pajamas, curled up on the couch together in a rare moment of sisterly peace, one that I'm paying Rose to provide.

I give her the usual instructions on being home alone with her sister, the things I could recite in my sleep, the things that have to be said even though she's heard them dozens of times.

Bending down to kiss them both good-night, I'm swept into the sweet coconut cloud of their shampoo. It makes me want to settle down on the couch beside them where it's safe. Spend the evening pressed against the soft cotton of their pajamas, inhaling their scent. They feel like the only thing I've done right in the world—it makes me proud and sad at the same time.

*　*　*

The plates have been cleared away, replaced by a small sampling of desserts. I think the dinner was good. I haven't really tasted anything other than the wine, which I've drunk far too much of, even for me.

I pull a crème brûlée toward me and crack its polished surface, releasing the creamy insides. I don't want to eat it. I just want to break something. Evan's droning on about some fishing trip he took a million years ago with his college friends. He finally takes a breath to ask Thomas a question.

"So how long have you been back in town?"

"Since around mid-July," Thomas's answer sends a current of annoyance through me. He'd been back for months before getting in touch.

"And what part of town are you in?" Evan asks.

"I'm still looking for the right place. Living out of a suitcase at the moment."

Evan starts telling Thomas the best up-and-coming neighborhoods to get into and I drain what's left in my wineglass.

Thomas reaches across the table and gently nudges my hand. "Are you going to eat that?" He nods at the crème brûlée.

I shove it hard toward him, half hoping it ends up in his lap. "No, I don't want it." His eyebrows come together in a quizzical look, but I ignore it. My annoyance is not at him, it's at myself. For caring that Thomas didn't get in touch with me the minute he got back to town. I wouldn't have been able to be in the same town as Thomas for a day, not to mention months, without trying to see him. Realizing that fact in the moment makes me realize I'm no more over him than I was sixteen years ago.

Thomas nudges me with his foot under the table, but I refuse to look at him. Evan has gotten quite animated with a story about our own home renovations and bumps me in the shoulder with an elbow. Thomas nudges me again, and it sends me right out of my chair. I try not to sway with the sudden movement.

Evan looks up in concern. "What's wrong?"

"Nothing. I just need to get some fresh air. I'm getting one of those headaches. You know. When it's too stuffy?"

Evan stares back at me with annoyed confusion. I don't get headaches and never have. He starts to get up from his chair. "I'll come with you."

I put out a hand to stop him. "No that's okay, I'll just be a few minutes." I leave before he can say anything else.

Moving slowly so as not to stumble, I feel them watching me go. It was ridiculous to make such a scene, but I can't turn back now. I wind through a small crowd of waiting patrons at the front door. They move aside, hoping my departure means a free table.

It isn't the type of place Evan and I would ever go normally—trendy, expensive, dimly lit with candles on each table. It's the kind of restaurant for people with double incomes and no kids. Or people with kids and incomes big enough that they can go out for the evening and pretend they don't have kids.

I find an alley to duck into beside the building. It's as trendy as the inside of the restaurant, with brick walls covered in colorful graffiti. It's cold out, and I wish I'd brought my coat. My head is fine. I don't need the fresh air. I just needed to get away from them both. The whole night has been a tsunami of emotion rushing through me—wanting Thomas, hating myself for wanting Thomas, feeling pathetic for wanting Thomas, feeling guilty for wanting Thomas while sitting next to my husband. Meanwhile, the two of them are laughing away and enjoying the goddamn crème brûlée!

I'm drunker than I should be. My head feels like a fishbowl, my brain sloshing around inside, the rest of my body hanging there numb and detached. I lean against the wall for support.

It's happening all over again, and I'm letting it. He's already gotten under my skin, and now I'm feeling hurt because I wasn't his first priority when he got back after sixteen years, which is absolutely ridiculous considering I'm married with two kids.

"Henny?" Thomas's voice ends my mental tirade, a flush of embarrassment rising into my cheeks, as though he heard my thoughts.

He walks over, grabs my hand, and pulls me deeper into the alley. "Evan is time-sucking the waitress with questions about how they marinade the steaks, so I thought I'd duck out and check on you."

Thomas lets go of my hand and turns away from me. He unzips his pants, and I watch as his pee washes across bands of blue-and-green graffiti.

"Seriously, Thomas?" I fake my disgust. I don't really mind that he's peeing—I mind that naked bits of him are right there and it excites me.

"Sorry," he says, sounding anything but apologetic. "I told him I was going to the bathroom, so I figured I really should." He finishes, zips his pants up, and turns to face me. "What's the matter, Henny?"

"I have a headache," I say flatly.

"I don't believe you."

Even after so much time apart, he knows me too well. "Why did you take so long to get in touch when you got back here? I can't imagine living close to you and not trying to see you after so many years, so clearly, I still care more about you than you do about me." I hate myself as soon as the words are out of my mouth.

"I had a lot to work out when I first got back. And I wasn't sure you'd even want to see me. It took some time to work up the courage to approach you."

His words work like a soothing balm on my insecurity and petty annoyance. I push myself off the wall so that we're only inches apart.

"And that part about you caring more than me," he continues. "That's not even close to being true. Never was."

I laugh self-consciously. "That was a stupid thing to say. I sounded like I did back in college whenever I got jealous of you not spending enough time with me."

He leans in closer. "I've been thinking a lot about college lately. All the fun we had."

He's only inches away—close enough for me to rise on the balls of my feet and kiss him. A thick block of energy thrums in the space between us. "Which kind of fun do you mean, exactly?"

He bends down to whisper in my ear. "The Daring Game."

Footsteps and a shadow at the end of the alley cause Thomas to take a step away from me, and I cross my arms over my chest, suddenly shivering with the cold.

"Hannah?" Evan calls out.

Thomas puts a hand on my back and leads me toward him. "She's fine. I wanted some fresh air myself, so I thought I'd come check on her."

Evan nods. "We should think about getting home, Hannah. It's already eleven. And if you're not really feeling well . . ." He trails off, giving me a questioning look.

I put on my most sober expression, wide eyes and forced smile. "Okay. Let's just settle the bill and we'll go."

"It's been taken care of," Thomas is quick to interject. "I gave them my card when we got here."

Evan puffs his chest out slightly. "No need. We'll chip in."

Thomas waves the comment away. "Don't be silly. I asked you. I picked the restaurant. I get the bill."

I can tell by Evan's expression that he's going to protest, so I jump in. "That's very generous of you, Thomas."

"We'll get the next one," Evan makes sure to add. *Where to?* I want to ask him. *Our favorite family pizza place?*

Evan turns and heads back to the restaurant for our coats. I start to follow, but Thomas grabs my arm. "Are you in?" His breath smells of garlic and wine. I nod without hesitation. He smiles a slow, satisfied smile, then squeezes my arm. "Good. Be ready. Your dare could come at any time."

They're Scarlett's words, said whenever we started a fresh round of the game. He winks, releases my arm, and moves back toward the restaurant.

The illicitness of the proposal makes my nerve ends tingle. I should stop him, tell him that on second thought I don't want to play our juvenile game again, remind him of how it ended last time, but I don't. I ignore my good sense because I want to laugh out loud, skip back into the restaurant, beg him to give me a dare right there on the spot. My thirty-six years slip away like dry skin, the boredom, the responsibility, the roles I'm so sick of playing gone in an instant.

* * *

At home Evan charges inside and starts the process of getting the girls up to bed. He was silent the whole cab ride home, which is unnerving. All he has to do is say that he isn't comfortable with me seeing Thomas, that he doesn't like how close we were in the alley, that it felt inappropriate, and it's all over.

I lock myself away in our bathroom and brush the evidence of wine from my teeth. Scrub the carefully applied makeup from my face. Release my body from a bra that was hiked up so high the straps dug into my shoulders and underwear that promised to flatten my stomach but did nothing but carve a line from the waistband into my soft flesh.

I put on my flannel pajamas and instantly feel more like myself. Sliding into the cool sheets of my bed, I put my head on the pillow and hope the spinning won't be too bad.

Evan comes in and sits down on my side of the bed. "What the hell is wrong with you?"

I open my eyes and struggle into a sitting position, which takes way too much effort. "What are you talking about?"

"Maybe your friend didn't pick up on it, but I know you, I know you better than anybody."

My skin crawls at the ownership in his statement. "Pick up on what?"

"You were drunk, Hannah! Before we'd even left for dinner."

"Drunk?" It's not the offense I was expecting to be accused of.

"You barely ate anything. You didn't even try to act interested in what I was saying." He ticks each thing off on his fingers. "Then you jumped up from the table and staggered outside for no apparent reason."

"I had a headache!" I say loudly.

"Maybe from all the red wine you drank." His voice matches mine, and I worry the kids will hear.

"My god, Evan, it's a Saturday night. So I had a bit too much wine. I was nervous, that's all." The last part slips free from my fuzzy mind, and I instantly regret it.

His eyes narrow. "Nervous about what?"

I shrug and fall back against the pillows, my lips tightly sealed. He eyes me suspiciously and I wait for him to push me for an answer, but he only exhales and runs a hand through his hair. "It was embarrassing, Hannah. And it's not just because it's a Saturday night. It could be a Wednesday or a Thursday or a goddamn Tuesday." He pauses to see the impact his words have had on me. When I give him nothing, he continues, "I've had enough of the drinking, and clearly our conversation the other night had no impact. Maybe more drastic measures are needed."

"What are you going to do, Evan, force me into rehab for having too much wine on a Saturday night?"

He slowly stands up from the bed so that he's looking down on me. "If that's what it takes." He pauses for effect. "Embarrass me like that again and you will regret it." Before I can even respond to his ridiculous-sounding threat, he turns dramatically and storms out of the room. I wait for a minute or two to see if he's coming back and am relieved when I hear him rustling around in the linen closet, getting sheets for the guest bed.

I slide back down under the duvet and pull it up under my chin. I did have too much to drink tonight; most of the evening is a bit hazy. But not the last part, not me and Thomas in the alley. That part is as clear as day, the thought of it creating a warm band of satisfaction that wraps itself around my chest.

I reach out from under my sheets to grab my phone. Tapping on the Facebook app, I go right to Scarlett's page. There's a new post of her in the bath, bubbles carefully arranged to keep it from being pornographic, with candles all around her, the ones she sells through her business. Then a hashtag about romantic bubble baths. Obviously, someone was there taking the photo.

I go to my messages and reread her last one before starting my reply. *Evan and I had dinner with Thomas tonight. We all had a wonderful time together. I understand your concerns but please don't worry. College was a long time ago and we've all grown up. I can handle having Thomas in my life again. It's nice to connect with an old friend and I could really use the company right now. He actually suggested starting the Daring Game up again, just for fun. I'll keep you posted! xoxo*

The message is calculated, meant to make Scarlett feel like I'm not completely disregarding her concerns but also make her feel a bit jealous that Thomas and I might become close again, without her here to ruin it. I hit send and then curl up and fall into a deep wine-fogged sleep, oblivious to what I've set in motion.

* * *

It feels as though something has woken me, but the house is still costumed in the silence and darkness of the middle of the night. It was probably the dehydration that woke me; my mouth is coated in dryness. I forgot to bring a glass of water to bed. Glancing at the clock, I'm surprised to see I've been asleep for only about forty minutes. I'll never make it through the night without water. Throwing back the covers, I quietly make my way down to the kitchen, where I fill a glass to the brim at the sink.

Taking it into the living room, I go to the picture window to look out onto the backyard. It's supposed to be a full moon tonight, and I'm hoping to catch a glimpse of it. But there's too much cloud cover to see anything, and I'm about to turn and head back up to bed when a flash of movement at the back of the yard catches my attention.

Light from the kitchen behind me makes it hard to see into the darkness of the yard, so I put my glass down on a side table and cup my hands around my face up against the window. I'm sure I see a shadowy figure at the very edge of the property line, but it's so still I can't tell if it's a tree or an actual person. I've almost convinced myself it's just my imagination when the thing moves—an arm slowly rising in what looks to be a casual wave.

I jump away from the window and duck behind the curtain. My brain is still foggy from the wine and my movements are slow and clumsy, making it all feel like a bad dream. Once my heart slows, I step over to the kitchen to shut off the light so I can get a proper look without being seen myself. When I peer around the curtain, the shadow is gone. Nothing but trees swaying slightly with a wind that's picked up.

"You're drunk." I whisper the admonishment to myself, hoping it dispels the sense of being watched, the feeling that someone was out there. Grabbing my glass of water from the side table, I slowly make my way back up to bed, swearing to stop drinking so much.

THEN

I kept my feelings for Thomas hidden well, under a thick blanket of indifference, but when random girls flirted with him at parties, I felt as though I might puke, and when his skin brushed mine, I thought I might melt. Scarlett didn't seem to feel anything for Thomas other than friendship. She burped around him, shoved her face full of pizza, offered to get girls' numbers for him.

I was jealous of her platonic attitude toward him, of her control of the situation. I said nothing to her about my feelings for Thomas, and it wasn't until well into the Daring Game that I realized she'd known all along.

Scarlett was the one who came up with it. It was a Friday, and we were at Thomas's apartment passing around a bong with only weed dust in it and no plans for the night. I suggested playing truth or dare, hoping it meant I'd get to kiss Thomas, and it sparked something in Scarlett. She told me truth or dare was for little kids and then went looking for a pen and pad. We spent the rest of the night coming up with the rules of a game that would change our lives:

1. Everyone in the group would take turns being the darer, the one to present a dare to another in the group.
2. The one who did the dare would then present the next dare, and so on.
3. If a person failed to complete a dare that had been given to them, then the darer would serve them a punishment. It could be anything the darer decided was fitting.

4. *There would be no more than one dare given a week.*
5. *All dares would be logged in a notebook that was to be kept in a hollowed-out tree at St. James Cemetery, the Daring Tree, which was located halfway between the campus and my house. (It was the tree Scarlett and I had found when we were kids and used to hide contraband items in, like cigarettes and* Penthouse *magazines.)*
6. *When a darer was ready to dare, they were to call the others to the tree with a message of* Do you Dare?
7. *The game was not to be talked about with anyone outside the three of us. If it was discovered that one of us had broken this rule, then that person would be banned from the game and the group for eternity.*

The dares started out simple at first—petty theft, light vandalism, practical jokes played on unsuspecting students—but in typical Scarlett fashion, she got bored. The dares became tougher, with more at stake, just like she liked it.

OCTOBER 8, 2018

That lost feeling I get when the girls leave for the day hasn't even had time to settle in before the text comes. It's Monday morning; the school bus has only just pulled away.

I stare at the screen in confusion for a few seconds: a text from Lucy. *Ready for your first dare?* Then I remember I saved Thomas's number under that name for secrecy's sake. I reread the words several times. In the bright light of reality on a Monday morning, I'm no longer so sure. I watch a few cars pass by the front window, people on their way to their busy days.

Scarlett replied to my message on Saturday night, and no matter how hard I tried, I couldn't keep the warning of her words out of my head. Every time I read it, I could hear her voice in my head, her bossy, threatening tone, the way she enunciates each word so clearly when she's scolding me.

Does Evan know about your history with Thomas? I doubt that he does since he went out for dinner with you both. Should I be filling him in??? Don't fool yourself Hannah, "just friends" with you and Thomas can't work. If you need a friend, find someone without all the baggage and sexual tension, and please god DO NOT PLAY THE DARING GAME!!! Love, your very concerned, true friend, Scarlett

Pick you up in ten minutes? Another text from Thomas comes in.

This morning I made a point of getting up early, showering and dressing before everyone else. Then I made a Sunday morning kind of breakfast with eggs and bacon and toast. I even made a fruit salad for the girls' lunches. After I spent most of yesterday, after the dinner with Thomas, in bed nursing my hangover, the guilt and sense of failure were choking me to death, and I felt I had some making up to do.

A few domestic acts have helped loosen that chokehold, but now Thomas's text has arrived, offering me a full escape. I drift into the kitchen, still clutching my phone, and sit down at the table. The house is so quiet I can hear the ticking of the grandfather clock in the front hallway.

I could go and nobody would even know—the realization is freeing. I don't have to tell Evan everything I've done with my day, and I certainly don't have to tell Scarlett. I can have pockets of time that are just my own. The weight of the day stretching ahead of me lifts.

My phone buzzes on the table with another text—just a single question mark.

Yes! I text right back, afraid the offer may suddenly disappear.

Wear a light jacket and shoes with good treads. Will pull up out front. His reply grips at my stomach with a fist of excitement. I delete the conversation, starting the habit of secrets, and head upstairs to get ready.

I'm outside waiting when a silver BMW SUV rolls to a stop in front of the house. I run out to the car, feeling as though every neighbor is watching, and quickly jump into the passenger seat.

"Since when did you become a BMW guy?" I ask as he pulls away from the curb. I'm a little impressed but feign disdain. When Thomas was in college, he hated all things yuppie, mostly because his uncle was one.

"They're nice cars," he snaps back. "And I can write it off."

"Oh, well then, if you can write it off."

He gives me a gentle shove. "Wasn't that a Volvo I saw in your driveway?"

"An ancient one with a million kilometers on it and about five pounds of goldfish crackers crammed into the seats from the toddler years."

"What the hell are goldfish crackers?"

I shake my head. "You don't wanna know."

He tosses something onto my lap. A notebook with a black-and-white speckled cover—the very same kind that we used to keep track of our dares in college.

"Inside is your first dare," Thomas says, glancing away from the road to give me an excited smile. "We'll start leaving it in the tree after this one."

"You know we could just set up a secret email account and do it that way. It would be way more convenient."

He pretends to be appalled. "Where's your sense of ceremony? And tradition?"

"To be honest," I say. "I'm surprised you want to play this game again, considering how it ended for you the last time we played."

"I only want to play again because Scarlett isn't a part of it. And I thought it would be fun, make things interesting in our boring old adulthood. It may have ended badly, but it was fun while it lasted."

"My life could definitely use some more fun." I crack open the brand-new notebook. His writing is on the first page. *I, Thomas Sutton, dare you, Hannah Warren, to climb the Westville water tower.*

"You can't be serious!" I slam the book shut. "That's not fair."

There was only one dare I wasn't able to complete back in the day. It was to climb the Westville water tower. Westville was a small town that had at one point become swallowed by the growth of our city and turned into a soulless suburb. I'm not sure if the water tower is even in use anymore, but it still stands tall, visible from most places in the east end of the city.

I'd pretty much kept my fear of heights a secret until Scarlett gave me that horrible dare. I did try to push through it, clinging to those metal rungs with sweaty hands, moving one step at a time, not once looking down. It was the wind that got me. About halfway up you start to feel it caressing your neck, whispering into your ear, playing with stray strands of hair. I froze and couldn't move up or down. Thomas had to come get me, coax me from my trance and guide me back to the ground. And of course, Scarlett made me pay for it. Those were the rules—*Don't complete the dare, suffer the punishment.*

"You can't do that," I protest, shoving the book back at him.

He pushes it away. "I absolutely can do it, and I have. It's the perfect first dare."

"I'm not going to do it." I shake my head. "This was a stupid idea."

"Isn't there some part of you that wants to conquer that water tower? Do something that you couldn't do in youth instead of the other way around?"

"What are you talking about?"

He signals and turns onto the road that leads to Westville. "As you get older, you can't do stuff that you used to do when you were young. Doesn't that bug you?"

"You mean like cartwheels and front flips off diving boards?"

"Exactly."

"No. It does not bother me."

He laughs and gives the steering wheel a little slap. "Come on, Henny. Live a little, will you?"

His scent fills the enclosed space and goes straight to my head. I watch his hands slide along the steering wheel, and it makes me think things that I shouldn't.

"Fine," I say, just to distract myself from my thoughts, then immediately feel the dread of my submission. "But you may need to come rescue me again."

He reaches out and pats my knee, letting his hand rest there. "I will always come rescue you, Henny."

The skin under my jeans burns with his touch. I gently swat his hand away. "I'm going to get you back for this. I should have known when you told me to wear shoes with treads that I was in trouble."

"You won't regret it," he says with authentic enthusiasm. "It. Will. Wake. You. Up." He practically yells each word at me.

"Who said I was sleeping?" I challenge him. I don't tell him that just being in this car with him is waking me up to something. Shifting my wife-and-mother molecular structure into something different, something I'm not sure I recognize.

He concentrates on navigating along the dirt road that leads to the tower. Only when he comes to a stop and puts the car in park does he turn to face me.

"We're all sleeping, Henny. It's called adulthood. Sleepwalking through life, wondering what the hell happened to the real you. Wishing you could go back in time to when it was all laid out in front of you and do things differently." He glances out the window. "I know you know what I'm talking about."

There's a pressure in my chest that makes it hard to breathe. Maybe it's shock that he knows something I've barely even admitted to myself; maybe it's the pain of knowing I'm not hiding it as well as I thought I was.

I open my car door and get out, breathing the fresh air in deeply, relieving the pressure in my chest. I walk to the front of the car and stare up at the water tower. Thomas gets out and comes to stand beside me.

"I'm gonna do it." The declaration ignites my adrenaline.

Thomas claps me on the back. "I knew you would."

We walk around the perimeter of the fence until we find an opening—part hole in the ground, part peeled-back chain-link. I get on my stomach and wiggle my way under, not caring that I'm smearing dirt all down the front of me.

As I stand at the bottom of the tower, my courage springs a slow leak.

"I'll be right behind you this time." Thomas bends down and cups his hands together to boost me to the first rung. In a kind of trance, I lift my foot and let him propel me up. Using all my strength, I'm able to get my feet onto the first rung. I'm not as strong as I used to be, which makes me even more determined.

Somehow, I get myself into position—sweat collecting in my armpits, my breathing heavy. I move up the ladder to make room for Thomas and watch in awe as he jumps from the ground to the first rung and then heaves his body up without even the slightest bit of struggle.

"I work out," he says, in answer to my shocked expression.

"Who are you?" I can't help but ask. In college, Thomas thought exercise was a bourgeois waste of good energy.

I try not to think about anything as I climb each rung, one foot at a time. I ignore Thomas's words of encouragement. I take long, deep breaths. I don't look down. Even when the wind arrives to caress my neck, I keep going, telling myself it's just wind; I will not be blown off the ladder.

When I do let myself think, it's of my girls. Would they be proud of me in this moment, see me as brave, fearless, able to do anything? Is it a story I'll one day tell them when they have to conquer their own fears? Will they be shocked, feeling that maybe they don't know all there is to know about their mother?

I finally reach the top, and an odd combination of a grunt, scream, and laugh escapes me into the sky above us—struggle, fear, and elation. I crawl up onto the platform and freeze on all fours. Thomas arrives right behind me and helps me into a sitting position. We're safely penned in by the metal railing but able to let our legs dangle.

My feet swing weightless below me like a separate part of my body. The entire suburb of Westville stretches out in front of us, miles and miles of uniform gray roofs, top hats to the cookie- cutter houses that sit beneath them. A subdivision has never looked so beautiful to me. Green squares of manicured lawns with well-planned-out patches of growing trees, all dissected and disrupted by the gray pavement and yellow lines of straight roads. From up here it looks like a child's play mat.

Thomas puts his arm around me and pulls me in close. "I knew you could do it, Henny. I knew it."

I suddenly burst into tears. No warning. Like a dam breaking. The harder I try to stop, the uglier it gets.

He keeps his arm around me tightly, saying nothing. Only when the sobs stop being convulsions do I try to talk. "I'm sorry."

He squeezes me even tighter. "Don't be sorry."

"I've just been really unhappy and lonely lately." The words come out tentative. When he doesn't recoil in disgust or pull his arm away, I continue. "Evan and I are having problems, and I just feel like I'm failing at everything in life right now." I again think about telling Thomas about the miscarriage and my stay in the hospital, but the shame is a fist, holding those words tightly.

"Don't say that, Henny." He shifts so that he's facing me. "You're a great mom. I can tell that just from being in your home for an hour.

And besides that, in my opinion, just keeping your kids alive this long means you win."

I laugh through my tears. "You don't think I'm crazy? Loving my life and hating my life at the same time?" I search his eyes for even the slightest hint of aversion.

"No crazier than you've ever been," he answers with a straight face.

I laugh again and give a reluctant nod. "Fair enough."

He pulls his legs in and gets to his feet. "Come on." He holds out his hand.

I tuck my hands in my jacket pockets. "I'm good down here."

"Come on, Henny. Trust me."

Reluctantly I reach out for Thomas's hand and let him pull me to my feet. A blast of wind knocks into me, and I have to grab the metal railing to steady myself.

"Scream," he commands. Then he lets out a wild, whooping yell that gets carried away on the wind.

I take a deep breath and expel everything that sits inside of me unsaid—a guttural yell that turns into a cry of joy. When I have no breath left, I turn to Thomas, who quickly snaps my photo with his phone.

He looks at it and smiles. "There she is." He passes me his phone so I can see for myself.

It's me, all right, but a version I haven't seen in a long time. There's no posing, no attempt to show my best angle, no concern for the whiteness of my teeth, a double chin, or laugh lines. I'm tearstained, my hair's a mess from the wind, but I'm smiling with abandon, my eyes wide and wild.

Climbing down from the tower is even harder than going up. The closer I get to the ground, the closer I am to returning to real life. I don't want the dare to end, or the feelings it's given me. Mostly I don't want my time with Thomas to be over.

He drives home slowly, as though he doesn't want our time together to end either. We sit mostly in silence, comfortable to be back in each other's company again. When we pull up in front of my house, he hands me the black-and-white notebook.

"Your turn."

I run my hand across the smooth cover. "My turn to get you back, you mean?"

He laughs, slow, relaxed, and familiar. The absence of it in my life for so many years suddenly creeps up on me and whacks me with a painful fist of nostalgia.

"I missed you, Henny," he says, as though the very same nostalgia has hit him too. He leans over and pulls me into an awkward hug, both of us suspended over the hump of the center console.

"I missed you too, Thomas." My words bounce against the skin of his neck, so close to my lips I can feel the warmth. I force myself out of the hug and notice that my neighbor Libby is standing beside the car, looking into the window.

"Shit," I mumble under my breath before slowly rolling the window down.

"Hannah," she says. "So glad I caught you."

I gesture to Thomas. "I was just out with an old college friend." I hope it's hint enough to tell her she should come back later to talk, but instead she reaches a hand into the car.

"Libby Green."

Thomas politely returns the handshake. "Thomas. Pleased to meet you."

"Sorry, I didn't catch your last name?" she says, smiling even wider to mask her nosiness.

"Sutton," I reply flatly, hoping my tone will ward her off.

"Well, pleasure to meet you, Thomas Sutton." She then turns her attention fully to me, her blue eyes laser focused. "I have some important neighborhood news to discuss."

"Just let me hop out, then, and Thomas can be on his way." I shoot him an apologetic look and slide out of the car to face Libby. He gives one last wave, then pulls away, and I'm right back in the middle of my boring life.

Libby shoves a piece of paper with some writing and a crudely drawn sketch of a hooded figure on it at me. "Not sure if you heard, but there have been reports of someone—around six feet, medium build, wearing a black windbreaker, hood up—lurking around the neighbor-hood at night. Appears to be a male, based on the descriptions. I made these and am passing them out to families so they can be well informed and keep an eye out."

I have a flash of the shadowy figure I thought I saw in our backyard a couple of nights ago, and a shiver runs through me. I go to say some-thing but stop. I'd had too much to drink that night and can barely even remember what I saw. The whole thing feels like a dream now.

Instead, I take the flyer from her. "I haven't heard anything about this."

"We did discuss it at the community meeting last week, but you weren't there, so . . ." She trails off, pausing for a moment to let the full inference of my neighborly neglect sink in. "The first sighting was actu-ally several weeks back, but it was only once we all got together for the meeting and someone mentioned it that we realized how often he'd actually been in the neighborhood lurking about."

"He's just lurking? He hasn't done anything yet?" I ask. Libby's the type of person who loves to incite fear in everyone just so she can orga-nize the rescue.

"Lurking now, but Hannah, you know how these things go. It starts with the little stuff, and then before you know it, a child has gone missing."

"I'm not sure of that pattern statistically, Libby." She gives me a tight smile, as though she expected that kind of response from me. I can hear Evan's voice in my head: *Why don't you at least try to get along with the neighbors and fit in?*

"But"—I quickly recover—"I'll be sure to let the whole family know about this, and we'll be keeping an eye out."

"Thank you, Hannah. We all have to do our part to keep our chil-dren safe, to protect our precious families, don't we?"

I smile toothpaste commercial wide and give a nod of my head. "We sure do, Libby."

"Your friend Thomas Sutton is very handsome." She gives me a mis-chievous smile. "Does Evan know you're spending your day with another man, a good-looking one at that, in a BMW?"

I stammer nonsensically, completely caught off guard by her question. She swats me on the arm playfully. "I'm just joking, Hannah. And you certainly don't strike me as the illicit-affair type. You have a hard enough time getting cupcakes to the street party, let alone manage a secret rendezvous. Am I right?" Her high-pitched laughter lodges in my eardrums like a sharp splinter.

I want to give her a hard shove, shock the smile off her face, but instead I force out a weak laugh. "Of course I'm not. He's just a friend from college. Evan and I had dinner with him on Saturday, actually."

Libby's only half listening, her attention grabbed by a neighbor across the street who's pulling into their driveway. "Better push on with these flyers," she says, giving a wave over her shoulder as she marches off to ignite fear in someone else.

Walking up the driveway, I scrunch the flyer into a ball with relish and toss it into one of the garbage cans that sits at the side of the house. When I turn to go up the path to the front door, I glance over and see Libby and the other neighbor watching me. Based on the narrowed squint of her eyes and the deep downturn of her lips, I know she saw me throw it out.

I quickly unlock the front door and hurry inside, embarrassment turning my cheeks bright red. I've committed yet another faux pas with the neighbors. I just hope that Evan doesn't hear about it. The renewed sense of myself that Thomas's dare gave me is quickly draining away.

Walking into the kitchen makes it worse when I come to face-to-face with the mess of this morning's elaborate breakfast, which I abandoned for the dare.

I'm too hungry to tackle it just yet, so I make myself a sandwich and take it into the living room. My book sits on the coffee table, so I grab it to read while I eat. There's still lots of time to clean up the kitchen and organize things for dinner, I assure myself.

* * *

I don't hear him come in the front door. It's only his deep sigh that alerts me to his presence. I drop the book and shoot off the couch.

"My god, Evan, you scared me." I look at my wrist, which doesn't have a watch, which never has a watch. "What time is it? The girls, they're not even—"

"I'm home early," he interrupts to explain. "I'm playing golf after work and forgot my shoes."

He goes into the kitchen, and I cringe as I hear another one of his deep sighs. He mutters something indecipherable under his breath and then stomps up the stairs to get his shoes.

By the time he comes back down, I have hot water running over the pans in the sink and am loading the dishwasher. He yells out something about being late for dinner and then the front door slams, sending a tremor of his annoyance through the whole house.

"At least I wasn't drinking," I call after him, then go to the fridge and take out a beer.

Reaching for my phone, I open the Facebook app to reply to Scarlett's earlier message. *I appreciate the concern, but I think you're being a bit melodramatic. I'm not the twenty-year-old girl who was obsessed with Thomas back in college. I proved that today when I climbed the Westville water tower. It was the first dare, and I climbed all the way to the top!!! So, you see, I'm no longer Henny Penny, afraid of everything and I'm no longer under Thomas's spell. Please just be happy for me. xo*

I hit send, and nervousness flutters through my gut. Even from across the world I find it hard to disobey her. I wonder if she'll detect the insincerity about no longer being under Thomas's spell. She always could see right through me. That was the problem.

THEN

The dare was to break into Professor Moretti's basement and steal some of his homemade wine. Both Thomas and I had him for different history courses, and he often bragged about his delicious stockpile. It was Thomas's dare for me.

We did our usual thing: met at the tree, read out the dare, made a plan. Then, as soon as it was dark, we headed to Professor Moretti's house. Thomas climbed down into one of the window wells and jimmied the window open, holding it up for me as I slid over the cement windowsill, scraping a thick line down my back, and landed on both feet on the cement floor. I could hear footsteps above me and the low rumble of Professor Moretti's voice.

I imagined him clomping down the stairs to find me standing in his basement. He'd be shocked and confused but still find some way to reference history. "Ms. Warren, what do you think you're doing down here? Hiding from the Nazis?"

I had no problem finding the wine. There were shelves stocked with the stuff. I handed two bottles out to Thomas and Scarlett and then scurried back to get a third—one for each of us.

To get me out, Thomas grabbed both of my wrists, and I walked my way up the wall and through the window, scraping a thick line down my stomach to match my back.

We took our steal to Thomas's. Scarlett uncorked the first bottle with her teeth while Thomas chose a record to listen to. He considered himself a purist—no tapes or CDs for him, only vinyl. Scarlett took a few slugs from the bottle. "It's not that bad," she said, as though she were suddenly a wine connoisseur.

PJ Harvey's voice took command of the room and then Thomas joined us, flopping down on the couch beside me and taking the bottle from Scarlett for his own turn with it. "It tastes like he grew the grapes in his basement."

Scarlett reached out and grabbed it back. "Who cares? It's free alcohol. You won that round, Hannah. Well done!" She saluted me with the bottle and then tipped it back to drink from it.

A dribble of red wine escaped down her chin. Before she could wipe it away, she had a moment of looking vampiric, the shadows of the basement making her cheeks look hollow, her eyes black, her teeth and chin stained red. A shiver ran down my spine as she finally passed the bottle over to me.

The wine was sweet and sour at the same time—earth, grapes, sugar, vinegar, each taste presenting itself on the way down. I didn't so much like the taste as I did the feeling of warmth and fluidity that it spread through my body. The heady, loose-limbed feeling of wine made it an instant friend.

We spent the night passing the bottles around until not a drop was left in any of them, taking turns playing records, sometimes forcing ourselves up to dance if the song called for it.

Late into the night, Scarlett passed out at one end of the couch. I made my way over to the record player, weaving as I went. Getting down on my knees, I rummaged through the pile of records that littered the floor until I found Pearl Jam's Ten album. The pink cover made it easy to spot.

"It's that time, is it?" Thomas asked, standing over me.

I handed him the record to put on. "It sure is." I played it every time I was there.

I lay down on the floor in front of the stereo, and Thomas disappeared into the kitchen. I must have passed out for a little while, because the next thing I remember, Thomas was shaking me awake.

He held a glass of water out to me. "You might want to drink some of this."

I sat up, and the room spun. My mouth was dry and had a terrible sickly-sweet taste. I gratefully took the water from him and drank it down in almost one gulp. "I think I need some fresh air."

It was a walkout basement, and Thomas and I stood just outside the entrance, leaving the doors open so we could hear the music. It was the end of November by then and the air was cold. We could see our breath, but the chill worked to sober me up and I liked the quiet that happened only that late at night.

"What time is it?" *I asked.*

"Around three, I think," *he answered.* "Are you feeling better?" *He reached out to give my back a rub. I cringed and sucked in my breath.* "What's wrong?"

"I scraped my back when I was going into Professor Moretti's basement." *I lifted my shirt just a bit.* "And here too."

He reached out and very gently stroked the angry red scrape down my stomach, his finger leaving a trail of fire as it moved. The music went from steady drums and Eddie Vedder's angry scream to the melodic, emotion-drenched lamenting of "Black," the perfect song for a first kiss.

Before I could overthink it, worry about rejection, or consider the rules of our friendship, I stepped closer to Thomas so that his whole hand pressed up against my bare skin. He slid his hand out from between us and used it to pull me right up against him. I leaned up as he leaned down, and our lips met, soft at first. There was a tentativeness to it, as though we both thought the world might implode on contact. But when it didn't, the kiss deepened.

I let loose every repressed urge, unresolved flirtation, and raging hormone, and the kiss went from tentative to frantic. Teeth colliding, tongues searching. His hands found their way back up inside my shirt, and a herd of butterflies raced from my stomach to my skull and back again.

My hands went up into his soft, thick hair, then down the length of his back. They couldn't move fast enough or take in enough of his body at once. I could smell each facet of his day right there in the kiss, his body odor only partly masked by pine-scented deodorant, fruity shampoo, and pizza for dinner. The words This is actually happening *ran through my head on repeat as the song came to a crescendo worthy of a movie scene.*

"What the fuck are you two doing?" Scarlett's words were like strong arms pulling Thomas and me apart. She stood there, squinting at us through bloodshot, puffy eyes, her long blond hair a tangled mess, one hand on her bony hip. I waited for her fury at us for breaking the rules, for tipping the balance of our newly formed friendship, but she just laughed. Then took a step toward me. "I want some love."

Before I knew what was happening, her lips were on mine. We'd kissed before, when we were younger, but it was practice for when we kissed boys, not practice for when we kissed with boys. She forced my lips open with her tongue and pushed in deeper. I should have pulled out of it, ended it there, but her lips were soft and familiar, and it had happened so fast, and I was so slow from the alcohol.

Just as quickly as she'd leaned into me, she pulled away and found Thomas, her lips on his, her hand on the back of his head keeping him there.

My first instinct was to push her away from him, to make it stop, but before I could protest, he'd pulled out of the kiss with her and turned back to me, and once again he was mine.

I should have stepped out of the circle in that moment, gotten mad at Scarlett for swooping in to claim what I wanted for myself, gotten mad at Thomas for going along with it, but I didn't. I rationalized that sharing him was better than not having him at all. That turning on Scarlett could mean I would lose both of them. And so just like that, the three of us slid from the friend zone into one of blurred lines and potential disaster.

OCTOBER 18, 2018

Scarlett's latest message makes me laugh out loud. She's the last person to be claiming the moral high road when it comes to the game, and yet she's warning us against the very thing she created.

Hannah! You can't be serious about resurrecting the game. Do you not remember what happened on our very last dare??? What are you guys thinking, you're both too old for this.

My reply is bold, more challenging than I've ever been with Scarlett, maybe because she's across the world, maybe because I finally have Thomas all to myself. Nevertheless, my hands shake as I type it, and the minute I hit send, I feel a shot of adrenaline course through me. The very same feelings I got growing up with her whenever I did the opposite of what she told me to.

Thanks for the warning but I think we'll be okay. Adulting gets boring, you need some adventure now and again, you of all people should know that. If you can't be happy for me then please don't message me again. H.

* * *

It's Thomas's turn for a dare. He completed mine with no problem at all—shoplift a pack of gum and a chocolate bar. It was lame, but I really couldn't think of anything.

I ignore the need to go grocery shopping and instead come to the tree to pick up the notebook. Inside I find that he's taped the photo of me at the top of the water tower beside the first dare and pasted in the chocolate bar and gum wrappers of the items he stole. He's keeping careful track of it all. I wonder if one day when we're old, we'll look back at this notebook and feel we were so young.

My new dare is to go to Miller's Pub and get a phone number from a stranger. It seems simple enough in theory, but the thought of flirting or being so bold as to ask for somebody's number is, in fact, terrifying.

Miller's Pub is downtown, in the financial district, a few steps below the street. Where people go on their lunch hours to have some drinks, maybe eat something, maybe meet someone who exists in the same corporate world they do.

The dare specifically says to be there at one PM. I go home and spend two hours slipping in and out of pieces of clothing. I never noticed how worn and drab and utilitarian my clothes have become. Everything is machine washable, cotton, and in shades that can be mixed and matched in the dark. When you don't have a daily destination for your clothing, all that matters is that it covers you.

In an act of desperation, I go into Evan's closet. As I flip through his ironed pants, his dress shirts, and blazers, a soft breeze of jealousy blows through me. He goes out into the world every day. The wardrobe is justified, important—just like he is. I used to know what that felt like.

I steal a white button-down shirt. It shifts the jealousy to satisfaction. Pairing it with my one pair of black dress pants, I tie it at the waist and blouse it. The outline of my black bra shows through the white fabric just enough to be sexy without being slutty. I pull my hair into a slicked-back ponytail just like I've seen on TV and put on some extra makeup. Not half bad, I muse, surveying the finished product in my mirror.

I decide to take the bus downtown so I don't have to worry about finding parking and can safely have a drink or two. As is my pattern, I have a slow leak, and the confidence I felt at home is practically gone by the time I step off the bus a block away from the bar. The walk there is too short. I pass my destination three times before finally forcing myself to go inside. I don't have to go through with the phone number part of the dare, I reason with myself. I'll just get a drink and go home.

Grasping the thick, brass door handle of the pub, I have a flurry of annoyance at Thomas. He's forced me from my residential street, my track pants, my Netflix-while-folding-laundry and shoved me into a strange world, all for the sake of a dare that I don't think I'll be able to accomplish.

I perch on a stool at the shiny wooden bar. "A Manhattan, please," I say to the black-shirted bartender. I've never had a Manhattan before, but it seems like a downtown-financial-district kind of cocktail.

"Rough day?" A man's voice reaches me from two stools over.

I glance in his direction. He's older than me. Made more attractive by the trim suit that he's wearing and the hair wax that keeps his thinning gray hair in a very deliberate tousle. Without the suit, he's probably paunchy in places, but he's not bad-looking overall.

The bartender sets a thick-walled glass down in front of me. The tan-and-brown ombre of the cocktail with its bright-red cherry on the bottom makes it almost too pretty to drink.

"May I?" the man asks, gesturing to the stool beside me.

I give an awkward combination of a nod and a shrug before taking a sip of my drink. The ice knocks against my lip while the liquid burns though my blood. I can't believe it's this easy. I haven't even said a word.

His name is Stu. I give my real name, then realize I probably should have given him a fake name. I'm definitely out of practice. We have some polite small talk, light stuff that means nothing at all. Still, he listens intently, laughs at the few jokes I make, which makes the interaction somewhat enjoyable. Those mornings on the couch listening to national radio have paid off. I'm up on current events, able to throw out pop culture references. I forgot I even had the ability to be charming.

He flirts unabashedly but with respect, which is what keeps me there. He compliments my eyes and steals glances at my lips. Then buys me another Manhattan.

I feel sexy. The kind of feeling that comes when somebody doesn't have a guarantee that you'll sleep with them but is willing to work for it. The very kind that evaporates with years of marriage, leaving you wondering where it went and how you can ever get it back. The kind you might have in a dream, leaving you still feeling like that person when you wake up, but fades away as you go about your day.

It's easy to believe he wants me because I'm pretending to be something else. I wonder if he'd feel the same way if he'd met me last Monday morning after I sent the kids to school. When the house was a disaster, and I was still wearing my pajamas because I hadn't gotten to the laundry and my hair was greasy because I hadn't had time to wash it.

"Hannah." I turn away from my suitor at the sound of my name.

My breath catches at the unexpected sight of Thomas. Dressed in a pale-gray suit with a black button-down shirt underneath and no tie, his tanned skin and dark hair standing out against the lightness of his suit, he's almost too handsome to bear. I look away, forcing the indifference I know I should feel.

He puts a hand on my shoulder, and I inadvertently lean in. "Sorry I'm late," he says, inserting himself into my charade. "Do you still have time for that meeting?"

His arrival has shoved aside all interest in the man at the bar but also ramped up the fun of the make-believe, so I decide to carry it on just a little bit. "My friend here." I gesture to the man beside me. "We're just in the middle of something. Weren't we, Stu?"

He knocks the bar with his knuckle and shoots Thomas a smug look. "We sure were." He thinks he's already won.

"Well, I apologize for interrupting, but we've got to figure out those numbers." Thomas thumbs in the direction of a booth off in the corner. "The ones for the Simpson account."

I sigh and put two fingers to my temple, as though Thomas is an annoyance I will just have to suffer. "Fine. Just give me a minute, please."

Thomas surveys the man beside me with narrowed eyes, then gives me a nod. "I'll wait over there."

The man's body language quickly changes. He leans away from me, looks like a deflated balloon. "Back to your shitty day, I guess," he says with a forced smile. What had he thought was going to happen? A blow job in the bathroom? The thought makes me feel powerful, but only because he isn't going to get it.

I hesitate. The dare still hasn't been completed. "I know it's a bit brash," I say, pretending to care. "But could I maybe get your number?"

I put a hand on his arm. "In case I need to share a drink with a stranger on another shitty day."

He reinflates and reaches for a coaster, then gestures to the bartender for a pen. "I have a condo not far from here. Call me anytime you're in the neighborhood." He hands me the slightly damp piece of cardboard, his name and number written among the deer antlers of the beer logo.

I hold the coaster up. "Will do." Walking away from him, I know he's watching me. It's the most attractive I've felt in years.

Sitting at a booth in the corner, Thomas pretends to tip his hat to me. "Well done. I wasn't sure you were up to the task."

I slide in next to him. "Neither was I."

"Feel good?"

"In a way. I mean, it's all just pretend." I lower my voice. "He thinks I'm a stressed-out, disgruntled career woman." Thomas chuckles softly. "If he found out I was actually a stressed-out, disgruntled stay-at-home mom, I don't think he would have given me his number."

Thomas widens his eyes at me in dismay. "You could have sat at the bar in your housecoat, and he would have given you his number."

My cheeks flush with the compliment. "Anyway. It was a fun dare. I have to admit it."

"I wanted to heat things up a bit. Give you a bit of sexy, albeit harmless, fun."

I sigh, because he's so right. An afternoon dressed up, enjoying a cocktail with a stranger, and the world seems fresh again. "I guess it's what this game's all about. Making life fun again."

He makes a fist and gently taps it on the top of my hand. "Exactly. We need this, Henny. I'm not liking this getting-old bullshit." He nods at something behind me. "There goes your conquest."

I glance across the room and give Stu a little wave. He returns it before slipping the leather strap of his messenger bag over his shoulder and leaving the pub.

With one finger I roll the edge of the coaster back and forth across the table. "Funny. I don't even feel the slightest bit guilty."

"About what?"

"Evan."

Thomas shrugs. "It's just a game, Henny."

"So then it doesn't count?"

He flicks the coaster out from under my finger. "Let's say it doesn't. It's us, after all. The same rules don't apply. They never have."

"Only the rules of the game."

Reaching into his suit jacket pocket, he pulls out a pen and picks up the coaster to write something on it. "This is the only number you need," he says, sliding it back to me. He's scratched out Stu's number and written his own.

I laugh and toss it back to him before taking the notebook out of my purse and putting it on the table. Thomas flips it open to the page where he's already written down the dare and tucks the coaster into the spine, then pushes it back to me. "Your turn. And make it risky this time. No more petty shoplifting."

I tuck the notebook back in my purse. "Risky? I'm not very good at risky. Remember?"

He slides closer to me, puts an arm around the back of the booth so that's it's just above me. "Risky is fun, though." He stares hard into my eyes. "Isn't it?"

I give a little nonchalant half nod. "I suppose so." He's so close I can see the open pores from his morning shave. There's a shift in our energy, and he made it happen. We've gone from light and friendly to intense and intimate. Exactly how it's always been between me and Thomas, but returning here after so many years, I don't know what to do with it.

"You know that man wanted to fuck you?" His words come out soft and quiet like the beginning of a bedtime story, but they shock me and set my nerves on edge. What Thomas was hoping for—I can tell from the look in his eyes.

"Maybe," I whisper back.

"He did." He leans in even closer, puts a hand on my thigh. "Trust me."

To escape the intensity of his stare, I look down at the table, brush at crumbs that aren't there. "Okay," I say under my breath.

He pulls away slightly but keeps his hand on my leg. "Are you blushing?"

"No." I put a hand to my face and feel its heat. "I don't know."

He squeezes my thigh. "Sorry. I didn't mean to make you uncomfortable."

I pick up my now-empty glass and roll the remaining ice cubes around, avoiding his eyes. "No, no. It's fine. I just don't really think of myself like that anymore."

"Hold that thought. I'm going to get you another drink." Before I can stop him, he pulls away from me and slides out of the booth, leaving me feeling as though I've been abruptly unplugged, the space around me suddenly cooler, the flush from my face draining away.

I don't want to hold that thought. The one of me no longer feeling like a sexual being. Of thinking more about my kids' needs than my own. Of the fact that Evan and I haven't had sex in over eight months. My total lack of motivation to do so. When you go long enough without doing it, the whole thing takes on so much baggage, becoming awkward and full of expectation, which makes you want to do it even less. How are you supposed to get over that? It's easier to just shut that part down in yourself and prioritize everything, everyone, else.

Thomas returns with another Manhattan for me and a glass of water for himself. He moves back in beside me but keeps a respectable distance this time. The last thing I need is more alcohol, but that doesn't stop me from drinking some. The warm liquid filters through me, maintaining the heavy buzz I have going from the first two.

"You're not having a drink?" I ask.

"I have a meeting in a bit, so better not." He takes a sip of water and pushes the glass away before turning to give me his full attention. "So, I don't mean to pry, and stop me if I am, but what do you mean you don't think of yourself that way? You're one of the most beautiful, most sexual women I've ever known, and if Evan isn't telling you that every day, keeping that part of you alive . . ." He throws up both hands with a huff of exasperation. "Well then, no offense to you or him, but I think he's failing miserably."

I can't help but laugh at Thomas's indignation on behalf of my lackluster sex life. I'm also not sure I've ever found him more attractive, his dark eyes stormy with frustration on my behalf, his lips pursed, waiting for my explanation. "You really don't understand marriage, do you?"

He shakes his head. "Not at all. Explain it to me."

"It's hard when you have kids. Things change. You don't see each other the same way or have time or privacy or the energy." I take another sip of my drink.

Thomas thinks about what I've said while rubbing his thumb through a trail of condensation on the table. "I see what you're saying." He looks up at me, right in the eyes. "I just can't imagine being married to you and not telling you every day how beautiful you are." He shrugs as though it's such a simple thing.

I don't know how to respond. It's a painful compliment, him proposing that such a thing is even possible and that I'm worthy of it. Like he's showing me the most beautiful, most fragrant flower that I'm not allowed to touch or smell for myself and letting me know that in other circumstances it could have been mine.

Thomas's phone buzzes on the table with a text. He huffs in annoyance. "Shit, I've gotta go," he says after reading it. "They've moved our meeting up." I nod, trying to hide my disappointment.

I expect him to stand up and rush out of there, so it catches me off guard when he slides in close again and cups my chin in his hands, staring right into my eyes with an intensity that only Thomas could have. He strokes my jawline with his thumb, sending a flush of heat down into my body, where it collects between my legs, turning to a steady throb.

"I'm not around to say it every day, so I'll say it now, as cheesy as it may sound." He's so close his words are breath against my skin. "You're beautiful, Hannah Warren, and always have been." He leans in, and for a brief second I think he's going to kiss me, but he lifts his head, landing a quick peck on my forehead before pulling away completely and sliding free from the booth.

My heart is pounding with the anticipation of what I thought was going to be an actual kiss between us, and disappointment that it wasn't is quickly flooding my veins. I resist the urge to grab for him, yank him back down to me. I want more. My encounter with the man at the bar, Thomas's closeness, and the complimentary words have combined to ignite a fierce fire of want in me, but the flames have only been fanned. There's been nothing to extinguish them.

He doesn't seem to notice the desperate way I look up at him as he slides his phone into his pocket and pulls the cuffs of his suit jacket over his watch. "See you soon?"

I nod, force my lips into a platonic smile. At the door he turns to give me a wave, and my whole body prickles with an agitated wanting like I've never felt before.

I drink the rest of my Manhattan and get up from the table. Asking the bartender to watch my things, I leave my coat and purse on the stool and go down a dark hallway to the restroom. It's empty. I lock myself in a stall painted all black. The lights are dim, and the small room is full of shadow.

Putting my forehead against the cool metal door of the stall, I run a hand down the front of my pants. I think of how easy it would be to lead someone down that hallway and into the empty bathroom. How easy it would be to do bad things in this dark cave, tucked away from my real life.

I put my hand down my pants and grip the top of the stall door. I think of Stu. I think of Thomas. One because he wanted me, the other because I want him. The heavy scents of bleach and beer fill my nose and throat as I gasp, open-mouthed, seizures of pleasure coursing through me as I finally come.

Letting myself out of the stall, I go to the sink. I can smell my own ripeness on my fingers. Rubbing my soapy hands together under the warm water, I look at myself in the mirror. It's me, but different. Hunger flushes my cheeks and plumps my lips. There are secrets growing behind my eyes. I know this girl, but I haven't seen her since college, since the game, since Thomas.

A woman comes into the bathroom, breaking through my reverie. I leave the restroom, put a tip down for the bartender, and collect my things. Leaving the shelter of the bar and stepping out into the fresh air and sunlight, I realize I'm a wee bit drunk. Three Manhattans in two hours will do that.

I get a window seat on the bus ride home and lean against the cool glass and close my eyes. As I move closer to home and reality, the guilt I thought I was immune to slowly begins to creep in. I haven't done anything wrong, officially, but I'm walking a fine line and I know it. It's mother guilt I feel more than wife guilt. Evan has chipped away at me for so long that I feel almost numb when it comes to him; I can barely muster any sense of loyalty. But how would I explain this kind of afternoon to my girls?

Before the guilt can build any further, do any real damage, I open my eyes, sit up straight, and give my head a shake. Rummaging around in my purse, I find a piece of gum and put it in my mouth. I take out my phone and open my Pinterest page to search for a nice dinner to make this evening. By the time the bus pulls up at my stop, I've planned the perfect meal with what little food we have in the house, sobered up, and slipped back into the worn skin of wife and mother. Stepping off the bus, I leave my guilt, along with my gum wrapper, on the seat and focus only on getting inside and getting dinner organized.

"Hannah!" As soon as I hear my name, I knows it's her.

I slowly turn. There's nowhere to hide. "Hi, Libby."

She looks me up and down with confusion. "You look nice. What's the occasion?"

I went to a bar to get a guy's number and then got myself off in the bathroom stall. The truth runs through my head, causing a blush of shame. "Just lunch with a friend."

She gives me a suspicious look, as though me having friends to lunch with seems like an unlikely excuse. "Sounds lovely. Anyway, the reason I'm bothering you again is that the man I was telling you about, who's been lurking around the neighborhood at night?" I nod to let her know I remember who she's talking about. "Well, he was spotted just last night in the Sinclairs' backyard."

"That's right across the street from us," I say with sincere concern. "Did he do anything, try to break in?"

Libby shakes her head, causing her short black bob to swing. "No, but Mr. Sinclair did call the police, but by the time they got here the person was gone. The police think he may be homeless and looking for places to sleep at night, so be sure to keep your garage locked."

"Yes, of course. Thank you for letting me know," I say, once again picturing the figure I thought I saw in my own backyard.

She gives me another suspicious look, probably for being so agreeable. "I'm not sure I buy the homeless theory, though. It feels more sinister to me." She shivers dramatically for effect. "And Halloween is just under two weeks away, so unless he's caught before then, we're going to organize a community trick or treat event, everyone out at the same time, kids and parents moving in one big group with a curfew, that kind of thing. I'll get it all organized and let you all know the details when I have them."

A community-wide Halloween sounds horrific to me, but I nod and smile. "Thanks, Libby. I appreciate your efforts." I wish Evan were here to see how neighborly I'm being.

She gives me a humble smile. "We all just want to keep our kids safe. Right?" Before I can answer, she turns to go. "You enjoy the rest of the day," she calls out as she walks away, her tight runner's ass barely moving in her black leggings. She's apparently a real estate agent, but I've never seen her do anything other than flit around the neighborhood, gossiping and telling people what to do. I just hope she's been too busy with the lurker to remember my comings and goings.

THEN

There were some rules. Or at least the guise of rules; who could actually put boundaries on what we'd created? No intercourse, no fooling around without all three of us present. We were free to be with people outside the group, but none of us ever were. We only wanted each other, the Daring Game, and our nights twisted together in Thomas's bed, one body of three.

We went to parties only for the free booze and to get dares done. Once we were sufficiently intoxicated and had stolen fraternity mascots and delivered them to competing fraternities, filched cell phones and sent rogue texts, or ignited drunken brawls, we left and went back to Thomas's.

Our favorite part of the night was listening to records, going over each detail of the dare we'd just executed while we finished whatever alcohol we'd been able to pilfer from the party or smoked whatever drugs we'd been able to find in random dresser drawers. We were like pariahs among our own kind—college students. We looked like them and for the most part acted like them, but only to get what we wanted. For the first time in my life, not fitting in with the masses felt like something I'd chosen. I felt superior to everyone who wasn't having the kind of fun that Scarlett, Thomas, and I were having.

By early morning, drunk or high or both, we always ended up in Thomas's bed, stripped down to our underwear, never fully nude—Scarlett's rule. We kissed, rubbed up against each other, licked, moved our hands over every bit of exposed skin until somewhat satiated. Like innocent teens in high school, we kept it on the outside. Scarlett said that the rules kept things from getting too out of hand. I didn't agree—the rules made us creative, perverted, and me, hungry for more.

*   *   *

Almost overnight, I went from a mostly sober, quiet, school-focused over-achiever who preferred high ponytails and baggy sweatshirts to some-thing entirely different. I drank too much, did drugs too often, gave more attention to coming up with dares than my schoolwork, and didn't care that my grades showed it.

I was slowly turning into the devil I'd been the night Thomas met me. I started wearing bright-red lipstick and going to the thrift shop to buy my clothes, trading in my flared yoga pants and zip-up hoodies for band T-shirts, ripped jeans with fishnets underneath, Doc Martens, and anti-capitalism buttons on my backpack. I was becoming the female version of Thomas, dissolving into him, leaving almost nothing of myself. I'd had crushes on boys before, had one-night stands with sloppy sex, boyfriends who lasted a few weeks, but I'd never felt the way I did about Thomas. Scarlett called it an obsession, I called it love.

My father made comments now and again, about my grades, about my appearance, about staying away for nights at a time, but I didn't have a mother, so as long as I still passed my classes, covered up the majority of my body, and eventually came home, he didn't push things with me.

Scarlett made her own fair share of comments about my changes, but they bounced right off me, making no impression at all, for the first time ever. And it was because, for the first time ever, I had a secret from Scarlett.

Thomas and I were breaking the rules of the threesome every chance we could. We sat together in our shared art history class, in the dark, my binder held up like a shield as his hand found its way under the waist-band of my pants and into my underwear. I kept my gaze steady on the Matisses and Cézannes that flashed across as the screen as his fingers found their way inside me. Each time I came, it was only a controlled body shudder and a quick closing of my eyes that would have given me

70

away, while on the inside a vibrant explosion happened, bright enough to match the postimpressionists' brushstrokes that blurred together in front of me.

*   *   *

One night after a keg party, after we'd had our customary threesome and fallen asleep, I woke up to Thomas pushed up against me, his hard-on vibrating against my back. I rolled over to face him. He smiled playfully and put a finger to his lips. Scarlett snored gently on the far side of the bed, giving me a false sense of security. I slowly slid down under the covers.

It could have been Thomas's soft moaning, the shuddering of his body when he finally came, or the rhythmic bobbing of my head under the covers. When I surfaced, Thomas's eyes were closed as he absorbed the pleasure of his first blow job from me. Scarlett's eyes were wide open, staring into mine, the cold jealousy turning them to cut stones of green.

This time she didn't force herself between us, just rolled over so that her back was to us and didn't say a word, which scared me much more than if she had.

OCTOBER 31, 2018

A pirate, a pizza slice, and a cat hold open their treat bags for candy; I give them each a handful. I'm in a generous mood. The night's warm and windy. Kids are having a hard time holding on to all the bits of their costumes.

I sit down on the front step of the porch with the bowl of candy and watch parents and trick-or-treaters pass under the streetlight in front of the house. The sweet scent of burning pumpkin wafts over, and I envision the black spot that's forming on the underside of the lid of our jack-o'-lantern. I consider shifting it, but instead unwrap another bite-sized chocolate bar and shove the whole thing in my mouth.

Evan has taken the girls trick-or-treating in the neighborhood group that Libby organized and left me to hand out candy. Following the trick-or-treating there's a block party at the Duncans', also organized by Libby.

I stare down at the message on my phone from Scarlett for the tenth time. She's clever, sending me a warning that we were given back in college from one of the victims of our dares. One we should have listened to but didn't. *It's a dangerous game you're all playing. People will get hurt, it's inevitable. I just hope it's not something that ruins lives, but I have a feeling it will be.* I leave it unanswered and close the app, doing my best to ignore the sense of foreboding it's planted in the pit of my stomach. Leave it to Scarlett to get under my skin.

Gracie comes running up the driveway, tugging at the crotch of her two-sizes-too-small Supergirl costume from last year, worn only because by the time I took her to the store for a new one, they only had adult costumes left that were way too big for her. There were tears, yelling, and a truck ton of guilt on my part, but she eventually agreed to just go as Supergirl again, despite the growth spurt she'd had over the summer and the fact that she called it a costume for little kids.

"Mom, look how much candy I got." She holds up her bulging pillowcase.

"Good job, Gracie!" Inside I'm cringing at the amount of sugar intake, but on the outside I'm very good at playing excited.

Rose saunters up behind her wearing a very lame, thrown-together cat burglar costume, created only for the sake of collecting candy. I told her last night that she was too old to be trick-or-treating, which of course turned into an epic battle, which she, of course, ended up winning.

Evan's right behind her walking with Libby, who's wearing a witch hat and black cape and carrying a broom and a mini plastic cauldron, and her eight-year-old twin girls, one in an Alice in Wonderland costume, the other as the Cheshire Cat. Libby's husband Rob hangs back, standing at the end of the driveway, looking at his phone. I'm surprised Libby didn't force him to dress up like the Mad Hatter.

"Great costumes, ladies," I say, dropping candy into the twins' open treat bags.

"I was up well into the night putting the finishing touches on them," Libby brags.

"You made them?" I ask, legitimately impressed.

"I did. I make their costumes every year. I just can't stand those tacky store-bought ones." Gracie gives the crotch of her ill-fitting, store-bought costume a self-conscious tug, and the comment feels like a slight directed right at me.

"Well, not everyone has the time, or the interest for that matter, to make their kids' costumes by hand, but kudos to you." I drop a mini Kit Kat bar into her cauldron, and she startles at the thud of it hitting the bottom.

"Hannah's far too busy reading to put much effort in on the costume front, or the cleaning-the-house front or gardening," Evan chimes in, his words like a kick to the stomach.

Libby laughs awkwardly. "Well, we all have our priorities, don't we? I personally hate doing laundry." I can't imagine the laundry in Libby's house piling up, but I do appreciate her attempt at lessening Evan's harsh remarks.

"Are we going to the Duncans' now or not?" Rose asks.

Evan claps his hands. "We sure are. Just put your candy inside and we'll go. Hannah, are you joining us?"

For a split second I pretend to consider it before saying, "No, I think I'll finish handing out candy and then go do some reading."

Libby gives another awkward laugh at my pointed words. "Well, enjoy your night, then, Hannah, and happy Halloween." She herds her girls away from the porch and starts toward the Duncans'. Gracie and Rose hand me their pillowcases of candy and take off.

"We won't be late," Evan says. "Probably ten-ish." No apology for his earlier insult.

"Take as long as you'd like," I reply. He gives a cross between a huff and a chuckle before turning to go.

* * *

I take the pillowcases into the kitchen and plop them down on the counter. In the dark and quiet of the house, the children out on the street sound like a distant memory. Leaves tap like fingers on the window to get in as the wind picks them up and throws them against the glass. At any moment a serial killer in a hockey mask will appear at the back door. The boring, antisocial mother will be the first to go.

The ding of my phone rings out in the silent kitchen and I jump, then put a hand to my chest and laugh at my own idiocy.

Good dare! Are you coming? The message is from Thomas, still disguised as Lucy. Earlier today I left a dare for him in the Daring Tree. I wasn't sure I'd be able to meet him, though, so I told him to take photos as evidence.

I chew a hangnail until it grows into a pinprick of blood, debating what to do while staring out the kitchen window. The wind's picked up, making the night a proper, blustery Halloween. I can still hear the faint calls of people outside, and I suddenly want to be out there with them. Moving through the streets, out to have my own mischief.

Be there in fifteen, I text back—a surge of excitement easily banishing the effects of Scarlett's message and Evan's rude remarks.

I run upstairs and throw on some black leggings and a black sweatshirt.

While digging through the hall closet for my black windbreaker, a text from Evan comes through—a photo of Gracie bobbing for apples. It fills me with sticky guilt for not being there to see it in person, but I use blame to push the guilt away. If he hadn't made that comment about me only having time to read, I probably would have gone to the party. Blame comes in handy that way.

*   *   *

Weaving in and out of costumed children and their parents who follow close behind, I turn a blind eye to a group of teenagers using a pumpkin like a soccer ball in the middle of the road. The energy of the night heightens my anticipation, and nervous adrenaline buzzes through me. I've forgotten what it's like to be out on Halloween moving through the city streets, trying not to be seen.

The square is well lit and more crowded than I thought it would be, mostly with adults and older kids milling around. Am I crazy to go into a cemetery on Halloween night by myself? My answer comes in a gust of unseasonably warm wind that moves trash across the cobblestones, whips my hair across my face, and carries the scent of rain.

I cross my fingers that Thomas is already there and force myself away from the light of the square and into the black of the cemetery. The flashlight on my phone is a meager sliver cutting through the darkness, illuminating the path ahead of me but nothing on either side—not comforting at all.

"Boo!" Thomas steps out from behind the tree, sending me reeling backward. He's dressed all in black and already holds a carton of eggs in one hand—otherwise I would have shoved him, hard.

"Not funny, Thomas," I yell.

"Oh, come on, Henny, it's Halloween."

"I'm quite aware of that. Why do you think I gave you the dare to egg houses?"

"And a perfect dare it is. Let's go cause Halloween mayhem."

"Fine but if I get caught and charged, you're paying the fine."

He huffs with indignation. "As if we're going to get caught."

"And I only have an hour."

He loops an arm through mine and starts walking. "We can do a lot of damage in an hour."

"That's what I'm afraid of."

* * *

Thomas insists on going to the most affluent neighborhood in the city, inhabited by old Victorian mansions with manicured lawns and pools in the backyard. Thomas's rationale is that they can afford to pay someone to clean the egg off, so we needn't feel as guilty.

It isn't the first time we've egged this neighborhood. Another Halloween, a lifetime away, Thomas dared Scarlett to do the same. Back then his motivation was a display of anti-wealth sentiment, not just the fun of it. Scarlett egged houses, and then Thomas littered the lawns with flyers proclaiming the social benefits of communism while I watched from the bushes.

At thirty-six, standing in the cover of a tall, hundred-year-old boxwood hedge, things feel very different—I admire the curtains hanging in the window just seconds before Thomas launches the first egg at it.

He does two more in quick succession, surprising me with the accuracy of his aim. The tight smack it makes against the window fills me with a strange kind of satisfaction.

We linger only seconds to watch the yolk paint a sticky yellow trail down the paneled bay window before we set off running. I blindly follow Thomas as he weaves across lawns and around thick-trunked old maples.

I haven't run like this in years. My neglected muscles tighten in resistance, the loose flesh around them shaking with each pounding step until a hot itch burns along my skin. My lungs ache as I gulp the cool October night air, but it doesn't slow me down.

Only once we're blocks away from our first victim do we stop and crouch down behind a low stone wall. A painful stitch is stuck in my side like a thorn, and my left hip throbs with a foreign ache.

"My god. I'm too old for this," I whisper between my heavy breaths.

Thomas laughs and peers over the stone wall to survey our next target. "We'll have to get a bit closer this time. We won't be able to hit anything from here." He takes a few eggs from the carton before handing it to me and then steps out of the cover of the stone wall.

"Thomas, wait," I hiss at him, but he keeps walking, right out onto the lawn. I have no choice but to follow.

Lights are on upstairs, but the downstairs of the house is in total darkness. The grand entrance is just begging to be egged. Two planters flank the large front door, both overflowing with seasonal greenery, and a perfectly round pumpkin nestles in the middle of it all. I want to mar its superficial perfection. Make some mess so it looks a bit more like my life.

I glance around to make sure nobody's watching and then take two eggs from the carton and throw them as hard as I can at the entrance. They land like a loud knock on the front door, and the sound of a dog barking erupts from within.

Thomas looks back at me in surprise, then wastes no time in rocketing his own eggs at the front window just as a light comes on downstairs. The sound of a large lock being slid back reaches us out on the lawn, and suddenly there's a figure emerging from the front door.

Thomas grabs my hand. I drop the egg carton and let him pull me into a run across the damp, cushy grass.

"I called the police, you little assholes," the figure at the door bellows.

We jump over the low stone wall and run right out into the street for a full block. Then Thomas veers across a few lawns and leads us down the side of a house and into somebody's backyard. Only then does he slow down. We cut through a couple of backyards and then find a driveway that leads back to the sidewalk.

Just as we step out into the light of the streetlamps, a police car turns onto the block and rolls past us slowly, the officer in the car giving us a careful once-over. Thomas nods and once again takes my hand, as though we're just a law-abiding married couple out for a Halloween walk.

We don't say a word to each other and continue holding hands until the streets have narrowed and the houses have shrunk and we're back in middle-class territory.

"Can you believe how fast the police came?" Thomas is the first to speak.

"They must have been just hanging out there. On the ready to protect the rich people." I gesture to the houses around us. "I bet we could egg twice as many houses in this neighborhood before the police showed up."

"We can go get more eggs if you'd like?"

"Absolutely not! I'm not risking arrest again. No matter how much fun it was. Besides, I have to get home."

"But it's still so early," he whines.

"Thomas!"

"Fine." He points at a small park. "We'll cut through there. It's faster."

We leave the sidewalk to walk along a dimly lit path. The park's empty. A tired-looking playground sits at one end and has been expertly wrapped in toilet paper.

I point it out. "The city delinquents have been busy tonight."

"Us included," Thomas laughs.

Wind blasts through the park. The rusty swings move back and forth with its force, making a high-pitched, eerie squeak. The trees above us crack and groan, their branches bending low and snapping back like disapproving fists.

"It's creepy here," I say with an actual shiver. Thomas drapes his arm across my shoulders. "Don't worry. I'll protect you." His arm feels heavy, consequential, like a loaded gun.

I should slide free, but instead I move my body just a little closer. "I don't need your protection."

Two older kids on bikes suddenly appear on the path, one in a rabid bunny mask, the other a killer clown. Thomas pulls me in closer, moving us both out of their way. They roll slowly by, looking us up and down, one of them whistling a sinister tune.

"Are you sure you don't need my protection?" he asks with a laugh as soon as they're gone. "They look like they're out for more than just egg throwing to me." Another blast of wind sweeps through the park, kicking up the leaves around us and setting the swings alive again.

"Things are getting creepy," I say with an exaggerated shiver.

Thomas pulls me in for a full hug. "Don't be such a Henny Penny. It's just Halloween."

I'm caught off guard by the sudden closeness, the warmth of his body, the firm wall of his chest against me, his smell, the tight wrap of his arms. He rubs my back and then releases me, but I feel desperate for more. Without thinking I take hold of the collar of his jacket and pull him into me, lift onto the balls of my feet and bring my lips to his. I feel him stiffen at first, as though he's about to pull away, but I push in deeper and he stays there, his body softening into mine. There's so much flesh to the kiss, his full lips, his tongue. Every kiss we've ever had comes rushing back.

Like an alarm going off, my phone rings out with a text. I step out of the kiss as though we've been caught in the act.

"I'm sorry. I shouldn't have done that." I'm flooded with embarrassment and shame. My phone buzzes again. I take it out to find a recently delivered photo of Gracie blindfolded, whacking a pumpkin piñata. The sight of her magnifies the ugliness of what I've just done. Wind as angry as a scorned lover rushes through the space between us. Some drops of rain follow close behind, large ones, heavy with wet and the promise that more will surely follow.

"I have to go," I say, glancing around for the best escape route.

"Henny, please don't feel bad. I—"

Holding up a hand, I stop him from continuing. I can't take the pity he must have for me—an unhappy stay-at-home mom throwing herself at her college obsession. "Can we just forget about it, please? It was a lapse in judgment. It won't happen again."

He shoves a hand through his hair and frowns deeply. Looks as though he's about to say something, but before he can, I start to walk backward away from him.

"I have to go. Good job on the dare." I fake a smile and give him a thumbs-up before turning away and starting a slow jog out of the park. I hear him call out to me, but I don't turn back.

Halfway home, the real rain starts—pounding down on the pavement and jumping back up to splash across my pant legs. In my neighborhood I pass the Duncans' house and see people in the front window watching the torrential rain come down. Pulling the hood of my windbreaker in tighter, I look away, unsure if any of my family members are watching. Some people are leaving the party, running out into the rain, laughing and screaming. I quicken my pace. Shame rises again, a brick of it this time that sits uneasily in the pit of my stomach. There are so many kinds of shame— some tickle the back of your throat and are easily swallowed away; others get inside you and are hard to dislodge.

In the house I pull off my sopping coat and shove it to the back of the closet along with my waterlogged sneakers. Wet drips from my hair down into the back of my sweater, so I head straight upstairs to run a bath. It will be a good explanation for my wet hair.

Peeling off my wet clothes, I slip into the warm bath, sinking down under the water to complete my disguise, then popping back up to rest my head against the tub. The tops of my breasts float like lush hills above the soapy water. My mind wanders right back to the kiss. I feel foolish and guilty for having done it, but remembering the sensations causes a throb low in my groin. A whisper of butterflies in my stomach. The firmness of Thomas's lips, the warmth of his breath, the fleshiness of his tongue . . .

A knock at the door shocks me out of my thoughts. "Mom?" Gracie's voice breaks into the bathroom, and every other sensation is replaced with a flood of mom guilt.

"I'm here, baby. Just one second." I step out of the bath and slip on my robe, shoving my wet clothes deep into the laundry hamper. Unlocking the door, I'm confronted by a very tired Supergirl.

I guide her toward her room. "Let's get you out of that costume." My illicit thoughts of Thomas drain away with the bathwater.

I help Gracie out of her too-tight costume, listening to every detail of the party. How it took twenty-six hits before the piñata broke, and how a girl shoved Gracie over in the rush to get the fallen candy, and how the boy with the peanut allergy had to give away most of his candy, and about the new dog that the Duncans just got, a French bulldog who slobbered all over Gracie's leg.

While I'm brushing the tangles from her hair, Gracie asks if I'll stay with her until she falls asleep. Rose told her that ghosts come out more on Halloween night than any other night, and she also overheard Libby talking to Evan about the man who's been seen lurking around the neighborhood. I tell her I'm happy to lie with her but Rose doesn't know what she's talking about and the police will take care of the lurker, so not to worry.

Spooning her thin body, stroking the soft skin of her arm to help her fall asleep, I wonder if there's something seriously wrong with me. Something that makes me able to sneak out into the night to play games and kiss other men, only to come home as though nothing has happened and do the mom things. Can good people do bad things and still be good people? Or more specifically, can a woman do bad things and still be a good mother? Does my desire for Thomas mean I love my children any less? Would a man contemplate the same things in the same situation?

The questions keep coming, suspended in my mind like hooded figures hanging from the gallows.

THEN

Scarlett didn't say anything about what she saw happen between me and Thomas that night we were all in bed together. I questioned her in a roundabout way, concluding that she must have been asleep the whole time, that she'd opened her eyes only momentarily but not really registered what she'd seen. I should have known better.

Scarlett never handed out her punishments right away after failing a dare. She waited, made you sweat, worked you up into a frenzy until you were scared that something was lurking around every corner. I think she enjoyed the punishments even more than the dares.

It was no different when I failed her dare to climb the Westville water tower—coincidentally only a few days after giving Thomas a blow job. It was a dare she knew I'd fail; she was the only one who knew how afraid of heights I was. She pocketed the punishment, waiting until the perfect opportunity, striking weeks after the failed dare so that I'd started to relax.

There was a party, a big one; flyers had been passed out. There was going to be a DJ. Scarlett called us to the Daring Tree and told us to come party ready. I got there first, and she was leaning against the tree, an unnerving smirk on her face as she watched me approach.

"What the hell is up with you?" I asked, trying to play it cool, even though the crackle of energy around her was unsettling.

She beckoned me closer and then opened her hand. Sitting in her palm was a plastic baggie containing three tiny pills, all bright yellow.

"What are those?" I asked, a knot of trepidation already forming in my stomach.

"E," she whispered.

"Ecstasy?"

"Yes, dummy, ecstasy. We're going to take it tonight. Thomas already agreed." She closed her hand over the pills.

"You talked to Thomas about it?"

"Yeah, he came with me to buy it. I didn't want to go alone."

"Why didn't you ask me?" My voice whined slightly with jealousy, and I hated myself for it. Being left out of anything with those two, even buying drugs, stung.

"I just thought taking a guy with me would be safest. No big deal, Henny."

"What does it do exactly?" I asked.

"Gets you high," Scarlett shot back with a condescending laugh.

"What kind of high?" I was used to mushrooms and weed, natural stuff. The chemicals scared me.

"Apparently a really good one. Like you love everybody around you and just want to dance and hug and have a good time. The guy who sold it to me said it was the best drug he's ever done."

"Is this a dare?" I asked, because at that point, it felt like everything was with Scarlett.

She threw her head back and laughed. "No, Henny!" she practically screamed. "Not everything has to do with the game." She threw her arms out to the sides. "It's for fun."

Thomas sauntered up behind me. "What's for fun?" Scarlett opened her palm to expose the little baggie, and he nodded.

"You're good with this?" I asked, half hoping he'd say he wasn't and we could just stick to the usual stuff.

He shrugged. "Sure. I've heard good things about it. Apparently, you get pretty off your face."

Scarlett didn't need any more encouragement. She dropped a pill into Thomas's palm and then pulled a bottle of water from her bag and handed it to him. He swallowed it down without a second thought. That was Thomas for you, always ready and willing to alter his state of consciousness.

"Hold out your hand," she directed me.

"I don't know about this," I waffled.

"Come on, Henny," Thomas encouraged. "We'll have fun together, I promise."

That's all it took. I held out my hand, and Scarlett smiled as wide as a Cheshire cat and dropped a pill in my palm, then handed me the bottle of water. As soon as it went down my throat, a surge of panic rose in me. There was no going back.

Scarlett put the lid on the water bottle and stashed the small plastic baggie with the remaining pill back in her bag.

"Aren't you going to take it?" I asked.

"Later," she answered. "You heard Thomas. It gets you off your face. I'll make sure you guys are okay first, and then I'll take mine. That way we won't all be tripping hard at the same time, and I can take care of you and then you can take care of me." She put a hand on my shoulder. "Good?"

I nodded but wasn't sure I bought it. Scarlett was not the mother-hen type, which meant she was up to something.

By the time we got to the party, I could feel the drugs gaining traction and my suspicion of Scarlett was long forgotten. I felt like I had warm honey pulsing through my veins, and there was a gentle electrical current running along the outside of my skin. The world became crisp and clear, brighter and softer at the same time. I'd never felt anything like it.

I took off my black jean jacket so that I had just a tank top on, desperately wanting to feel the air on my bare arms. Scarlett reached out and brushed my shoulder, and it felt as though her fingertips were feathers, spreading warmth and pleasure all across my skin.

"Do that again," I said.

She laughed. "I think somebody's high."

I glanced over at Thomas, and his beautiful full lips slowly spread into a smile, the pupils of his dark eyes as wide as saucers. He reached out and took my hand, sending a tidal wave of desire through me.

"I want to dance." The words came out as soon as I heard the pulsing of music from somewhere deep in the large house. We followed it down into a basement that had been transformed into a mini rave, complete with a DJ in the corner and a blanket of darkness. There was just one revolving light that swung back and forth across the room, illuminating the shadows for only a split second before moving on.

"Let's dance," I said, leaning into Scarlett.

She nodded back toward the stairs. "Thomas and I will just go get drinks, and I'm going to take my pill. Find us a spot and we'll be right back."

If I hadn't been so high, the idea of being on a dance floor by myself would have been horrifying, but I had taken a drug that made everyone my friend and banished all self-consciousness.

I turned away from Scarlett and Thomas and stepped into the throng of people dancing. They welcomed me, parting so that I could fit, smiling back at me with equally enlarged pupils and hearts. The music charged inside me and took control, the repetitive thump of it burying deep down into my chest. I let it move me, swaying gently when it was quiet, getting down low as it began to build, jumping up when it reached a peak that lifted me off the ground.

* * *

It was thirst that finally drove me from the basement. I'd lost all track of time, not sure how long I'd been down there or how long Scarlett and Thomas had been gone. The high had calmed into an enjoyable low hum, but my throat was dry. I felt as though I'd been dancing in a desert without water.

Climbing the stairs out of the darkness, I kept an eye out for my friends. In the kitchen I filled a red Solo cup full of tap water and drank it down, then filled it up again.

"Hey, Hannah." A girl from Scarlett's dorm suddenly appeared at my side. I smiled and nodded.

She gave me a curious look. "My god, what did you take?" she asked with a laugh, suddenly making me self-conscious. I wanted to race back down to the darkness of the basement where people understood me, but first I needed to find Thomas and Scarlett.

"Have you seen Scarlett anywhere?" I asked.

"I think I saw her heading upstairs a while ago," she answered. I thanked her and slid away.

The house became cramped upstairs, just a long dark hallway with doors off it. I peeked into the rooms that were open and found small groups of people lying across beds and on the floor talking, but no Thomas or Scarlett. When I ran out of open-door options, I debated going back down to the basement to wait for them there, but something pushed me on—an unsettling curiosity that told me to open doors.

I saw the white blond of her hair first and knew it was her, then the bare skin of her back. She stopped rocking back and forth to turn and look right at me. There was no shock on her face; it was as though she'd been expecting me. I stepped farther into the room. I needed to see who was beneath her.

Thomas's head lifted from the pillow; he looked right at me as well. There was a flash of confusion on his face, as though he wasn't sure who he was looking at. "Hannah?" he said. Then he looked up at Scarlett and appeared even more confused.

I slowly backed out of the room. The liquid honey had turned to ice-cold mercury, and I was certain I was going to throw up. I ran to the end of the hallway, where I could see a toilet through the crack of a door, and fell to my knees just in time for a bright-yellow stream of vomit to escape me.

Scarlett found me in the bathroom. She closed herself in with me, and I could smell Thomas on her. I dry-heaved into the toilet, but nothing more came out.

"My god, Henny, are you having a bad trip?" she asked, with forced-sounding concern.

"What about the rules?" I managed to get out, my voice husky from dehydration.

She shook her long blond hair off her shoulders and then lasered me into focus with her bright-green eyes. "We're really high." She shrugged. "I guess we just got carried away. You know how that can happen, don't you, Henny?"

I knew in that moment that she'd been awake the night I'd slipped under the covers at Thomas's apartment. A sharp chemical taste bit at the back of my throat, threatening to make me sick again, but I swallowed it down and took a deep breath to calm myself. Hot tears burned my eyes, so I looked away and reached for her bag. "Do you have any more water, or some gum?"

"I think so," she answered, suddenly looking bored. I'd not given her the dramatic response she'd been hoping for, no sobbing or yelling. It was right there, sitting under the surface, but I kept it at bay. I wanted to beg her to just let me have him to myself, but I knew that would never happen and it would be like rolling over to expose my soft underbelly, making it easier for her to rip into it. If I had Thomas, it meant she had neither of us. She'd destroy all three friendships before she'd let that happen.

She stood up to look in the mirror and smooth down her sex-tousled hair.

Rummaging around in the bag, my fingers brushed a small plastic baggie. I pulled it out and saw a single yellow pill still inside. I slid the baggie back in her purse, then shoved it away from me and got up off the ground, realizing in that moment the lengths that Scarlett would go.

I bent down over the tap and cupped water into my horrible-tasting mouth. I took my time drinking, wondering what to say to Scarlett.

"I'm going home," was all I could come up with.

"Are you mad at me?" Another attempt to get me to engage, open the wound so that she could push into it.

"No, just tired."

She let me leave the bathroom, which surprised me.

I passed Thomas sitting on the stairs, his head in his hands. He jumped up when he saw me, but I just kept walking.

"Henny, what happened?"

"You and Scarlett had sex."

He followed me right out of the house. "It was so messed up, Henny. She said you were going to be there; I was so high. I was so confused, and it felt so—"

I spun around and held a hand up. "I don't need to hear about it, Thomas. We broke the rules first. We should have known that Scarlett would find a way to punish us for it. Punish me." I added, knowing it wasn't really about Thomas at all.

"But Henny," he said, his eyes begging for forgiveness. "You know it's you I want, right?"

I shook my head. "It doesn't matter. She's the one who makes the rules. She always has."

NOVEMBER 9, 2018

I get out my funeral clothes—a knit black dress, black heels, and a wool coat that belonged to my mother. I put on mascara and eye shadow, which I never normally do on weekdays. It's all for Thomas's dare, which is to go to a hotel and charge drinks to someone else's room. The Somersby Hotel—the swankiest, most expensive place in the city. It's a classic Thomas dare: steal from the rich. He seems to have missed the irony that as an adult, he's become rich enough to afford drinks at the Somersby.

I don't bring that up. The dare gives me another excuse to get out of the house for the afternoon and see Thomas, who has insisted on coming to make sure I go through with it. I also haven't brought up the kiss that happened on Halloween, and fortunately neither has he. Thinking about it gives me a hot flush of embarrassment. My memory of it has morphed into a version where he stands there stiffly while desperate, lonely me throws herself at him. I just hope we can forget it ever happened, and I plan to be on my very best behavior. *Just friends*, I remind myself while getting ready.

* * *

Walking up the street from the bus stop, I catch sight of Thomas sitting in the window, scrolling through his phone. For a split second I slip myself into an alternate reality where he's my husband, waiting for me to return from some very different kind of morning than the one I've really had—sweeping up toast crumbs and plunging the upstairs toilet.

I spin through the revolving door and am ejected out into a lobby full of heavy chandeliers, peacock-blue velvet couches, and large potted palms. It heightens the fantasy in my head, and I glide across the marble floor.

The ability to *not be me* is starting to come very easily. Escape was what I'd been craving, and it's certainly what I'm getting. All in enough time to get home and welcome the girls after their day at school, no harm done, I keep telling myself.

He watches me walk toward him, and I resist the urge to adjust my coat or fix my hair.

"Well, don't you like nice," he says as he pulls out a chair for me.

"If we're going to keep this game going, I might need a new wardrobe." I slip out of my coat and relax back into the club chair.

He signals for the waiter. "Maybe after this we'll go buy you some clothes with somebody else's credit card."

"Shh," I hiss.

Thomas smiles up at the waiter. "I'll have your best bottle of champagne."

"It's only eleven thirty, Thomas," I interject.

"We'll have a side of orange juice with it, then," he's quick to add.

"And will you be charging this to your room, sir?"

"Yes, please. Room 1202." The waiter simply nods and then hurries away from the table.

"I thought this was my dare." I glare at him, pretending to be mad but actually quite grateful that he did the lying and not me.

He shrugs in his typical Thomas way. "Playing along with the lie is just as important a part of the dare as the lie itself."

I flinch at the dishonesty of it all but quickly convince myself that anybody staying here can afford a couple of extra drinks on their tab. They probably won't even notice. "So, you're playing hooky from work?" I ask, to get my mind off the deception.

"I told them I was taking potential clients out for lunch. I've done well for the company, so they give me quite a lot of freedom." The statement stirs something in me. I never thought power and money would be sexy to me, but on Thomas it is.

"Did you ever think you'd end up in commercial real estate?"

"Did you ever think you'd be a stay-at-home mom?"

I know the question is just him trying to make a point, but it stings nonetheless. Of course I didn't. But then again, I didn't ever think I'd be any one thing. I just let life happen to me and thought that was how it had to be. Then woke up one day and honestly couldn't remember how I'd gotten there.

The waiter arrives with the champagne and a small carafe of freshly squeezed orange juice. He puts small white cocktail napkins down on the table before placing tall clear champagne flutes on them. "Something specific you're celebrating, Mr. and Mrs. Beverley?" he asks while pouring the sparkling golden liquid into my glass. I raise a finger to correct him but then remember we're under aliases. We are the people staying in room 1202.

Thomas slaps the arm of his chair in exuberance. "We sure are. Growing old. Unrealized dreams and ending up where you never meant to."

The waiter works hard to conceal his confusion before bowing politely and walking away from the table.

"So much for being inconspicuous," I say, before taking a sip of my very expensive and delicious champagne, ignoring the juice completely.

The sadness in his expression deepens. "Speaking of unrealized dreams. I often wonder what would have happened if that final dare hadn't gone so wrong, if I hadn't had to leave school like that." He takes a sip and then studies the fast-moving bubbles in the glass before looking up at me. "Hell, we might have gotten married or something crazy like that."

His words are like a kick in the stomach. I want to laugh and cry at the same time. The heavy weight of lost opportunities settling on my shoulders makes me question my entire world.

He lifts his glass, oblivious to the storm he's caused in me. "Here's to a day of being somebody else. The happily married Mr. Beverley and his beautiful, clever, and daring wife, Mrs. Beverley."

The laugh that comes out of me is a cross between a sob and a chuckle.

As we sip champagne, we create details of the imagined life of Mr. and Mrs. Beverley. It's much safer than talking about real missed

opportunities and regret. I go on safaris in Africa and help build librar-
ies in Nepal. He travels around removing land mines from postwar
countries and proposed to me at the top of the Eiffel Tower.

When the waiter comes back around, Thomas flicks his hand at the
ice bucket. "I'd like another bottle of champagne sent up to our room,
please." I give him a look, but he ignores me.

"What are you doing?" I lean forward to whisper as soon as the
waiter has left.

"Part two of the dare." He stands up from the table, buttons his
dark-gray blazer, and holds his hand out to me. "Come on."

Gathering up my coat and purse, I foolishly reach up to take his
hand. He leads me over to the front desk, but all I can concentrate on is
the feel of his skin against mine. It moves blood through my body so
fast my heartbeat thumps like a heavy rock in my chest.

Thomas leans up against the counter and pulls me in close, letting my
hand go and sliding his arm around my waist. Our closeness, the champagne, the make-believe—it all culminates in a heady rush of lust. So heady
that I barely register what he's saying to the woman behind the front desk.

"Not to worry, sir; we have customers leave their keys in the room all
the time." She slides a plastic room key toward him, and he takes it with
his free hand, holding tightly to me as though I might drift away. Does
he not know that his body works like a magnet to mine and always has?

"Thanks so much." With key in hand, arm still wrapped around
me, he moves me across the lobby, my shoes clicking loudly on the shiny
floor, and onto a waiting elevator.

"What the hell are we doing?" We're close enough for me to whisper
into his ear.

He turns his head so that our faces are only inches apart. "Just wait
and see, Mrs. Beverley." His dark eyes shine, and I know I'm in trouble. I
know I should step away from him and get ready to hit the button to go
back to the lobby. I know I should end the make-believe before it goes
too far and we get caught and have to explain our silly game to the police
or, worse, to Evan. But I don't. Instead, I absorb the sexual tension that
vibrates between us, that I know I'm not imagining. Soak in his attention
and closeness. Let the excitement of the dare keep reality at bay.

The elevator doors open to the twelfth floor. Thomas listens at the door of room 1202 before sliding the key card into the lock.

Inside the room, things become more real to me. There's a large suitcase in the corner, a coat draped over a chair. The cleaners must have already come, because the beds are made and look as though they haven't been slept in in.

Seeing the evidence of the real people we're impersonating wakes me up to how wrong the dare really is. "Thomas. This is crazy. We should go."

"It's Mr. Beverley, and I'm not going anywhere."

He takes off his blazer, tosses it on the bed, pulls his tie out through the starched neck hole of his shirt. "Come here, Mrs. Beverley." He gestures me over. I can tell from his loose movements that the alcohol is affecting him.

I take four steps closer. "We should really go, Thomas. Before this dare involves the police."

He completely ignores me, reaching up and embedding his hand in the tangle of my hair, making every nerve in my neck jump to the surface. "Who's Thomas?"

"What are you doing?" The words come out a whisper.

"When you kissed me on Halloween, I realized that you want me as much as I want you. I wasn't sure. I was keeping my feelings to myself, but if we both feel it"—he leans in close and puts his mouth up against my ear—"why fight it?" His voice is low and hoarse with want.

I lean into him, feeling as though my body is no longer my own. A dull ache permeates every part of me, one that can only be relieved by having what I want—Thomas. "We shouldn't do this." There's no conviction to my words, and it's too late for good sense, but I feel better for saying it. I've at least tried to do the right thing.

The stubble on his face brushes against my cheek. "Enough regrets, Henny."

I turn my face in such a way that he knows he's convinced me. Our mouths brush against each other, tentatively at first, and then he pulls me into him, crushing his lips against mine. I grab the sides of his shirt so there's no way he can escape from the kiss he started.

He pulls my dress up around my waist, then reaches his hand into the back of my underwear and grabs at my flesh greedily.

I fumble his belt open and then the button of his pants before pulling back the elastic waist of his underwear and sliding my fingers inside to take him in my hand.

He tugs my underwear down and pushes my legs apart with one hand so that he can move his fingers up inside me. My legs begin to tremble, and I grip him tighter to keep myself up. Instinctively my body rocks back and forth, creating pressure against the palm of his hand, starting a fire there that builds slowly.

All the while I work my hand up and down inside his pants to the rhythm of my own pleasure. He moans and pushes his face into my neck. The entire lower half of my body throbs with the rawness of my need to have him inside me. Our lips are still connected, our hands still working, Thomas begins moving me over to the bed, and I let him.

We've just untangled ourselves so that I can fall back onto the mattress when a knock on the door invades the space. I freeze, my body dropping from hot to cold in an instant. Thomas steps away from the bed and I scramble to pull my underwear up, my dress down.

"Jesus Christ, Thomas," I hiss. Fear deadens all desire in me.

"It's okay, Henny." Thomas drapes his shirt over the top of his undone pants and saunters toward the door while I sit there, holding my breath.

"Your champagne, Mr. Beverley." I hear a voice say.

"Ah, yes, thank you," Thomas replies calmly.

For some unknown reason Thomas lets the waiter come right into the room, where he slowly begins to arrange an ice bucket, set out glasses, and uncork the champagne. His arrival reminds me that we're in someone else's room, a fact that was forgotten in the heat of the moment with Thomas. The waiter glances over at me sitting silently on the bed, my dress twisted, my cheeks flushed, and gives a small knowing smile that makes me want to push him out of the room along with the champagne. *Please god don't let him remember my face*, I think to myself.

I can't tell if I feel relief that we were interrupted before it went any further or frustration that we were interrupted before it went any further. I'm a contrast of emotions. Appalled at what just happened and excited by it at the same time. The swinging back and forth between each version is making me nauseous.

The waiter leaves and I get off the bed, my legs still shaky from the adrenaline of what we almost did. "We should go." My voice comes out weak and sounds like somebody else's.

Thomas comes over to me. "But we're not done yet, Mrs. Beverley. The champagne just got here."

"Thomas, stop." It comes out loud, like somebody suddenly turned the volume up on me. "This is not our room. If we get caught—"

"This *is* my room, Henny." He stops me midsentence.

"What do you mean?"

"It's my room. I'm staying here while I find a permanent place to live. Nobody is going to bust in and catch us at something."

"Who's Mr. Beverley, then?"

He hits his own chest. "Me. It's my uncle's last name. I started using it instead of my parents' name after college. For anonymity because of what happened."

Relief and anger battle each other for the right to be my reaction. Relief wins, but I still hit him hard in the shoulder. "Goddamn it, Thomas. Why are you always fucking with my head?"

He reaches for a glass of champagne and holds it out to me. "Aw, come on, don't be mad. It was fun. Wasn't it?"

I take the glass from him, thinking it might ease the guilt, calm my nerves. Instead, the sweet fizziness churns in my stomach like slippery eels, and I worry I might bring it all right back up onto the expensive carpet. "I really should go," I say as much to myself as to him.

"Don't go, Henny." His pleading makes him look young and boyish. Almost enough to make me cave. "We have this room all to ourselves. Don't you want to take advantage of it?"

"Thomas." I give him my own pleading look. Wishing he'd stop tempting me. Wishing he'd let me make one right decision today and leave. I don't want to. Not at all. I just know I should.

He sinks down onto the end of the bed, looking defeated. "I'm sorry," he says, his voice flat and unreadable. "It's selfish of me. Wanting you. Pressuring you to be with me." He throws one hand up. "You're a mother, for Christ's sake."

The comment works like a hammer, striking a very specific nerve in me. "Me being a mother has nothing to do with this. Me being a mother is none of your business." The guilt is easily masked as anger and directs itself right at him. "I'm a good mother, but that's not all I am, and not everything I do is as a mother. If I want to fuck you, that's my choice as an adult, not as a goddamn mother. I can be more than one thing!" I'm convincing myself as much as him.

He shakes his head, his eyes wide. "I wasn't saying that you're not a good mother. I just meant—"

I point at him. "No man would be reminded that he's a father seconds after he commits adultery. Only a man would do that to a woman."

Thomas holds up both hands as if to surrender. "You're right. I just did a total man thing, and I'm sorry. It is your choice as an adult to fuck me, not as a mother, and selfishly I wish you would." He drops his hands into his lap, and everything in his face softens. "Couldn't it be like before—our secret, our rules, we forget about the other stuff when we're together?" He shrugs. "I mean, I had you first."

His words are clever, challenging me to prove my sovereignty and giving me a warped kind of reasoning to do it. He watches me closely, as though he can see my internal debate. I stand on the precipice of becoming a full-blown adulterer. Everything in my body and heart wants it, but the strong code of monogamy that society conditions into us is holding firm.

"And I love you," he says, turning both hands up, as though there's nothing that can be done about it. "I've never stopped."

Nails in the coffin of my fidelity. You can justify anything in the name of love. I move so that I'm standing only inches away. Thomas gets up off the bed to meet me, and before I can change my mind, his mouth is on mine. There's a franticness to the kiss, as though something could once again pull us apart at any moment. He starts pushing at my clothes, working to free me from them, and it becomes a flurry of hands, undoing our own buttons and zippers while also working on each other's. I stand there naked, marveling for a split second at my lack of self-consciousness. Thomas's desire for me leaves no room for my customary insecurities. Through the lens of his wanting, I'm perfect.

He gently guides me to lie back on the bed, and I sink down into the luxurious bedding, the white duvet molding around my body. He lies down next to me, his skin a line of heat against mine, and begins to run a hand over me. Taking an inventory, studying the parts of me that are new to him. He traces the stretch marks on my stomach, and I don't shift away, try to hide them like I do with Evan.

A trembling begins all over my body and a small chatter in my teeth. "Please," I say, impatient to have him inside me, desperate for a release from the intensity he's building within the walls of my skin. "Please."

He rolls on top of me, the weight of him already causing me to moan in pleasure. As he gently guides himself inside, I push up to meet him, wrapping one leg around his hips to bring him in as far as I can. He meets my urgency with his own, gripping my shoulders as he moves himself in and out, whispering my name. My hands on his lower back, I feel his muscles ripple with a shudder, and then he lets out one long, loud moan and collapses onto me, and it's over as quickly as it began.

"I'm sorry," he mumbles into my neck. "It's been a while." I pat his shoulder, relieved to hear him say it.

Seconds later, his head snaps up, his eyes full of fear. "My god, I didn't even ask if you were on the pill, or if we needed protection."

I gently slide out from under him. "It's okay. I can't get pregnant." He rolls onto his side, and I pull the side of the duvet over my naked body.

He reaches out and rubs my arm. "Not that it would be the worst thing in the world if I got you pregnant."

His words shock me, and a yelp of nervous laughter escapes. "Well, I can't anyway, so no need to even discuss it." I want to quickly put a lid on this conversation.

He sits up and slides down to the end of the bed, reaching out for the bottle of champagne on the dresser. He gets under the covers and leans against the headboard, so I do the same. After taking a swig right from the bottle, he passes it to me.

"You've had two kids. Why can't you get pregnant now? Did something happen?"

I know he won't let the pregnancy discussion go, so I take another long sip of champagne to ready myself for the explanation. "I had a miscarriage almost two years ago, and they had to perform an emergency hysterectomy." I force the words out, fast and curt. It's still not a comfortable story to tell. I doubt it ever will be.

Thomas's face scrunches in sympathy. "My god, Henny, that's tragic."

"And then Evan had me committed." The words just fall from my mouth. I've never told anyone that before. Maybe being in bed with another man will do that, or I'm just a sucker for somebody's sympathy.

We pass the bottle back and forth as I tell him what happened with the painkillers, about being in the hospital for a month, what it's done to our marriage. When I finish telling him everything, the champagne is done, and I feel as though my insides have been scraped clean. He tosses the bottle onto the floor and pulls me down to lie beside him. He didn't say much while I was talking, mostly nodded so that I knew he was listening.

Now he pulls me in close, our faces only inches apart. "I'm sorry you went through such a horrible thing." His voice is almost a whisper, as though anything louder might break me. "Evan was wrong to send you away. You needed to be taken care of, not alienated. Because it wasn't your fault. You know that, right, that none of it was your fault?"

I give a slight nod of my head, afraid that if I speak, I'll cry. He leans in and kisses me, and the scraped-out parts inside suddenly feel full again. I move my body up against his.

The second time is slower, allowing time for hands to explore and mouths to venture. The urgency is replaced by emotion, and I feel my heart dipping into dangerous places, pleasure and sensation letting all my guards down.

When we finish, I realize there's only an hour before the girls get home from school. "I have to go," I say, sliding free of his body.

"Can't you call in sick or something?" he says, taking hold of my arm.

"There's no such thing as calling in sick when you're a parent. Or more specifically when you're a mother." I gently pull free of his hold and shift to the end of the bed, where my clothes lie in a pile.

Thomas stays in bed, watching me get dressed, and for the first time I feel self-conscious. Reality begins to eclipse the heady abandon of lust. "I'm going to need a bit of time," I say, pulling on my coat.

"What do you mean?" Thomas props himself up on one elbow, the covers slipping down to expose his bare chest.

"I have a lot to lose. I need to figure out how this can work. *If* this can work," I quickly correct myself. "Just let me get in touch, okay?"

His expression clouds over, but only briefly, before he gives a half shrug and nods. "Yeah, of course. I totally get it." He pushes the covers up and gets out of bed, not self-conscious at all about his nakedness.

Taking me into his arms, he pulls me in for a hug, and I can feel every bit of his lean body through the fabric of my clothes. "This can be whatever you want it to be, Henny." He leans down to whisper in my ear. "No pressure, okay?"

"Okay." The word comes out muffled against his chest. I tilt my head up and give him a quick kiss on the lips before pulling away.

"You know where to find me," he calls out as I slip through the door and into the hallway.

I feel as though the adultery is stamped all over me for anyone to see—my black clothing wearing the impression of his bare skin, glowing as though under a black light. Pulling my coat tight around me, I make my way to the elevator. I'm the only one in there and stare at my reflection for any evident signs: Are my lips too swollen? Is my hair too messy? Are the secrets showing themselves in my eyes?

As I step out into the busy lobby, the effects of the champagne are suddenly magnified. My brain is muddled, my thoughts swinging all over the place. The world now feels like an obstacle course I must get through with an egg on a spoon. Should I let it fall and break, all my secrets will be released.

I'm so focused on getting out of the Somersby that I don't even notice her until halfway across the lobby, when I hear someone say my name. "Hannah?"

Spinning around, I come face-to-face with Libby. She's wearing a tailored navy-blue pantsuit with a crisp white shirt, looking like she belongs there. Did she see me get off the elevator, or earlier standing at the reception with Thomas's arm around me?

"Libby, hey." Too much emotion and anxiety are churning through my body for me to sound anything but caught off guard and guilty. "What are you doing here?"

"Well, I could ask you the same thing," she says with a light chuckle. She thumbs toward the dining room. "I just had lunch with a colleague." Her eyes widen in expectation of my explanation for being at the Somersby in the middle of the afternoon.

"Sounds lovely," I say, putting a hand on her arm. "Well, I'd better run. Have to get home in time for bus drop-off." I give her arm a friendly squeeze to confuse her and try to make a quick escape, but she grabs hold of my wrist, keeping me there.

"I'm going to be sending around a petition to everyone to have cameras set up all through the neighborhood. The police don't have any leads on the man lurking around at night. We have to take our own safety into our hands, don't you think?"

I think it sounds like something out of George Orwell's *1984* and complete overkill, not to mention an invasion of privacy, but it's not the time to take her on. "Sure, drop it by, and Evan and I will mull it over."

She cocks her head in confusion, sending her black bob swinging. "What is there to mull over? It's about the safety of our children."

I glance over at the elevator, afraid Thomas will appear at any moment. The lobby feels suffocatingly warm, which my thick wool coat is not helping; a thin trickle of sweat runs down the center of my back, and I start to feel light-headed.

"Talk soon," I say with a curt smile, yanking my wrist free then moving briskly away, sliding into a section of the revolving door with another woman to escape faster, feeling like discovery is nipping at my heels.

THEN

Once again, nothing was said after the party where Scarlett and Thomas had sex. We all tried to act like it didn't matter, each of us having our own reasons for doing so, making the friendship suddenly feel more like a chess game than a relationship. In truth, it was only me and Scarlett playing. Thomas was a pawn on the board. Only after the game was done did I realize we hadn't even been playing for the same prize.

The Daring Game itself became a game within a game, each dare strategically planned to damage the opponent in some way. Scarlett almost won it all when she dared Thomas to seduce his Modern Philosophy professor. He'd mentioned a few times that she was always flirting with him, and Scarlett had tucked that information away until she could use it.

She dared him to get his professor back to his apartment, where we would be watching from the closet. He only needed to get a kiss or cop a feel—"nothing more than that," Scarlett had explained, as though she were doing him a favor. She gave him a week to set it up.

Only two days in, Thomas leaned close to me in art history class and said, "I'm going to pass on the dare with my teacher."

"Don't!" was my whispered warning back to him. "She'll only come up with something worse. Just get in and get out quickly with minimum damage." He gave me a confused look, not understanding that when I said minimum damage, I meant to me.

"This is getting fucked up," he hissed back at me. I wanted him to clarify which part, but the lights were thrown back on for a surprise

quiz. He left in a hurry after class before I had a chance to talk to him about it.

* * *

It wasn't hard for Thomas to get his professor back to his place. He told her he had a decent vinyl collection. It was exactly the opening she'd been waiting for, and she told him she'd love to see it sometime, outside school hours, then gave him a quick wink. When Thomas relayed this to me and Scarlett, I felt embarrassed by her shamelessness, her desperation. I was so used to male professors and their unabashed flirtation with students that a woman doing it seemed so much more perverse and unethical. I hated myself for thinking like this, but mostly I hated the professor for wanting Thomas.

* * *

Scarlett and I went over to Thomas's apartment half an hour before the professor was due to arrive. Thomas was unusually quiet. I figured it was just because he was nervous, so I didn't say anything. I was quiet because it was a slow torture that I was enduring, one I'd vowed to get through just to spite Scarlett. She was oblivious to both of us and rambled on about herself until there was a knock at the door and she grabbed my arm and yanked me into the closet.

She and I stood side by side, Thomas's clothes pressed up against us. It was like having a crowd of him all around me, emitting his scent, the soft fabric of his favorite shirts brushing against my skin. The closet had louver doors, and Scarlett and I got a dissected view of the entire room. Even with her body fragmented by the slats, I could see that the professor was attractive, with a round girlish face, freckles, and long red hair. She could pass for early twenties, though there was no way she was.

A flutter of nausea rose in my stomach as I watched her survey Thomas's place. I could see the hunger in her eyes even from my vantage point, and it scared me.

She pretended to be interested in Thomas's record collection while he got them both beers from the kitchen, pulling records from the shelf to inspect the covers. "Mind if I put one on?" she asked.

"No, of course not," he called back. His voice and movements were stiff.

She chose the Disintegration album by the Cure, and my stomach clenched. It was one of Thomas's favorites.

"Good choice," he said, handing her a beer.

She clinked hers against his. "Here's to getting out of the classroom." He nodded, and they both took a sip. "But remember, this has to stay between you and me." He nodded again, and my nausea intensified. "I've actually never done this before," she continued. "Seen a student outside of school." She shrugged. "You just seem older, smarter than the rest." She cocked her head to the side and gazed at Thomas. "Different."

Scarlett nudged me in the side, and I had to suppress a surprised grunt. I glanced over at her, and she rolled her eyes. I assumed it was a signal that she thought the woman was full of shit.

The closet quickly turned claustrophobic; it was too hot, and I was finding it hard to breathe. I closed my eyes to block it all out—Scarlett, Thomas, the unsuspecting professor. That only made it worse, being faced straight on with my conscience. What had we been thinking setting this woman up like that? It was downright cruel.

Scarlett gave me another nudge, gentler this time. I opened my eyes and looked over at her. She gave me an annoyed look and nodded her head toward the room, mouthing the word watch.

The woman had her arms around Thomas's neck, and they were kissing. I willed him to stop—he'd won the dare, gotten her there and gotten in a kiss; that's all Scarlett had required—but he didn't. He let her pull open the top of his jeans and slide her hand inside.

Stop her! The words raged through my head. He didn't. I closed my eyes again, but Scarlett pinched me only seconds later, and they flew open. Thomas had pulled out of the kiss; he was staring right at the closet, his mouth slack with pleasure but an angry glint in his eyes. I knew then that I'd made a big mistake. I shouldn't have told him not to pass on the dare. He'd wanted me to not be okay with it, to stop it for our sake, but I'd been so focused on what Scarlett's next move might be, trying so hard to beat her, I'd lost sight of the fact that he was in the game too. And as a result, he was punishing me for it. I half expected Scarlett to call out checkmate.

Thomas started to pull the woman's skirt up, still staring right at me, his vengeful glare penetrating the wooden slats of the door. It was escalating too fast, too far. I was sure I would be watching them have sex in only a matter of minutes. I couldn't breathe; the scent of Thomas was choking me, the sight of him with her scraping away at my insides, and I could feel Scarlett's body beside me, buzzing with satisfaction. I needed it all to stop.

Without thinking I pushed open the closet doors and stumbled out into the room. "Stop," I said loudly. Thomas's eyes went wide in shock, and his professor pulled her hand free of his pants and whipped around to face me, frantically pulling at her skirt.

"What the hell," she said, working to tuck her shirt back in. She swung her head back and forth between me and Thomas, who stood there speechless, not even bothering to do his pants up. "Is this some crazy ex-girlfriend shit?" she asked Thomas, thumbing in my direction. Before he could answer, Scarlett stepped out of the closet, glaring at me.

"There are more of you?" the professor said.

"It was a dare," I blurted out. "He doesn't like you. We dared him to do it." Scarlett grabbed me by the arm, her fingers digging into my flesh to stop the bleeding of information.

The woman looked over at Thomas for an explanation, but he said nothing, choosing instead to finally zip his pants. We all stood there in a moment of silence, the only sound the woeful wailing of Robert Smith as the Cure album played on.

She gave Thomas a push on the arm to get his attention. "This was just a game for you? I risked my job and reputation for some immature prank. Is that true?"

"It's a game, not a prank," I felt the need to clarify.

"Shut the fuck up, Hannah," Thomas spat at me, sending a dagger of pain through my heart. He'd never spoken to me like that.

"You three are really messed up, you know that?" she said, suddenly seeming her actual age. "And sadly immature. I mean, playing truth or dare, at your age?"

"It's not like that. It's—" I tried to correct her, but Scarlett's grip tightened to silence me.

"Whatever it is exactly, it seems like a dangerous game you're all playing," she continued in her lecture-y professor voice. "People will get hurt; it's inevitable. I just hope it's not something that ruins lives, but I have a feeling it will be." She shot Thomas an ice-cold glare. "It just better not be mine." She grabbed her purse from the coffee table. "Or I'll make sure you all go down with me."

Only then did Scarlett step forward to say something. "Speaking up about this will cause you greater trouble than it will us, and I'd advise you not to forget that."

The woman shook her head, and for a split second I admired the way the light danced across the red of her hair. "Fuck you," she said before storming out, slamming the door hard as she went.

Thomas walked over to the record player and pulled the needle off, ending the wailing. "Way to go, Henny," he said as he replaced the Cure with the Strokes. "I'm guessing I can expect a pretty shit mark in that class now."

"What the hell were you thinking, Hannah?" Scarlett chimed in. Her hands on her hips, her sharp chin jutting out. "That's by far one of the most idiotic things you've ever done. You jeopardized the game and made us look like a bunch of voyeur creeps."

"The dare was your idea, Scarlett." Thomas surprised me by quickly coming to my defense, and he used her full name, which meant he was really mad. "Including the voyeur part. It was a fucked-up dare to begin with."

Not having Thomas wholly on her side visibly reduced her level of aggressiveness. She let her hands drop to her sides and sighed dramatically. "They're supposed to be fucked up. That's the point, isn't it?" It was hard to tell whether she was serious or joking.

I just stood there staring at them both, still in shock that I'd broken out of the closet like that and ruined everything. I'd thought I could keep my feelings for Thomas in check, but clearly I'd been wrong. "I'm sorry." I finally managed to say, not directly to Thomas or Scarlett but to the room, to myself.

"It's no big deal," Thomas said. I looked over at him, and the look in his eyes contradicted his words. It was a big deal; I'd shown him how I *really felt, and he was finally seeing what I'd been working so hard to cover up.*

Scarlett didn't say anything. She walked over to where the professor had left her beer and picked it up, taking a long, drawn-out glug of it. When she finally pulled it away from her lips, she turned to look at me. "Technically you broke one of the most important rules of the Daring Game." She paused for dramatic effect. "You talked about the game with an outsider. The punishment is to be banned from the group and the game." She narrowed her eyes at me, waiting for me to beg for forgiveness.

My heart was beating fast, and a soft tremor started up my legs. It was what I'd feared all along—to be cast aside by her, friendless and lonely—but I was not going to beg. I forced myself to shrug, the only nonchalant body gesture I could muster. "Then do it. Ban me from the group, Scarlett." We were playing a game of friendship chicken, and I was not about to let her win.

"Don't be ridiculous, Scary," Thomas said. "It's a fucking game."

Scarlett let a wide grin slowly spread across her face, erasing the hostility completely. "I'm just messing with you, Henny." Her voice was suddenly light and playful. The beating of my heart began to slow, and I exhaled with relief. "I'd never kick my best girl out of the group." She crossed the room and threw her arms around me in a tight hug. "Friends forever," she whispered in my ear, before flicking her tongue against the lobe, sending an electric shiver down my spine.

NOVEMBER 14, 2018

Where has Thomas been all these years? There isn't a trace of him any-
where and then he suddenly just shows up on your doorstep. Who doesn't
have social media these days??? Something doesn't seem right Hannah.
I'm telling you!

I didn't respond to Scarlett's last message, so I guess she thought
she'd try another tactic. It does start my mind wandering, trying to
recall if he ever mentioned anything he'd been up to in the past sixteen
years other than work. I stop myself before I go too deep down the rabbit hole she's trying to create and compose my reply.

No social media? Then he must be a serial killer in hiding. I'll keep
you posted if I find any body parts in his freezer. And what about you?
You message me about three times a year, but then Thomas arrives back
in town and you're messaging every few days. That doesn't seem right
either!

I'm getting bolder when it comes to Scarlett. Maybe because she's
across the world. Maybe because I'm becoming a different person. Since
Thomas has come back and we started playing the Daring Game, I feel
braver, like I can be more than what I've settled for in myself.

It's been five days since I had sex with Thomas at the Somersby. I
think about it constantly, and even when I'm not thinking about it, a
visceral memory of it will flash through my mind without warning,
sideswiping my brain. Several times a day I've gone to text him but then
forced myself to put my phone down. I'm trying to be smart about it;

frequency and hastiness is what will get you caught. Time and a bit of distance will keep you safe, or so I tell myself.

Putting my phone away, I pull out my book. Dinner is in the oven and needs another forty-five minutes; the girls are in their rooms doing homework; the house is clean; even the lunch kits have been cleaned and are ready for tomorrow. I feel like I've earned a glass of wine and some reading time before I have to set the table.

I hear the front door open and close, and then Evan calls out for me. "Living room," I call back, my stomach clenching at his arrival home, as it always does these days. He appears in the living room, and I brace myself for his look of exasperation at my glass of wine and open book, but his eyes skim past both without registering.

He leans in and plants a rough kiss on the top of my head, a habit he just won't let go, no matter how out of sorts we are. "Dinner almost ready? I'm going out tonight."

"It needs about forty-five minutes. I've made a roast chicken with vegetables."

"Hmm, don't think I'll have enough time." He starts to leave the room.

"Wait," I call out to stop him. "Where are you going? Was I supposed to know you wanted to eat early tonight?" I work to recall what Evan said to me this morning on his way out, but I'm sure it didn't include the request for an early dinner.

"Having drinks with Tom. It's a last-minute thing. He texted this afternoon while I was at work."

"Tom?"

Evan huffs impatiently. "Yes, Tom. Your college friend."

"You mean you're having drinks tonight with Thomas?" My voice cracks on his name, and I can feel the blood drain from my face. I reach for my wineglass.

Evan shrugs. "Yeah, Thomas, Tom, same difference. We exchanged phone numbers at dinner that one night. I told him to get in touch if he ever wanted advice on where to buy in the city. Apparently, he has his eye on a place, wants to see what I think."

"He works in real estate, Evan." I don't even try to keep the condescension from my voice. Hopefully it masks the panic that's there too.

What is Thomas doing hanging out with my husband only days after we had sex?

Evan rolls his eyes with such exaggeration that I'm sure they're going to disappear into his skull. "Whatever, Hannah; maybe it's just an excuse to get together. People do that sometimes, you know, when they're trying to become friends. That may be a hard concept for you, considering you seem to be above having friends."

"Thomas is my friend," I practically yell.

"Oh, so that's it. You're feeling possessive of him. Did you want him all to yourself?"

The accusation causes me to shrink back into the couch, take another sip from my wine. "No. I was just pointing out that I do have friends. I know how to make friends." The last sentence is almost a whisper.

"You should be happy, Hannah. That I'm getting to know your old college friend. And if you're feeling left out, then next time we can all go out together. Okay?" Evan thinks he's being generous. He really must have no clue about Thomas and me, which is reassuring but also makes it that much more of a betrayal.

"Yeah, sure, whatever. It's fine with me. Honestly."

He gives a brief nod, as though my reassurance isn't that relevant. "I'm just going to go change, and I'll grab a bite downtown," he says on his way out of the room.

I sit there in stunned silence. Mechanically sipping my wine, staring out the picture window at the purple of dusk that's started lowering like a heavy velvet curtain over the sky. I wonder if I should have stopped Evan from going. Would that have been a smarter tactic? Pretended to be angry about the nice dinner I'd prepared, about not getting to spend the evening with him, guilt him into staying home? No. That probably would have made me look more suspicious in the end. I've never been the clingy type and quite enjoy dinners with just the girls.

I reach for my phone to text Thomas. *Drinks with Evan???*

He responds right away. *It's all good. Trust me.*

I'll be expecting an update tomorrow, I'm quick to reply.

Can I give you one in person?

The three ellipses hang there as he waits for my reply.

Text me tomorrow is all I'm ready to give.

I'm annoyed at Thomas and not sure if I do trust him. What kind of game is he playing at? The slam of the front door alerts me to Evan's exit, no good-bye. A stone of dread sits heavy in the pit of my stomach, one that not even wine can wash away.

* * *

The sound of the front door wakes me. I push myself out of the awkward slumped position that I fell asleep in and retrieve my book from the floor where it fell. I did my best to have a good night with the girls and not think about Thomas and Evan out for drinks. After dinner we watched some TV of their choosing, a reality show full of people who never stop talking but don't seem to have anything important to say. Then, after a bedtime snuggle with Gracie and a quick check-in chat with Rose, I went right back to where I started: to the living room couch with a book to wait for Evan's return.

"Evan?" I quietly call out.

I hear him rummaging around in the kitchen, the taps running, and then he appears in the doorway with a glass of water in his hand. "What are you still doing up?" he asks before moving into the room, bringing the fumes of whatever he consumed earlier tonight with him.

"I fell asleep reading."

He carefully lowers himself into a chair across from me, working hard to disguise how drunk he is, which only makes it more obvious. Bringing the glass to his lips, he gulps down the water, his throat pulsing with the rapid intake, like a man who's just come through the desert.

He lets out an exaggerated *ahh* after draining most of the glass, then nods in my direction. "Have you been there all night?"

"No." The word is accompanied by a glare. "I fed the girls a nice dinner. Watched some TV with them and then got them both to bed. And then came back to read."

He chuckles. "I was only joking. Just because you were in the same spot when I left." He doesn't realize that in this moment it might be a joke, but flip it over in another moment and, like the rusty side of a coin, it's an accusation.

"You're home late for a work night." I make sure my voice is thick with disapproval. It's rare that Evan's on the wrong side of responsible behavior.

He leans back in the chair with a huff, sending a cloud of alcohol fumes in my direction. "Things got a bit away from me. Tom bought us shots."

"You had fun, then?"

He leans forward, putting his elbows on his knees and resting his face in his hands. His head bobs slightly, making him appear extra drunk. "I don't know."

I put my book on the coffee table, my hands suddenly slick with sweat. "What do you mean, you don't know? Either you did or you didn't."

He gives a half nod. "At first I did." Pausing, he drains the rest of his water and sets the glass on the ground. "Then the drunker we got, the less fun I had. He kept asking questions about us and the kids and our family."

I give a purposely incredulous snort. "And you don't enjoy talking about your family with other people."

"Not at a strip club."

My mouth drops open at his inadvertent confession. "You went to a strip club?"

He moves his hands up to rub at his temples. "It was Tom's idea. Clearly, I'm too drunk to keep any secrets."

"I don't care, Evan. You don't have to keep it a secret. I'm just surprised that you went. It's not like you."

"Speaking of secrets." He stops rubbing his temples and suddenly seems more sober than he was only seconds before. "Why didn't you ever tell me that you slept with Tom in college? I thought you guys were just friends."

My whole body clenches. I shift positions to mask it. "We were friends. The sex was just stupid drunken stuff. Nothing serious. He was only at school for a year anyway. Scarlett slept with him too. When they were both high." I'm rambling, throwing everything at him to make it less incriminating. My voice sounds like it's coming from outside of me and has a tinny echo.

A look of disgust crosses his face. "That sounds grossly incestuous."

You have no idea, I think to myself. "Yeah, it was a bit messed up, but you know, typical college stuff." I roll my eyes as though I'm so above it now. As though I'm not still playing the very game that got us all in trouble in the first place.

"That wasn't my college experience," he's quick to say. *Of course it wasn't*, I think to myself. "Weird, though," Evan continues. "Thomas made it sound like he was in love with you."

Once again everything in me constricts. I reach for the mug of mint tea I was drinking hours ago to avoid his eyes, taking a sip of the now-chalky, cold liquid.

Evan pushes himself up from the chair, wobbling slightly but no longer trying to hide it. He stands there for a few seconds looking down at me, and I know he's adding it all up—Thomas's version, my version, things I've told him in the past. Then he gives a sloppy shrug. "He obviously couldn't have been in love with you, though, if he ended up sleeping with your best friend."

"Well, exactly," I'm quick to confirm. Evan's black-and-white mind, his inability to see the nuances of people, make allowances for shadows and mistakes, usually drives me crazy, but in this instance, it saves me.

We say good-night, and he weaves his way to bed. I stay downstairs until well after one AM, replacing my tea with wine, wondering what Thomas was thinking—waiting for Evan to fall sleep. Hoping everything about tonight is a blur when he wakes up in the morning.

NOVEMBER 15, 2018

Evan's skin was the color of ash this morning, and his usually sharp hazel eyes were red-rimmed, murky pools of water. The sight of him made me feel enough pity to make him eggs and toast for breakfast and dig out an extra-large travel mug for his coffee. I did what I could to get him out of the house and to work. Then as soon as the house was empty, I texted Thomas, demanding an explanation for last night.

He responded immediately, saying he could explain everything but wanted to do it in person, asking if I'd go out to a property with him that he needed to look at for work. *We can talk in the car*, he wrote. I agreed, of course. Even confused by his behavior and angry, I relish the idea of seeing him.

* * *

It's only been six days since I last saw Thomas, but standing at the front window watching for his car, I feel starved for him, like I could take big bites of his flesh and still not feel fully satiated. When his car appears, I step out onto the front porch and glance up and down the street to make sure it's clear before running out to meet him, the whole time feeling as though eyes are locked on me like a gun barrel to a target, even though nobody's even in sight.

Sliding into the car, I'm greeted first by the rich scent of him, which immediately ignites all other senses. My eyes search for his, quickly falling into the deep brown of them, like they're bottomless holes in the earth. My hands itch to reach up and plant themselves in the thick mess of his hair, to take hold of his tanned hand resting casually on the gearshift and put it against my cheek.

I keep these feelings in check, smile tightly, remind myself of my annoyance at him for Evan's night out. Look out the window to break the spell. Only when he begins driving do I glance back at him.

"You're looking in much better condition than Evan this morning," I point out. "Is it because you can hold your alcohol better, or did you purposely get him drunk?"

Thomas shrugs, a mischievous smile slowly spreading. "Maybe a bit of both. I mostly drank soda water, which he assumed was a cocktail."

"It's not funny, Thomas," I snap back, erasing the smile from his face. "What on earth were you thinking? Taking my husband out, getting him drunk, asking too many questions about my family, then telling him that we had sex in college and making it sound like you were in love with me." I throw my hands up in the air. "You literally could not have made things any more incriminating than you did last night."

Thomas looks stunned by my tirade. He opens his mouth to say something, then shuts it, then opens it again. "I'm sorry. I thought being friendly with Evan would make us seem less guilty." He takes his eyes off the road to glance over at me. "And for the record, he got himself drunk. I didn't pour shots down his throat. Also, I only asked questions to keep the conversation going."

"And taking him to a strip club?" I add with a shake of my head. "Were you out to corrupt him or something?"

He looks back at the road, his apologetic expression disappearing, and laughs heartily. "But he was so easily corrupted. I couldn't help myself." He winces, but with a smile. "And I admit it, I did like the idea of tarnishing his wholesome image, just a little. Getting him to undo a few buttons on that button-down of his."

I groan loudly. It's the old Thomas, thinking he needs to teach people how to be. "We're talking about my husband here, the father of my children. The person I live with and have to explain it all to after a night out with you."

"Henny, I'm sorry. I didn't think it would be such a big deal. And if I'm being honest, I got a bit desperate when you didn't contact me after being together at the hotel. I kind of saw Evan as my back door in to see what was going on, how you were doing. Force you to get in touch with me."

I glance out the window. We're on our way out of the city. I vacillate between flattery that my silence turned Thomas into a desperate man and pure frustration at how reckless he's being because of it. "This is not a game, Thomas, where you make a move, then I make a move. It's not college, and Evan is not Scarlett. If you were upset about my silence after the hotel, then you should have just gotten in touch with me. Not found some back door through my husband." I slap my leg. "And what was with telling him about us being together in college?"

He winces for real this time. "I thought he already knew. Isn't that what married couples do, confess about all their past relationships? No secrets, that kind of thing."

"Secrets are the backbone of a marriage, you fool," I answer, joking but not joking.

He laughs and shakes his head. "A very romantic sentiment."

"And you didn't have to make it sound like you were in love with me."

"But I was. I am." There are those words again. He gives them away quite easily. I want to ask him how he knows after all these years that he's actually in love with me and not just the idea of me that's left over from college, but I'm too afraid of the answer, so I don't.

"Will you forgive me?" he asks, after a minute or so of my silence. He reaches out to put a hand on my thigh, making the skin under my jeans vibrate. "Please?" He slides his hand down to the inside of my leg. My annoyance is quickly burned away by the heat in my body.

"I forgive you," I say, looking out the window at the passing coun-tryside, purposely avoiding looking right at him. I was never not going to forgive him. I was angry at him when I thought he was just being careless and stupid, but the sick truth is, finding out that he did it just to get closer to me makes me feel good. "Just don't do anything like that again," I add for good measure. "Unless you want us to get caught."

"I don't mean to sound callous or ignorant, but why do you care? I mean, after what he did to you and how unhappy you are together. Would it be the worst thing in the world if your marriage ended?"

I slide his hand away from my leg, not liking how it feels coupled with his point-blank questions. "It's complicated."

"What's complicated about it? You're unhappy with him, so you leave."

"We have children together, Thomas. Divorce can be devastating to kids. I just don't know that I'm able to do that to my girls."

He doesn't respond. I'm hoping it's because he knows not to push me when it comes to my kids, but I have a feeling it's because he's formulating a new argument. Then he puts his turn signal on, and I spot a FOR SALE sign in the ground and figure it's only because we've arrived at our destination.

The driveway is long, slicing through thick forest until you suddenly enter a clearing with a massive house sitting in the middle of it. I let out a little gasp at the awe of it. Entire walls made of windows, supported by a foundation of stone that could have been pulled right from the ground the house now sits on. The glass of the windows reflects the trees back out to you so that it appears as though there's no division between the land and the structure.

"This place is amazing," I say, as the car rolls to a stop. "The kind of place I could write my award-winning novel."

"Since when did you want to write an award-winning novel?" he asks with a chuckle.

"Since always; I just never say it out loud. You know how much I love books. Of course I want to write one too." I point at the house. "I thought you dealt with commercial properties, not residential."

"I'm just helping another broker out with this one. He broke his ankle, so I said I'd walk the property for him and come up with a description for the listing." He opens his car door and gets out, so I do the same.

The chilly November air takes a bite out of me as soon as I leave the warmth of the car, and there's a light mist falling from the steely gray sky that doesn't help. "Are we going inside?" I ask with an involuntary shiver.

"I don't have a key."

I point at the large front door, where a lockbox hangs from the handle. "Aren't they usually in there? You just need the code."

Thomas glances over at the front door, then shakes his head. "There wouldn't be a key in there yet. The listing isn't going up for a couple of days. We're just here for the outside anyway."

"But it's so cold," I whine.

He reaches out and grabs my hand and starts walking me toward the forest. "If we keep moving, we'll be fine. I'm going to show you something really cool about this property, better than anything inside."

We walk along a thin path for a little while and then reach a ridge of higher land. He was right; moving makes the chill more bearable, and it's a beautiful property. "You're sure you know where you're going?" I ask as he leads me up the incline.

"I've studied the aerial shots of the place, so I have a pretty good idea. The lake should be just over this hill."

As soon as we crest the hill, the lake comes into view. You can see from one side of it to the other, it's that small, but it's beautiful. Trees and rocks surround the shoreline, and the water is a deep brownish green, rippled only by the light rain falling.

We find our way to a point of land that juts out into the lake. The trees are thick there and create as much shelter as we can find from the wet. I lean against a large gray rock that sits near the shore and take it all in while Thomas studies the shoreline up close.

After taking a few photos, Thomas comes over to where I am. "Do you remember going into the woods behind the college during art history class?" he asks with a sly smile.

"I have some vague recollection of it, yes." I don't admit I've thought of those times a lot over the years, dreamt of them even.

He moves right up to me, leaning his body into mine, so that I can feel the jagged surface of the rock digging into the back of my legs. "We're in the woods now." He stares down at me with an intensity that only Thomas can pull off, and those moments from years ago flash through my mind.

"What exactly are you proposing?" I raise one eyebrow with the question, and he reaches up to run his finger across it.

"Lie back," he orders. I do what he says, and he hooks his fingers into the top of my leggings and pulls, taking my underwear along with them, right down around my ankles.

The jagged surface of the rock bites into my bare skin, and the damp chill numbs me right through to the bone. Thomas gets down on his knees in front of me and wraps his hands around the backs of my thighs before leaning forward to put his face between my legs. The quick movement of his tongue works like the rays of the morning sun, spreading warmth outward to the rest of my body. I grip what I can of the unyielding stone to hold myself in place.

Opening my eyes, I look up into the canopy of trees and watch the rain fall from the gray sky, the drops seeming to move in slow motion as the sensations inside me build. Each impression is heightened: the feel of the cool rain on my face, the hard rock beneath me and Thomas's warm tongue, the sound of the water rolling across the rocks on the shore, the earthy scent of fallen leaves, wet bark and mud filling my nostrils with each deep breath in. All of it works in divine unison, bringing a climax so forceful I call out, shattering the peaceful silence around us.

Thomas stands up, pressing his body against mine, holding me there in place. My legs are jelly, and all I want to do is slide down onto the ground.

"I've always loved the way you taste," he says softly, before leaning down to kiss me lightly on the lips, giving me my own taste of myself.

We walk back slowly. I no longer mind the wet or the cold now that my body is insulated with endorphins.

"Want to look in the windows?" Thomas asks, when we arrive back at the house.

We walk up onto a deck that runs the whole length of the back of the house, and I cup my hands around my eyes against the glass of the large door that leads out onto it. It's one large room that must be the living room, leading onto a kitchen with a restaurant-sized fridge, an island the size of my entire kitchen at home, and a shiny gas stove that looks as though even the worst cook could make gourmet food on it. The ceilings are high, littered with pot lights that would make the space glow warmly in the evening, shiny polished concrete floors, and views into the woods at every turn.

"I think this might be the nicest house I've ever seen in person before. It must cost a fortune."

Thomas comes up to stand behind me, the warmth of his body penetrating my damp clothes. He pulls my hair away from my neck and leans down to kiss me gently. "Should I buy it for you, then?"

I laugh. "Yes, please, and a maid to go along with it."

He takes my shoulders and gently turns me around to face him. "I'm not joking, Henny." There's nothing light to his expression; it's all deep, dark seriousness. "We could be happy here. You, me, and the girls. Swimming in the lake in the summer, having barbecues out here on this deck, waking up each morning surrounded by the trees; you could write that award-winning novel, and—"

I take a step away from him and hold up a hand. "Stop. Please." He's instantly wounded, looking as though I've just stomped on a beautifully wrapped gift he's presented to me. "It's an amazing sentiment, Thomas, but I'm not ready for this kind of talk." I want to tell him that including my girls in this adulterous fantasy of his turns what just happened at the lake into something that makes me want to peel my skin from my body. I cannot be a mother and an adulteress in the same breath.

"Can we just keep things light for the moment? Play the game, have fun? See how our feelings develop before I leave my husband and drag my kids to a mansion in the woods?"

He takes a step away from me, his eyes narrowed, the dark brown suddenly looking like hard stone. "Wouldn't it be better than growing up with unhappily married parents in a boring cul-de-sac with houses that are all trying to be the same?"

I move toward the steps off the deck, but Thomas reaches out and grabs my arm. "Sorry, I'm sorry. That was out of line." I pull my arm free but don't say anything or move. "You're right, I'm moving too fast. I got carried away. It was the look in your eyes when you saw the inside of this place, and I thought, *I can give her this. I can make her dreams come true, make her happy.* But that's not my job, not right now." As always, he says just the right thing to explain away whatever I'm upset about.

"That's sweet of you, Thomas. It really is, and a fantasy that part of me would love to just dive right into, but it's not realistic. I didn't hear from you for sixteen years, then you arrive back in my life without warning and within weeks we're playing the Daring Game again and having an affair." I throw my hands up in the air. "That in itself is crazy to me, and I'm working hard to make sense of it. But I want it and I want you. I really do. It's made me happier than I've been in years, but that doesn't make it right. My marriage being shitty doesn't make it right either. And no matter what, I can't blow up my life because of it. I can't do that to my girls. I just can't."

"So, what, you'll never leave Evan, then?"

A tired sigh escapes me. "I don't know right now, Thomas. This is all new to me, I've never done anything like this before. I need time. Okay?"

"Like time apart?"

I know I should say yes. Alarm bells are going off in my head, but I quiet them by moving up against him and wrapping my arms around his torso. "Not time apart," I say, looking up into his face. Relief floods his eyes, and it makes me hug him tighter. "Let's just take it slowly and not get carried away. Do our best to limit the number of casualties."

He nods. "Okay. Go slowly. I can do that. Do you still want to play the game?"

"Yeah, sure. We're having fun with it, so why not?" I think that playing the game seems less illicit than hotel visits and sex in the woods. I think I'm making the safer choice, but the game has never been the safer choice.

* * *

Driving back into town, getting closer to my real life, I imagine telling Thomas that I was wrong, I do want that house in the woods, I do want that fantasy. I bite down hard on the inside of my cheek to keep the words from escaping me, until I taste the hint of blood and the sting tricks me into thinking I'm showing some willpower.

The rain has let up, but Thomas insists on dropping me at my front door. As we drive up my street, we pass Libby out for a run. She looks directly at me sitting there in the passenger seat next to Thomas.

"Shit," I say under my breath. "That fucking woman is everywhere."

"Who?" Thomas asks, leaning forward to peer out the front windshield.

"My neighbor Libby. You met her after the water tower dare. I'm not sure she even saw me just now, but I keep running into her when I'm with you."

"Are you friends with her?"

"No. Not at all. She's a gossiping busybody."

"Then you know what you have to do?"

"What?"

"Become friends with her, so that if she does think something is going on with you—"

"Which it is," I'm quick to add.

"Then she'll talk to you about it and not someone else."

"Great, thanks for the advice."

"Anytime." He squeezes my hand and then lets it go. Pulling up to my house, he puts the car in park and turns to face me. "Expect a dare very soon. Today gave me some ideas. And I promise"—he holds his hand up, as if taking an oath—"no more nights out with Evan. Or lofty propositions of mansions in the woods."

I hold up one warning finger. "And no mention of my girls at all."

He salutes me. "Got it. Won't happen again."

I want to lean forward and kiss his soft, pink lips, to run my hands through his thick hair and inhale one deep breath of his smell. I want to stay right there in the car with him—this man who'll get down on his knees in the mud for me.

"You'd better go before your neighbor and new best friend come running back this way," Thomas warns. He's right. The last thing I want is to have to talk to her. I blow him a quick kiss and get out of the car.

Once inside, I go upstairs to the bedroom and strip out of my damp clothes, shoving them into a laundry basket and taking them downstairs to the washing machine. Then I get into a hot shower and soap every inch of me. It's like cleaning up after a crime scene, but the body is mine.

THEN

Something happened between me and Thomas after I upended the dare with his professor. We stopped pretending there wasn't something greater between us than friendship or the threesome, but it was fragile and not fully formed, so we protected it by keeping it a secret from Scarlett. Neither of us was sure what would happen if we brought it out into the open.

There were woods along the back of the campus, and some days Thomas and I would slip out of art history to walk into them. There were trails, but on either side was thick, dense forest. We'd go off the trail and find as much cover as possible. It was late November by that point and cold, so we had to be strategic, slipping our pants down only so far, sliding our hands up into each other's shirts to keep them warm.

Thomas and I didn't have any rules out in the woods. Underwear went down, my bra came unclasped, each body part was explored. As I stood against a tree with my pants around my ankles, Thomas used his tongue in ways that made me grip the rough bark, the cold air turning my breath into thick plumes. We took turns, him on his knees in front of me, then me on my knees in front of him. We both came, sometimes more than once, using our mouths and our fingers.

One day it was really cold; my fingers were numb, my teeth chattering. I didn't think I could endure it enough for both of us to get off. I turned around and bent over, using the tree for support. "Fuck me," I ordered, surprised at my own boldness. He brought it out of me.

Thomas ran his hand along one cheek of my bare ass. "Not here, Henny," he said, pulling me away from the tree to face him. "I don't want to have sex with you for the first time out in the woods."

I pulled my pants up with a frustrated huff. "Fine, but I need to go inside. It's too cold for drawn-out foreplay."

"Why does it have to be like this?" Thomas zipped his coat up and shoved his hands in his pockets. "It was fun at first, the three of us fooling around, but now it's weird, the way we have to hide the fact that we want to be together, like we're cheating on Scarlett or something. It was you I liked in the first place. I only talked to you guys in the parking lot on Halloween because I wanted to meet you."

Happiness bloomed in my chest at his words.

He pulled a hand free from his pocket to run it through his thick brown hair. "Then things got all messed up, like that night I had sex with Scarlett when I was all high. She totally seduced me, you know?"

I held a hand up to stop him. His reminder of that night had turned the blooming happiness in my chest to piercing jealousy, but then I reminded myself that he was in the woods with me and not her. "She's more fragile than you'd think," I said, enjoying, for the first time ever, a sense of superiority over Scarlett. "If she knows about us, it will destroy her." It was more like she'd destroy us, but I didn't say that out loud. I wanted to look like I had the upper hand for once.

"You know, Hannah, the only reason I put up with Scarlett's rules and fucked-up mind games is you. I'm afraid that if I stand up to her, tell her how things really are, how I really feel, and make her mad, it'll be you that I lose. But I've just about had enough, so what am I supposed to do?"

"I don't know." My answer came out short and curt. I was torn between two places, not believing how lucky I was that a guy like Thomas wanted to be with me, but also afraid of losing the only best friend I'd ever known.

He threw up his hands. "Well, let me know when you figure it out." He turned and stomped back to the trail. I followed him, but we were silent the whole way back, and when we reached campus, he gave a backward wave and headed off in the direction of the library.

That weekend I was supposed to go away with Scarlett and her parents for her cousin's wedding, but I called her Friday morning and told her I was sick. The contained fury in her voice scared me. I gave her some graphic details of the stomach flu I was pretending to suffer from, and she begrudgingly said she hoped I felt better before hanging up the phone.

Then I called Thomas. We hadn't spoken since the day in the woods, and when he answered and heard it was me, he still sounded mad. Only when I told him what I'd done—lied to Scarlett, gotten us an entire weekend alone—did he soften, asking me to come over that night.

Thomas and I spent most of the weekend in bed. When I got there on Friday night, he had cleaned up, lit candles, and opened a cheap bottle of wine. Suddenly, not in the woods or with the threat of Scarlett catching us, I was nervous. I drank my first glass of wine in two gulps, hoping it would steady my nerves. Then I rambled on about my annoying psych professor, who loved to give pop quizzes, while Thomas chose a record.

"It's strange to all of a sudden have the place to ourselves," I said, once he'd plopped down on the couch beside me.

"She has too strong a hold over you, Henny."

"Scarlett?"

He nodded.

Of course I knew that, but rather than try to defend myself, I tipped my glass all the way back to get the one sip of wine left.

Thomas slid up close to me, put his hand on the back of my neck, and pulled me in for a kiss, causing Scarlett to disappear from the room completely. We had all weekend ahead of us, but the waiting, the hiding, had made us frantic. We were out of our clothes in a matter of seconds and migrated from the couch to the floor. There was no foreplay; we wanted the one thing we hadn't had of each other yet.

My whole body tensed as he pushed inside of me and then melted all around him as he moved in and out. There is great intimacy in using your mouth as a sexual instrument, but there's a wholeness that comes only when another person fits themselves inside you. I finally had Thomas in every way, and it felt exactly as it should. The endorphins, the nerve endings, the blood pumping made everything suddenly seem so simple. There was no Scarlett, no betrayal, only us.

The feeling lasted right up until late Sunday afternoon, when I finally stepped out of the dark cave that Thomas and I had been in for almost forty-eight hours. The sun burnt my eyes, the wind chapped my swollen lips, and each step aggravated the inside of my thighs, which felt soft and bruised from the repeated rubbing of Thomas's hips between them. Despite the discomfort, I was on a high right up until I walked through my front door and found Scarlett sitting in the living room with my father.

She smiled wide at my entrance and cocked her head to the side. "There she is." The singsong tone of her voice made the hairs on the back of my neck stand up. "I came over as soon as I got back to see how you were doing, but your dad said you've been gone all weekend long." She got up from the couch and came over to give me a hug. "I missed you," she said. I kept my arms straight at my sides, sure I would feel a knife slide into my back before the hug was over. But she stepped away from me, and I was still alive.

"Well," my dad said, pushing himself up off the couch. "I'll take my leave. I know that even a couple of days apart for you two peas in a pod means lots of catching up to do."

I wanted to reach out and grab a handful of his cable-knit cardigan to keep him there, to move his body in front of mine like a shield, but I let him saunter out of the room, whistling as he went.

"You didn't have to lie, you know," Scarlett said as soon as we were alone. I finally looked right at her and was shocked to see sadness in her eyes and not anger. "If you wanted to be together, you should have just said so. I know you like him, Hannah." She chuckled. "You're really not that good at hiding it."

"I do like him. And he likes me too, but we didn't want to ruin the friendship the three of us have, so we didn't say anything."

"Hannah," she said loudly. "It's okay. Honestly. I understand. Only a pathetic loser would have an issue with their best friend getting together with their other best friend." She reached out and grabbed my hand, her long, cool fingers wrapping themselves around my hot skin. "I mean, what matters most is that you're happy and that Thomas is happy. Just don't become one of those lame couples who never want to do anything."

"What, no, never!" I was so fast to reply. "We'll always have the Daring Game, after all."

It was the worst thing I could have said—forgetting all strategy, ignoring the chessboard completely. Essentially handing over my pieces so that she could control the outcome.

"Well, obviously. I certainly wouldn't let you and Thomas ruin the game."

"So we're okay then?" I asked, tensing for the answer.

She squeezed my hand. "Of course we are, Henny. You're my best friend. Forever and always." She let go of me and held up a scolding index finger. "But if you ever lie to me again, you'll pay. Mark my words." The flash of something in her eyes confused me for a second, but then she laughed and pulled me over to the couch, and the feeling was gone in an instant. "Now tell me everything. And don't leave out any details. My weekend was lame as hell, so I want to at least hear about a good one."

Later that night I called Thomas to tell him about what had happened with Scarlett. There was silence on the other end when I finished.

"Are you there?" I asked.

"Do you trust her?" he finally replied.

"Yeah, why wouldn't I? We've been friends since fifth grade." My reassurance was met with silence. "Don't you?"

"I don't know," he answered. "I guess we'll find out."

NOVEMBER 22, 2018

A message from Scarlett has been sitting in my in-box for days. I'm afraid to open it but know I can't avoid her forever. I brace myself and click on it. *Did you know that Thomas's uncle died? It's the only thing I could find online with any mention of the Thomas Sutton that we know. Again, do you not find that strange for someone in real estate???*

She doesn't even apologize or reference the point I made in my last message about how she got in touch with me only a few times a year until Thomas showed back up in town. I honestly can't understand why she cares so much. She's across the world, living her best life, and yet still feels compelled to drive a wedge between me and Thomas.

I could write back that Thomas doesn't use the name Sutton anymore, that he goes by Beverley, but something stops me from giving her that piece of information. Is it because I'm afraid she might actually find something out about him that I don't want to know? I swipe out of the app without replying, annoyed at the sliver of paranoia she's planted. That is what Scarlett does best, get in your head, but this time it's fleeting. I have a dare date with Thomas.

I slip my phone away and stand in the middle of the kitchen, trying to decide what needs to get done most before I abandon all my responsibilities to play the Daring Game. There's not much food in the house, so I do need groceries, but the dishwasher needs to be unloaded and three baskets of laundry need to be done, and then there's Evan's dry cleaning that I told him I took in three days ago but is really stashed in the trunk of my car. I figure I can grocery shop tomorrow, but the other stuff will stand out more if it doesn't get done, and I can drop off the dry cleaning on the way to the zoo. There's a twinge of guilt at the overlap of an errand for Evan and a liaison with Thomas. Then I pull the dishwasher open and see last night's dinner plates still crusted with food due to the human error of my children, and the guilt is quickly replaced with annoyance.

*   *   *

Walking through the zoo, my entire body is agitated with wanting, like the worst itch that, if not scratched, will drive me insane. Thomas isn't at the penguin enclosure when I get there. Nobody is. It's late November, almost a month until Christmas, and a light snow has started falling. The place is populated only with zookeepers and the odd die-hard zoo patron.

Most of the animals are curled up in the warmth of their artificial habitat. Not the penguins. They climb up onto white rock formations and waddle around in circles before sliding back into their pool of aqua water. It's a continuous loop of restricted activity. I can relate. And the Daring Game is like being let out of the enclosure for the day to do other kinds of things. To be a swallow for a few hours instead of a penguin.

I turn away from the black-and-white birds and see Thomas coming toward me, his hands shoved deep into his blue pea coat and his collar pulled up against the cold. I resist the urge to move to him.

"Fancy meeting you here," he says once he's close.

"What a strange coincidence." I play along. The sense of something to come sits between us like a wrapped present. "So, a trip to the zoo isn't much of a dare."

"It will be." He nods in the opposite direction and begins walking away from the penguins. We follow the blue elephant footprints on the path until Thomas stops and motions me into the bat house.

The air is musty and stale but warm. A dim blue light illuminates the tree branches behind a pane of glass that holds small, brown hanging clumps of bat.

It's claustrophobic, and I can't help feeling that at any moment, something is going to land on me or crawl up my pant leg. "Is this the dare?" I ask.

"Do you remember when you, me, and Scarlett got really high and came to the zoo?" He turns away from the bats and starts walking me backward into a dark corner. "We came in here when Scarlett was in the bathroom and kissed, and I felt you up for a few minutes."

"Oh my god! I do remember that trip. Scarlett got mad that we went ahead without her."

Thomas pushes me right up against the stucco wall. "But she's not here now. Nobody is." He pushes up against me and puts his lips to mine, making me forget entirely the creep factor of where we are. I bring my hand up to his neck so that I can feel his skin.

He's started to slide one hand up into my coat when the sound of a lock turning echoes through the small building. We quickly move apart, and my breath catches in my throat with a guilty hiccup. A zoo hand steps into the enclosure, a bucket in his hand.

He stops and nods at us. "These guys won't be doing much at this time of day."

"That's okay. We're just taking a break from the cold," Thomas says. The zoo hand nods again and puts the bucket on the floor to rummage around in his pockets for something.

Thomas gestures toward the door, and we make our way back outside, squinting against the return to light. "Was that the dare? Making out in the bat house?"

"I was hoping we'd do more than kiss. That you might want to return the favor of last week in the woods." He stops for a minute and looks around. "Come on. I think I know where we can go."

I have to run a few steps to keep up. "Go for what?"

"To fuck around. At the zoo. Like we couldn't do back in the day because of Scarlett. That's the dare, Henny."

I laugh. "Seriously, Thomas?" He doesn't say anything, just keeps walking.

The handful of people I've seen suddenly feel like a crowd. I want to stop walking and convince Thomas to forget the dare, but I'm afraid it will mean our time is up. So I follow along behind, my eyes locked on the back of his blue wool pea coat dusted in snow.

The path we're on leads down to a tunnel with a bridge above it. Before we go in, Thomas turns back. "Are you okay with the cold?"

"In what sense?" I ask, but he disappears into the shadow of the cement hole.

Stopping halfway in, he turns to face me. "This should do." Using his body, he maneuvers me up against the stone wall of the tunnel.

"I haven't agreed to this yet," I whisper.

He puts the heel of his hand between my legs and starts to slowly move it in circles. "So you're saying you don't want to?"

Warmth travels up from my thighs to flood the lower half of my body. "No." My voice has that breathless quality that always seems to happen around him.

He takes my hand and places it on the crotch of his jeans. "See how much I want to." His hard-on pushes the thick denim taut, and I wonder if it hurts, being trapped inside like that. I want to release it, to feel it in my hands. I unzip his pants and gently pull it out, wrapping my hand around it.

He gasps as my cold hand touches his warm, soft flesh. Following my lead, he maneuvers his hand under my coat and down inside the waist of my pants. My knees dip as his fingers find their way inside me.

The sound of footsteps echoes through the tunnel, and we freeze, only to realize they're moving above us across the bridge. The scare hurries our movements, brings him in closer, his lips to mine with a frenzied aggression.

We're locked together, creating a cocoon against the cold as we work in unison to find pleasure. With my one free hand I hug his upper body to keep myself up as an orgasm turns my muscles to liquid. My soft moans bounce off the walls circling us, but I have no way to stop them.

When I finish, Thomas pulls his hand free from my pants. He looks up and down the tunnel and then gently guides me down to the ground. The cement is cold on my knees, but it doesn't stop me from taking him in my mouth.

I look up. His face is slack, his mouth partly open, his eyes closed. He groans softly, makes exclamations of pleasure when I deepen my hold on him.

He comes quickly. I stand up on stiff legs, my knees protesting. He pulls me in for a kiss, long and slow, the kind that comes after, not before. "That was good," he says into my hair.

"So I won that dare, then?"

He laughs a deep laugh, throaty with pleasure. "You most certainly did."

A sound at one end of the tunnel makes me pull away, and I catch a glimpse of the back of a hooded figure.

"Where did that person come from?" I ask.

"They were probably headed this way and then saw us and turned around. Maybe some employee wanting to smoke a joint or something." Thomas zips up his pants.

"Do you think they saw what we were doing?" A fist of fear clenches my gut.

"Even if they did, who cares?"

"What if it was someone I know? Someone who knows Evan."

"At the zoo in November? What's the likelihood of that?"

I slice a hand through the air. "No more in-public stuff."

Thomas laughs, and it echoes through the tunnel, sounding more wicked than fun. "But it's hot."

I shake my head and take a step away from him, suddenly feeling very exposed. "It's too risky."

Thomas buttons up his coat. "Okay, no more public stuff."

Leaving the zoo, I scan the entire area, looking for the hooded figure, but I don't see anyone. Thomas's theory makes sense, but what if he's wrong? What if that person was in the tunnel, watching us? It wouldn't be the first time a dare has gone wrong.

NOVEMBER 22, 2018

"Can we have just one piece before dinner?" We haven't been two seconds out of the store and already Gracie is harassing me for the licorice I bought in a moment of weakness. I've felt unsettled and on edge since the dare at the zoo earlier this afternoon and am doing whatever I can to just get to the end of the day.

"Would you just let us get home first?" I beg, shifting the shopping bag from one hand to the next.

Rose and Evan waited in the car while Gracie and I ran in to grab some things for dinner after Rose's school basketball game.

"But I'm starving right now," Gracie whines.

I ignore her. The declarations of starvation are an hourly thing with this one. She tries to take one of the grocery bags out of my hand, thinking that being helpful will secure her an early piece of licorice.

I let go of the handles, sure she has the bag, but somehow it slips between both of us and onto the ground. Two yellow onions roll away, disappearing under the cars, the box of pasta lands in a puddle, and the jar of tomato sauce cracks open, bleeding all over the pavement.

The car's only a few feet away and I look up, hoping Evan has seen it and will get out to help, but he's got his head down, staring at the glowing screen of his phone, oblivious to anything else.

"I'm so sorry, Mom," Gracie says, reaching for the broken jar.

"Don't," I yell, and regret it as soon as I see the wounded look in her eyes. "It's okay, sweetie. I just don't want you to cut your hand on the glass."

She gets down to crawl forward to retrieve one of the renegade onions, but I grab her sleeve and pull her up off the ground.

"Just leave it, Gracie. It's fine, really." I kick the broken glass over toward a garbage can, grab the wet box of pasta, and guide Gracie to the car. "At least we still have the licorice," I say, pulling it free from the bag I'm holding and handing it to her. "Just one piece."

She gives me a grateful smile and takes the candy.

"Licorice," Evan says, looking up from his phone as we get into the car. "Before dinner?"

"There was an incident," I say quietly.

"You give in too easily, I swear. You need to learn to say no. It's better for them in the long run."

I want to scream or run out into the night, away from Evan's constant disdain, but I just take a deep breath and buckle up my seat belt. "How does everyone feel about grilled cheese sandwiches for dinner?" I ask.

Evan starts reversing out of the parking spot. "What happened to spaghetti? Isn't that why we stopped at the store?"

"I dropped the shopping bag, and the jar of sauce broke."

"What? How'd you do that?" He doesn't even try to mask his irritation.

"It was my fault, Dad," Gracie says, coming to my defense. "Mom was passing it to me, and it slipped out of my hand." Rose jumps at the opportunity to belittle her sister and huffs loudly with disgust.

"That's okay," Evan says, peering into the rearview mirror to give Gracie a reassuring smile. "Accidents happen." I wonder if he realizes how obvious he's just made it, that when I make a mistake there's only condemnation, but when someone else makes a mistake there's only understanding. I bite my lip to avoid using the moment to make that point. It's not something the girls should be made aware of as well.

It's one of those nights when the only purpose I serve is as a punching bag for my family. The grilled cheese sandwiches don't have enough cheese in them, and there's not enough ketchup to go around. I didn't get the only shampoo that Rose will use, and she wanted to wash her hair tonight. I didn't police the licorice closely enough, and Gracie got more than her sister. I'm too terrible at math to help Rose study for her quiz tomorrow. I didn't pick up Evan's dry cleaning; that should have been ready days ago. I weather it all without comment, because the truth is, I deserve it. Not for the reasons they give, but for the reasons they don't even know about, and hopefully never will.

The girls have finally retreated to their rooms for bed and Evan is on his computer in the office when I pour myself a glass of wine and take it into the living room. My body feels heavy with everyone's disappointment, and sinking into the couch brings some relief. Sipping my wine slowly, I wait for the sense of failure to ebb, and my thoughts inevitably wander to Thomas.

"I figured I'd find you in here with a glass of wine." Evan stops my wandering thoughts short.

"First one of the night." I cringe as the words leave my mouth, hating how pathetic I sound. Hating him for making me feel like I need to clarify that fact.

He sits down on the gray ottoman, and I'm hoping it means he's not staying long. "What's up?" I ask, to hurry it along.

"Where were you today?" His question lands with a thud against my chest. A flash of me on my knees in front of Thomas in the tunnel at the zoo flies through my mind, then of the hooded figure who suddenly appeared out of nowhere. Is it a coincidence that Evan is asking me this on the day we may have been seen by somebody?

I wipe a hand across my forehead as though I can clear the images away while I mentally scramble for a possible excuse. I can't say I was out for a walk, because I had my car; I can't say I was grocery shopping because there's no food in the house; I can't say I was out with friends because the only real friend I have right now is the one I'm having an affair with. I take a slow sip of my wine. "Why?"

"I came home at lunch, but you weren't here. I figured you were grocery shopping, but there's no evidence of that having happened."

I raise one eyebrow, working hard to get a handle on things. "So now you're checking up on me?"

"Do I have to be?" I give him a casual shrug for an answer. He narrows his eyes at me. "Seriously, Hannah, where were you?"

I figure a sliver of truth telling is better than a bold-faced lie that might come back on me, even though I'm incriminating myself to some degree. "I was dropping your dry cleaning off."

He sits up straighter and gives his head a little shake. "The dry cleaning you told me you dropped off three days ago?"

"I forgot about it in the trunk of my car. When you asked me, I lied and said I dropped it off so you wouldn't get mad."

He sighs deeply and braces both hands on his knees as though he's trying hard to contain his frustration, which only makes it more evident. "I really don't understand what you do with your time, Hannah. You're home all day, but we're eating grilled cheese sandwiches for dinner, the laundry is in piles waiting to be folded, my dry cleaning doesn't get dropped off, the house barely stays presentable."

The irony of the moment is that this isn't the first time Evan has said this. He said it before Thomas, before the Daring Game. When my only excuse was simply that I hate laundry and grocery shopping and cleaning.

"Why do you stay married to me, Evan?" The question comes out of nowhere and lands in the room like a dangerous substance.

He scrunches his face up as though confused, but I know full well he understood the question. "What do you mean?"

"If I'm such a horrible wife and mother, such an all-round disappointment, why not leave?"

He leans back slightly with an exaggerated laugh. "You're so melodramatic."

"I'm serious," I say, refusing to back down, now actually determined to make him give me an answer. "I wouldn't say we're exactly happy together, so why stay?" More dangerous words deposited like land mines around us, but I can't seem to stop them. They've been in me for too long.

Evan drops the look of false amusement and is suddenly so serious his face becomes hard angles. "Because I don't believe in failure."

It's my turn to laugh now. Out of shock, mostly. No words of love or attempts to dismiss the idea that we're not happy, just his inability to accept failure. "You're saying, then, that people who get a divorce fail at marriage?"

He shrugs. "How else would you put it? If you can't make your marriage work, then you've failed at it. I'm not about to do that."

"Do I have any choice in the matter, then?"

He shrugs again. "You always have choices, Hannah. You can leave this marriage anytime you want, but it will be alone, and the failure will fall entirely on your shoulders, which the girls will be fully aware of."

The steely look in Evan's eyes is unsettling and happens quickly, as though it's always been there, sitting right under the surface. "That statement sounds almost threatening, Evan. Like you're saying you'll take my girls from me."

He slowly stands up from the ottoman and slides his hands in his pockets but keeps me fixed with that look. "I'm glad I was clear, then."

The room crackles with tension and hostility, making the house feel as though it's holding its breath, as though the tick of the clock has slowed, as though the lights have dimmed.

I place my wineglass down on the coffee table to get it out of my shaking hand. "You can't do that, Evan. That's not how divorce works these days. It's shared custody."

"I really don't know where this sudden talk of divorce is coming from, but maybe it's good for you to know, Hannah, that I would never accept shared custody, and there's no reason I'd have to." He takes his hands out of his pockets and begins ticking things off on them. "Attempted suicide, a stay in a psych ward, family history of mental illness, and alcoholism. And all of that on easily accessed records."

The blood in my veins is running cold, but there's a heat in my belly that makes it hard to resist picking up my glass and hurling it at him. I take deep breaths to try to find calm, to stop myself from doing or saying something I'll regret.

He takes my silence for surrender, and his mouth curls into a smug half smile. "I won't let you turn this family into an ugly statistic just because you've turned into a disgruntled housewife. You should appreciate my commitment to you and the girls." He puts a hand on his chest. "I'm not a monster, I'm the good guy. Working hard to provide for the three of you, coming home for dinner every night, doing things with the girls, working on this house whenever I get the opportunity. So we fight now and again, so I push you to be better, do better; that's what spouses are supposed to do. Sorry it's not the Hollywood version of marriage you have in your head. It's called real life."

He pauses, waiting for my response, but I clench my jaw to keep my words from escaping. "I think you need to do some serious self-reflection, Hannah," he continues. "Figure out your priorities. Is it this family, or is it yourself? Because you can't have both."

"Why not?" My words come out a whisper.

He leans in. "Did you say something?"

"Why not?" The words come out much louder this time.

He huffs, his eyes filling with disdain. "You're a goddamn mother, that's why. Stop being so selfish." He moves toward the door. "This conversation is over, and I hope it's the last of its kind." Pausing before he disappears from the room, he turns back. "Unless, of course, you want to lose everything."

Before I can respond, he's gone, leaving his words like an anvil sitting heavy on my chest, trapping me there, unable to scream, unable to move, unable to leave.

NOVEMBER 23, 2018

You'd think Evan's threats about taking the girls if we got divorced would scare me away from Thomas, but it does exactly the opposite. I need him more than ever. Evan makes me feel powerless, as though I have no real definition without him or the girls or this house. Thomas makes me feel powerful, as though anything is possible, and with him I'm the person I was before I started sacrificing bits of myself for the approval of others.

As soon as everyone is out of the house this morning, I text him. *Today? Hotel?*

He responds almost immediately. *Yes. Will cancel meeting. 12pm.*

This time I make sure I have an alibi and go grocery shopping, placing things in the cart without thought. Moving up and down the aisle at a slow, calculated pace, killing time. The eighties pop playlist that leaks through the speakers of the store works like torture, the Chinese water kind—Whitney Houston wanting to dance with somebody. My body is wound tight with the anticipation of seeing Thomas, every bit of skin more sensitive. Even bending down to reach a jar of pickles feels sensual.

Standing in the checkout line, I survey the other customers. The woman with a newborn in the car seat, who looks down every few seconds to make sure her baby is still there, alive, and asleep—I've been her. The woman with the toddler climbing up the side of the cart, his mother extracting him from it before he climbs right in—I've been her too. The man staring into space, beaten down by the tedium of his day-to-day tasks—I've been him. I wonder if any of them have secrets like mine, if their grocery shopping is a guise for something more illicit.

At the Somersby, before heading to the elevator, I do a very quick scan of the lobby. The last thing I need is Libby jumping out from behind some potted plant to catch me in the act again. Alone in the elevator, I reach into my new black lacy bra, which I purchased last minute in the clothing section of the grocery store and slipped on in the car, and lift each breast higher. It's official, I think to myself. There's no more denying it—I'm having a full-blown affair. I've bought lingerie and am rendezvousing in a hotel in the middle of the day.

The elevator reaches the twelfth floor, and the doors slide open. There's a brief tug of conscience, a bolt of fear, a split second of paralysis, before I step out into the hall, letting my desire lead me, leaving all good sense to travel back down to the lobby.

Thomas opens the door with only a towel around his waist, still damp from a shower, and I wonder if this whole thing could get any more clichéd. Not that I don't appreciate seeing so much of his skin, or smelling the sweet muskiness of his soap, or the ability to pull his towel free and have exactly what I want.

"Come on in." He waves me through the door. "I just got out of the shower after a quick workout."

"You weren't at work?" I ask, pulling my shoes off at the door.

"No, I canceled the whole day as soon as you texted."

I pause mid coat removal. "Thomas, that's too much. I didn't mean to interfere with your work that deeply. I just thought we could have a quick visit in between things."

He pushes my coat off the rest of the way and then pulls me in close to him. "Don't you mean quick hookup? Because that's the sense I got from your text."

"I just really needed to see you." I don't tell him that my urgency is due to a fight with Evan that makes me feel like I can never leave my marriage. I don't want Evan here in the room with us.

He reaches up and strokes the side of my jaw. "I like hearing you say that. I was worried that the zoo spooked you and you'd be too afraid to see me again."

I gently push at the sides of his towel so that it falls away from his body. "I should be," I whisper, before reaching down to feel him, already hard. "I really should be." He moans and pulls me toward the bed. I guide him to sit on the edge and then take a step back so that I can get my clothing off. He reaches up with one hand to cup my breast, his thumb stroking the lace of my new bra.

"You're so beautiful." His words come out soft and full of awe. And that's why I'm here. Why I'm willing to risk so much—to be seen, to be beautiful, to be free, if only for a few hours.

THEN

After things about me and Thomas came out, we had only a couple of weeks before exams and then the Christmas holidays. I'd promised my dad I'd bring my grades up, so I spent a lot of time at home studying. The only time Thomas and I really had together was when he would sneak over in the middle of the night. I'd let him in through the back door, and we'd have sex in the living room. My dad was a heavy sleeper, but even if he did wake up, I'd hear the footsteps and have time to get Thomas out before he made it downstairs. This also meant that we didn't leave Scarlett out in order to be together. We didn't admit it out loud, but bringing our relationship right out in the open still made us nervous when it came to Scarlett.

After Thomas got back from his Christmas holidays and school started up again, we did our best to go back to normal. We started handing out dares again and still ended up in bed together, all three of us, snoring drunkenly after a party. We just didn't do any of the extracurricular stuff, and Scarlett would leave in the morning to go back to her dorm room to give me and Thomas time alone. There was a stiffness to things and Scarlett often seemed more distant than usual, but I figured that it would work itself out over time. That it was a temporary adjustment period. And most importantly, I had Thomas, and that was all that really mattered to me.

If I'd known it would last only a few months, then I would have relished it more, guarded it better.

DECEMBER 22, 2018

There haven't been any more dares, just a couple of afternoon visits to Thomas's hotel room. The game was the gateway, and now that we're fully in the landscape of an affair, it's been forgotten. I stay away as long as I can, depriving myself, as though it makes what we're doing less wrong if I'm not taking it whenever I can. And I'm careful, very careful, always having an alibi, always looking over my shoulder.

Scarlett hasn't written me back since the last message. I check every day, relieved when there's nothing from her but at the same time unnerved by it. Silent Scarlett is as scary as vocal Scarlett, and I can't help wondering what she's up to and why she seems to have given up on the anti-Thomas campaign so easily. I've gone to write her a few times but always end up deleting it.

At home I've been working hard to compensate for my sins. I've made sugar cookies from scratch, decorated a gingerbread house with the girls, made wreaths for the windows from real greenery. As though the good mother in me can tip the scales—outweigh the adulterer in me.

Evan keeps remarking on how pleasantly surprised he is by my domestic accomplishments, I'm sure he thinks it's because I've decided to try harder to please him, be the wife and mother he thinks I should be. He has no idea that it's fueled by guilt. That I'm not working hard at our marriage, I'm working hard at being two different people living in two different worlds.

Ironically, it's Evan who brings my two worlds colliding together. It happens when we've just finished putting up the Christmas tree. I let him pick it without argument. I've let the girls put the ornaments wherever they want, still in makeup mode, just wanting to please everyone.

Evan has his back to me as he rearranges a strand of lights. "I think we should have a little Christmas get-together. Invite some neighbors, and you can invite Thomas. Would be fun, don't you think?"

His question catches me off guard. I wonder if it's a test. Does he suspect something? Is he setting me up? If I say no, will that sound defensive? If I say yes, will it sound too eager?

"Don't you think?" My silence has finally inspired him to ask again.

I stare at the back of him. His shoulder blades look like small moving wings caught under his plaid shirt. The red lights on the tree make his blond hair look auburn. Studying him in pieces almost makes him autonomous, something outside the marriage.

He abandons the lights and looks at me with annoyance. "What? You don't want to be social even at Christmas?"

He should wish for capriciousness in me when it comes to Thomas. "Sure," I say, with as casual a shrug as I can manage. "I'll get in touch with Thomas; you invite the neighbors."

As soon as I agree to it, the dread sets in.

*   *   *

Libby is the first to arrive, carrying a homemade yule log and looking Christmas ready with a festive red blouse, nails and lips to match, and a trim black skirt. And I thought I was dressed up for the night in dark skinny jeans, a silky white tank top, and a green cardigan.

"Your wreaths smell divine, Hannah," she gushes, leaning in for a half hug to protect her cake. "So lovely of you to have us." Her husband, Rob, stands behind her, already looking bored but as good-looking as ever, with his black hair and olive skin, and dressed impeccably. I can't help thinking of him and Libby as the Barbie and Ken of the neighborhood, the couple that could be on the FOR SALE signs for houses on the street, with their perfect twin girls. Rob hands me a bottle of wine and looks distractedly past me to see who else is here.

"So glad you could come," I say with forced enthusiasm, hoping they'll move farther into the house and Evan can deal with them, but she stays there, her smile growing wider.

"Exciting news, Hannah. The security cameras will be going up around the neighborhood in a matter of days. I managed to get the majority of the neighbors to sign the petition, outnumbering those who opposed it. Thanks in part to your signatures."

"My signature?" I had completely forgotten about her Gestapo camera campaign, but it quickly comes rushing back.

She cocks her head to the side, her smiling lessening. "Yes. Evan got the petition back to me with both your signatures."

"Did he now?"

"And good thing," she continues, oblivious to my shock. "There have been three more sightings of the creeper since I spoke to you last."

I remind myself that our neighborhood Christmas party is not the place to tell off both my neighbor and my husband and push the anger down deep to fester. "Please go on in. Evan will get you a drink," I say, reaching for their coats while directing them toward the living room, to get them away from me.

I take their coats into the office to make a coat pile. Normally Evan gets the girls to greet the guests and take their coats, but I suggested they sleep at friends' houses for the night, which means I'm on coat duty, but more importantly that my children and my lover are not crossing paths.

The room still smells slightly of my father's pipe smoking, despite Evan's many efforts to get rid of it. I take a deep breath to steel myself for a party I never wanted. Stepping back out into the front foyer, I almost collide with Thomas, who's just coming through the front door.

"Henny," he says, with as much excitement as I feel. His appearance makes me feel instantly better.

He leans down for a hug, and every bit of me jumps to life as his body meets mine, as I smell his smell, feel the cold from outside coming in with him. "I've missed you," he whispers.

I laugh. "It's only been a week and a half," I whisper back. Glancing into the living room, I see Evan deeply engrossed in a conversation with Libby and her husband, so I pull Thomas into the office and shut the door. "I'll just take your coat," I say, pulling it free from his body and chucking it on the small pile before moving right up against him so that he knows what I want and the urgency of it. My anger at Evan about the petition makes me reckless, as though I'm entitled to some payback.

We work quickly, our lips meeting, his hands up my tank top to pull my bra down and roll my nipple between his fingers, sending currents of warmth through my torso. Voices outside the door shove us apart like a strong hand, and I quickly shrug my bra back into place and yank my sweater down.

The office door swings open, and I step forward, this time almost colliding with Evan.

"Hiding from the party already, Hannah?" Evan says, his voiced laced with annoyance. He then sees Thomas standing off to the side, his hands strategically in his pockets. "Ah, Tom, didn't see you there," he says, turning friendly in an instant. "Glad you could make it."

"I was just putting Thomas's coat away," I explain, gesturing to the coats that are thrown over the back of the love seat.

Evan thrusts two more coats at me. "Can you add these to the pile, please, and then come do your best impression of social? The Tompkins are here now."

I don't dare look at Thomas as we leave the office and make our way into the living room, afraid of what a look between us might betray to anyone watching closely.

I bring Thomas over to the bar that we've set up and pour him a drink. "Is the busybody neighbor here tonight?" he leans in to ask.

"Across the room in the red sweater," I say under my breath. "She was the first to arrive."

Libby stands at the Christmas tree, a glass of wine in her hand, the other toying with an ornament—a round white globe plastered with Rose's baby face and the words *Baby's first Christmas* below it. I imagine it slipping from the branch, through her fingers, and smashing on the floor below. She turns away from the tree and looks right at me, as though she's sensed me staring. Our eyes meet and she lets go of the ornament, excuses herself from the group she's in, and heads right for me.

"Wonderful party, Hannah," she says, as soon as she's within ear-shot. "The food is delicious."

"That would be Evan's handiwork. He spent the whole day in the kitchen wrapping things in pastry and stuffing things with cheese."

Libby's eyes widen in shocked admiration. "Well, aren't you lucky having a husband who can cook and entertain. Rob is hopeless at both."

"Libby, this is my friend Thomas Sutton. We went to college together. Thomas, this is Libby from down the street."

Thomas smiles widely and holds out his hand. "Pleasure to meet you, Libby."

She smiles tightly and returns the handshake. "We've actually already met. That one day when you were dropping Hannah off?"

"Ah, yes, of course," Thomas says. I'm cursing inside. I'd hoped Libby had forgotten that meeting. How naïve of me; this woman doesn't forget a thing.

*   *   *

The night rolls past in a blur. I mostly stay in constant motion, going from one group to the next, excusing myself to go into the kitchen whenever the conversation bores me. I hide out as long as I can, pretending to fuss with the food, before Evan comes in to escort me back out there.

I keep an eye on Thomas all through the night. He does well mingling and charming the neighbors. We keep a safe distance, only coming together a few times while in the company of others, me taking every opportunity I can to put a hand on his arm or brush my body against his as I pass by.

My only interactions with Evan are curt discussions about ice or the need for more crackers or reminders to watch my wine intake—no touching. There's a poorly masked suspicion in his eyes every time we come together, as if he's afraid I'm going to do something to wreck his carefully crafted party.

By ten thirty I'm back to hiding in the kitchen with a topped-up glass of wine. I just want everyone to go home; I have no more small talk left in me to make. This time it's Thomas who finds me as I stand leaning against the counter, cramming a cold cheese puff into my mouth.

"Are you also looking for a place to hide?" I ask.

"No, I was looking for you." He stands beside me at the counter so that our arms are touching. "Although I could use some hiding from your neighbor Libby and her boring husband. She gave me the third degree, and then I had to talk real estate with her for way too long. She even asked for my cell number, saying she wants to invite me to some networking events she organizes. The whole time her husband just stood there, barely saying a word."

The cheese puff quickly turns to a stone in the pit of my stomach. "It sounds like she suspects something, Thomas."

He shakes his head. "No. It sounds like she's a super nosy neighbor." He bumps my hip gently. "And even if she did suspect something, she has absolutely no proof of anything except seeing you and me together a couple of times in my car, which can easily be explained to Evan."

As though saying his name has summoned him, Evan appears in the kitchen. "What about Evan?" he asks, the suspicion even more present in his eyes.

Thomas pops one of the cold cheese puffs in his mouth and chews hard. "*Tell Evan how amazing these things are* was what I was just saying to Hannah."

The compliment makes Evan relax and smile. "You wouldn't believe how easy they are," he says, then directs his gaze to me, the smile falling away. "People are leaving. Can you please play gracious hostess for just five more minutes and say your good-byes?"

"I'm going to get going as well," Thomas says.

"Don't go yet." The words fly out before I have time to catch them.

Only when I hear a snide chuckle from Evan do I realize what I've done. "Interesting," he says, with yet another chuckle. "All of a sudden the antisocial one is feeling social." There's an awkward beat of silence before Evan turns and leaves the room. Thomas looks at me with an exaggerated grimace, and I do the same back to him.

"I certainly appreciate you pleading with me to stay, but I get the feeling that he doesn't," he says, a satisfied smile on his face.

I wave my hand in the direction Evan went. "Whatever. He's always looking for something to be irritated with me about."

Thomas moves right up against me and puts his face in my neck. "Well, he's not wrong to be in our case." He gently bites my neck and I give him a hard shove away from me.

"Are you trying to get me a divorce for Christmas?"

He shrugs. "I could think of worse things to get you."

Evan's threatening words about taking everything come rushing back to me, and I shake my head. "Let's not even joke." I reach for my glass of wine and take a long sip.

Thomas holds up both hands. "Sorry. It was just a joke, though. I wouldn't intentionally blow up your life. You know that, right?"

"Of course I do."

"I do find it strange that I was invited."

"Evan told me to. I thought it could look suspicious if I didn't. As though I was hiding something."

He nods and puts his hands in his pockets and rocks a bit on the balls of his feet. "Will I be able to see you soon?"

"Not until after Christmas. When the school holidays are over."

He sighs and runs a hand through his hair. "I understand. It's family time." He moves in and kisses me on the cheek. "Merry Christmas, Henny," he whispers in my ear. "I'll be thinking of you."

He turns to go, and a dull ache of missing him starts before he's even left the room. "Merry Christmas, Thomas." He turns back at my words, and I blow him a kiss. He gives me a nod, his eyes full of knowing, before leaving the room.

* * *

I fill the compost with broken cracker bits and olive pits, the hollowed-out shell of Brie, and some remaining chunks of hardened cheese, then stack the dishwasher with dirty glasses. Evan disappeared upstairs as soon as everyone was gone, so I've stayed downstairs to clean up.

One wine bottle still has enough for a modest nightcap, so I find a juice tumbler and fill it before throwing the bottle in the recycling bin with the other bottles we've drunk. I turn off all the downstairs lights except the Christmas tree and sit down on the couch with my wine. Heavy snowflakes fall outside, illuminated in the window by the lights of the tree, making me feel like I'm in a snow globe of quiet and stillness.

"Hannah." Evan bursts that peaceful bubble, startling me so that I spill some wine onto my jeans. I rub it away with my thumb.

"I thought you went to bed."

"I can't sleep."

"Would you like some herbal tea?" I ask. "The kind I give Rose when she can't sleep." I put my glass on the coffee table and move to get up.

"No," he says firmly. "I don't want any tea. I want to talk to you."

I sink back into the couch, doing my best to ready myself for what I'm sure is round two of the last time we had a talk in the living room with me drinking wine. Evan sits down in the chair across from me, and when I see the look on his face, the preemptive defensiveness I was feeling drains away. He looks anxious, not mad or condescending.

"What's going on between you and Thomas?"

My head snaps back slightly at the question, and I'm hoping it reads as surprise, not fear. "What do you mean, what's going on?"

"Libby mentioned that she's seen you together with him, more than once."

Panic tears through my wine-foggy brain, quickly sobering me. I had predicted this exact thing from Libby, told Thomas I was sure she suspected something, so I should have been better prepared, but I'm not. I'm caught off guard, my stomach instantly knotting, a sickly heat wave spreading through my body.

"Together where? And when exactly?" Somehow I manage indignation and authentic confusion, not what I'm really feeling—terror.

"She said she's seen him drop you off at home a few times, in the middle of the day."

"Fucking gossip," I mutter under my breath, unable to help myself.

"What?" Evan asks.

"I went for lunch with him one day, and another day we went for a walk. Nothing serious, just catching up after years of not seeing one another." I add a shrug to further the charade of nonchalance.

He mulls over my answer, looking for holes. "Why didn't you tell me?"

"Why didn't you tell me about forging my signature on the petition for the neighborhood security cameras? The petition that I specifically said I didn't want to sign." My ability to deflect blame and focus terrifies and amazes me.

"It's not the same thing at all. One's about the safety of our children, and one's about you sneaking around with another man."

"If I was sneaking around, then why did I get dropped off in broad daylight? And why are you suddenly so close to our neighbor that she's reporting back to you about my comings and goings and you're helping to push her Big Brother agenda for the neighborhood?"

Evan gets up from his chair, the anxiousness gone, replaced by his usual annoyance. "She's our neighbor, Hannah. She's not reporting back to me, just mentioning some things, and the entire world is not one of your novels. Security cameras on the street are a good thing, for the safety of our children, not some dictatorship spying on us." He gives his head a shake and sighs heavily. "I'm going to bed."

Only when he leaves the room do I fully exhale. We just played a tennis match of accusations, and I'm not sure who won. What I am sure of is that it's not over.

My phone dings with the arrival of a Facebook message. I tap my phone awake. It's from Scarlett. I'm not sure I can take her and Evan in one night, but curiosity gets the better of me and I open the message.

Sorry for the delay in responding, I was in Vietnam on a "no phones" yoga retreat. I've been thinking a lot about things, and you were right in your last message, I should have been better at keeping in touch. I should have been a better friend. I'll lay off about Thomas but first please tell me he hasn't blown up your life or anything. Please tell me you're being careful.

I can't give Scarlett the answer she wants, so I toss my phone on the floor and lie down on the couch. Curling into a tight ball, I quickly drift off, suffering dreams of Libby, Evan, and Scarlett appearing around every corner, with Thomas always just out of reach.

THEN

Early April was unseasonably warm. The snow had melted by the middle of March, and by Easter weekend flowers were already bursting through the damp soil. It wasn't long before final exams. You could feel the frenzy in the air that comes when an end to something is in sight. There were parties almost every night, students out on campus and the streets at all hours. There was a low hum of anticipation in the air, and combined with the warmth of spring, it created the feeling that something big could happen at any moment.

It got to us too. Thomas and I couldn't keep our hands off each other. We felt the separation of summer pushing against our backs, which made us push up against each other even harder. We went into the woods between classes, into bathrooms at parties, into alleyways outside of bars. We didn't need a lot of time; we just needed a lot of each other. With his adept hands and hard, fast thrusts and my ability to contort into almost any position, climax came easily for both of us.

*   *   *

Scarlett decided we had time left for just one more dare before we had to start studying. It was her turn to give one to Thomas. She swore it was going to be a good one. The call to the Daring Tree came the day before one of the biggest parties of the year. One of the fraternities hosted an annual fund raiser at Berkshire Lakeside Camp, which was about twenty minutes out of town. Buses took people out, and there were cabins to stay in and some people brought tents. The party apparently lasted until the buses returned the next day to bring everyone back to the city. Tickets were hard to come by, but of course Scarlett found a way to get three, claiming she'd had to blow the entire fraternity to get them so Thomas and I should be very appreciative. I was pretty sure she'd just used her parents' money, paying way more than the original price.

* * *

Scarlett and Thomas were already at the Daring Tree when I got there. I could tell from the look on his face that he'd been given the dare and did not like it.

"Not another seduce-your-professor dare, I hope," I said as soon as I reached them.

Scarlett huffed indignantly. "I would never, especially now that you two lovebirds are an item." Then she pretended to puke before breaking into laughter that sounded like birds fighting.

Thomas didn't say anything, just handed me the notebook so I could read it myself. The dare was to slip a tab of acid into the drink of the school's star quarterback, Jefferson Smith, at the party. Tall, dark, and very good looking, he was one of the most popular guys at the school.

"That could end badly," I said, handing the notebook back to Thomas.

Scarlett thumbed in his direction. "That's what he said. But I disagree. That guy is a total douchebag and could really benefit from a little Daring Game therapy." She lifted both hands into the air. "Who knows, it may just expand his consciousness so much that he actually becomes a decent guy." She let them fall back to her sides. "So, in essence, we're doing the world a favor."

Thomas shook his head. "I don't think it's a good idea, Scarlett. Sorry to ruin the last dare of the season, but I'm out."

"Don't be hasty," she said. "Just give it some thought. I'll bring the acid, and you can decide later. Just hang out with the guy for a bit, and you'll be dying to fuck with him."

Thomas reached out and took my hand, and Scarlett's eyes narrowed for a brief second before she quickly recovered. "I think we should just call it on the dares for now," he said. "And pick up again in September."

Scarlett raised both eyebrows in shock and disgust at his suggestion. "Are you fucking kidding me, Thomas? That's not fair at all. Hannah and I both completed your last dares. You can't just call it."

"Fine, then give me a different one. But not at the party. I just wanna go and have a good time. Why don't we just take the acid ourselves and have a good laugh at everyone?"

Scarlett went to protest, her mouth opening but then snapping shut again as she contemplated Thomas's idea, and then she gave a nonchalant shrug. "Okay, maybe you're right. I'll bring it and we'll see how things go."

Thomas let go of my hand to reach out and pull Scarlett in for a group hug. "Don't be mad, Scary," he said into the huddle. "I just don't want anything to ruin the last bit of time we have together before I go home for the summer."

Scarlett gave him a quick peck on the cheek, and my stomach tightened. "You're a total chickenshit, but you know I love you."

I pulled free from the two of them, suddenly needing air. Something didn't feel right about the easily reached peace treaty between Scarlett and Thomas, but I couldn't put it into words. I just knew I wanted to get away from the Daring Tree and was happy that Thomas had forfeited his final dare.

*　　*　　*

Despite the camp setting, the party was formal. I borrowed one of Scarlett's little black dresses. Her parents were always dragging her to fancy functions, so her wardrobe of dresses was enviable. My dad had never forced me to go anywhere except the occasional faculty dinner, where only cardigans were mandatory.

Scarlett chose an emerald-green dress that electrified her eyes, and Thomas wore his customary black jeans but with a black button-down to dress things up.

The three of us crammed into one seat for the bus ride, passing a flask between us. It felt like old times again, before everything became complicated, and so I naively slipped my armor off and decided to just enjoy it.

The camp was made up of dozens of cabins, three tall boathouses that lined the shore, and a large hall where the main party was. As soon as we stepped off the bus, we could hear the music pumping through the warm, clear night, spreading itself out over the lake, turning the entire landscape into one big party.

A couple of hours into the night, Thomas and I ducked away from the party to one of the empty cabins. It smelled of damp pine and the many campers who had stayed there over the years with their wet bathing suits, smelly shoes, bug spray, and sunscreen. Climbing into one of the lower bunks, we had slow, sloppy, drunk sex, hidden by the thick darkness of forest, with the sound of the lake lapping up against the rocky shore coming through the open window. When I came, I let the sound of it carry out into the night, not caring who heard.

Lying there with Thomas when we were finished, I was happy, the kind that comes easily, that you don't have to work to summon up. I couldn't remember ever having had that kind of happiness before.

"Let's just stay here for the night," Thomas said, and I knew he was feeling the same way I was. He always did.

I wanted to say yes, but the tug of Scarlett being alone at the party found me. "We should get back. Make sure Scary isn't getting into trouble." He groaned, but we both knew it was the right thing to do, so we climbed out of the bottom bunk and got back into the bits of clothing we'd removed.

As we were leaving the cabin, a flash of green caught my eye from within the forest. "Scarlett?" I called out.

She stepped out in the open, tugging her skirt down. "There you guys are. I was just taking a pee. The lineup to the girl's bathroom is ridiculous." She gave us an exaggerated wink. "Sneak off for some fun, did you?"

"Yeah, sorry. Were you looking for us?" I asked.

She shook her head. "Not really; only noticed you were gone when I was looking for somewhere to pee." She turned her attention full to Thomas, grabbing his arm and pulling him up against her. "I haven't forgotten about the dare, you know."

"This again?" he responded, sounding annoyed.

"Just come talk to him, and you'll see what a total jerk he is. Then, if you still don't want to do the dare. you don't have to. Deal?"

Thomas huffed. "Fine." The word was barely out of his mouth before Scarlett was pulling him back toward the party, leaving me a few paces behind.

Thomas looked back over his shoulder for me, but I waved him on, not wanting to be part of the struggle around Scarlett's stupid dare. I knew Thomas wouldn't do it, so I'd just wait until he'd appeased her and then we could go back to having a fun night.

I took a path down to one of the boathouses. The night air was cool, and I wished I'd brought my sweater with me. There was a small huddle of people at the end of the dock, smoking a joint. They opened the circle for me to join and offered it to me. I took one quick puff and passed it on. I didn't want to get too muddled up that night; I wanted to remember it, to be lucid and get everything I could out of it. Maybe it was the fairy-tale lake setting, being there with my two best friends, or being in love, or maybe the combination of all three.

I wandered along the many paths for a little while, giving myself a tour of the old camp before heading into the main party again. Scanning the room, I spotted Thomas standing with Jefferson Smith, the quarterback, and a few other people I didn't know. They were laughing about something, looking as though they'd just shared an inside joke. I felt relief; clearly Thomas thought the guy was okay if he was still standing there talking to him. Scarlett wouldn't be able to convince him to go through with the dare.

Scarlett suddenly appeared at Thomas's side, three beers clutched awkwardly in her hands. She held one out to Thomas. He took it but then passed it to Jefferson before taking one from Scarlett for himself. Only as they clinked bottles before tipping their heads back to drink did I realize what Scarlett had done.

JANUARY 7, 2019

Christmas went by in a blur. Evan and I managed to keep it together. I pretended to be happy about the new vacuum he gave me; he ignored my wine intake. We even had a nice time at his parents' farm for the few days that we went there. And unless family obligation called for it, we kept a safe distance. He didn't ask me about Thomas again, and I let Libby's security camera petition thing go.

By the time the holidays are over, I'm exhausted by the constant company of my family, the charade with Evan. I'm desperate to see Thomas. We've planned a full day together at his hotel. I set up the alibi this morning, casually telling Evan I'm going to see if I can return a sweater we got Rose that didn't fit and maybe do a bit of shopping downtown for the day. I'm just on my way out the door when I get a text from Evan. He forgot his laptop at home, and on it there's something he worked on over the holidays that he needs for a meeting in twenty minutes. He asks if I can email it to him.

Following his instructions, I key in the password, find the document in his work folder, and email it to him, all within five minutes, not even getting a thank-you in response. I'm about to close the laptop and leave, but a file at the very bottom of his desktop catches my attention, titled *Proof*. I've never had access to his computer before and wouldn't have if it hadn't been a work emergency. He usually keeps his devices with him, password protected.

It's my own guilt that makes the name of the file stand out, and I know that, which is also why I click on it. Inside is a document titled *H*. I click on that. I know right away it's about me. The dates start all the way back to when I took too many pills and ended up in the hospital and continue right up to the present. The more recent entries are mostly a catalog of how many drinks I've had in a night. The dinner with Thomas is listed, the one that included Evan back in October. In the notes for that one, he claims public drunkenness, humiliation, and embarrassment.

The dates don't just include my drinking violations but also what Evan calls negligence of household duties. Days he returned home to a mess, or when there wasn't *an adequate amount of food* in the house; me lying about dropping his dry cleaning off; the time I forgot to send a permission form for Gracie and had to drive down to the school to drop it off. For the day I slept in, because Evan let me, and he had to get the kids off to school, his description in the log reads, *Unable to wake up and get kids to school due to heavy drinking the night before.*

Reading through the detailed cataloging of every minor offense I'd committed over the past two years twists my stomach into knots and brings tears to my eyes. Evan and I have our problems, but I'd still always thought of home as my safe place. I'd thought the neighborhood cameras were an invasion, not knowing that what was going on in my house was worse.

I click out of the document and open another one in the file, titled *H. Activity.* It's another log but much shorter than the first one, mostly the dates and times that Libby saw me coming and going from the house—the day Thomas dropped me off after the water tower dare, and then the day I'd gone to see that house in the woods with Thomas and she'd jogged past the car. There's also the time she ran into me at the Somersby Hotel. Evan's also included dates and times when he's come home and I haven't been here. It appears it's happened more than I realized. The log doesn't create conclusive evidence of anything, really, but it does show me that Evan and Libby are on the same team, closer than I'd imagined and with the same goal—to bring me down.

There are three other documents in the file. One is a scan of my admittance to the hospital psych ward when they thought I'd tried to kill myself. The other is a scan of the initial evaluation by the psychiatrist on my first day in the hospital. The third is the autopsy report for my mother, which makes it very clear that cause of death was excessive drinking.

I hit print on everything in the folder, then sit back in the chair in shock. The only sound in the room is the rhythmic chug of the printer, which works like a hammer against my brain. I could just delete it, I think to myself, but what if he has a copy of it saved somewhere else and deleting it just becomes another one of my offenses to add to the list? I decide to take my chances, right- clicking on the folder and hitting delete before I can change my mind.

It doesn't make me feel any better. For all I know, he's already sent the file to a lawyer. I'm suddenly aware of the lengths Evan will go to win, how methodical and calculated he really is. How careful I have to be until I can figure out an escape. One that won't cost me everything.

The buzz of my phone in my pocket makes me jump. It's a message from Thomas, telling me to text him when I'm on my way and he can meet me at the side door of the hotel. I stare at the message, the plan to see him suddenly seeming so much more perilous than it did twenty minutes ago. For all I know, Libby is sitting at her living room window waiting for me to make a move so she can text Evan.

I think about calling him, telling him what I just found, asking for his help, but the embarrassment stops me. If I did that, I'd have to explain to Thomas what Evan has so meticulously cataloged: my bad behavior, my failures. My marriage and choice of husband being one of them. Instead, I write back that I have to cancel. That I'm suddenly not feeling well at all and don't want to get him sick. That I'll text him as soon as I feel better.

It's not a lie. After finding that folder, I have a pounding headache. I feel sick to my stomach and feverish.

I want to get undressed and get back in bed. To sleep the day away and forget what I just found, forget the mistakes I've made, mistakes that could be the match to the fire Evan is building, should they ever get out. But I don't.

I collect what I've printed out and hide it in a shoebox in my closet. Then I put on an old tracksuit and start cleaning, wiping down baseboards, washing windows, cobwebs, scrubbing the tiles in the bath-room until my hands are pink and raw. I make sure every bit of laundry is washed, dried, folded, and put away. If I've been able to get rid of that incriminating file, there won't be a single infraction for Evan to start over with. And then, once I've established a cleaner record, I'll leave without risking everything. It's a long-range plan, but it's the only one I can think of. It means giving up Thomas, but he was something I shouldn't have had in the first place

When I'm finished cleaning the house, I go to the grocery store, where I buy every single one of Evan's favorite things, along with a roast for dinner, all the while forgoing the wine aisle. *Kill him with kindness*, I keep thinking, wishing it were a literal saying.

After unloading the groceries, I head out to the sidewalk to bring in the garbage and recycling bins. One of them has tipped over into a pud-dle of dirty, slushy snow beside the curb. I bend down to retrieve it and feel a hand on my shoulder, stopping me.

"I'll get it."

Straightening up, I see it's Rob, Libby's husband. His face is flushed from running, his clothes mud splattered and damp. It's the most unkempt I think I've ever seen him. He picks both bins up easily and starts walking them toward my house.

"How was your Christmas?" he asks, after placing them beside the house.

"Ah, it was good," I manage to get out, taken aback at his sudden friendliness. "How about you?"

"Wonderful," he says with conviction, but the sentiment doesn't show in his eyes. They still have that vacant look that I've come to asso-ciate with him, like he's Libby's Stepford husband. "It's always so good to spend time with family over the holiday," he adds.

"Depends on the family," I say, but he doesn't laugh. "Joking, of course. Family is what holidays are all about." Wetness from the snow on the front lawn is slowly seeping through the bottom of my running shoes. I shift from one foot to the other and rub my hands together, hoping he'll catch the hint: I'm cold, he's awkward, and I want to go inside.

"Family really is everything, don't you think, Hannah?" The tone of his voice doesn't match what he's saying. There's sadness to it, or is it regret, or possibly disapproval? He's impossible to read, and I can't tell if he's being calculated, like his wife is, or if he's just a very strange man.

"Thank you for bringing my bins up," I say, no longer willing to stand out in the cold and try to figure him out or make the exchange any less awkward. I give a little wave and start toward the stairs of my porch. Fortunately, he takes the hint and starts walking down the driveway, slowly, again looking more like a robot than a real person.

"That's what neighbors are for," he says, before he's fully out of earshot. *And in the case of your wife, for spying and reporting to people's husbands*, I think to myself as I hurry into the house, wishing suddenly that I lived anywhere but our quiet cul-de-sac.

*   *   *

When Evan gets home, the house is spotless and smells of roast beef and Yorkshire pudding. The girls are doing their homework at the kitchen table, and I'm cutting up vegetables for a salad with a glass of ice water beside me.

He kisses the girls on the tops of their heads. "Wow, something smells good," he says, surveying the stove behind me, his eyes flitting over my glass of water. "And the house looks great. You must have had a busy day."

"I did," I answer curtly.

"Well, it's nice to come home to after the day I've had."

"Will you go on record with that?" I ask, keeping my eyes on the red onion I'm cutting.

"What?"

I shake my head at his question. "Nothing."

"I'm going to go lie down on the couch until dinner. Call me when it's ready." He moves in to give me his customary after-work kiss on the cheek.

I hold the knife up between us, the wide, shiny blade only inches from his face. "I'm cutting onion; you don't want to get too close."

He gives me a puzzled look but steps back, then points at the glass with a little chuckle. "That's water, right?"

I smile wide, so wide I know it will unnerve him. "Nothing but."

He shoots me another look of confusion. Watching him leave the room, I try to remember what drew me to him in the first place. To latch on to some remembrance of the beginning feelings, the ones that trick you into believing you'll survive a lifetime of monogamy and companionship together, but there's nothing there. Just a loud echo of emptiness in the space that used to hold love for him.

JANUARY 15, 2019

I've been putting Thomas off for over a week now, claiming to be sick, then to be taking care of sick kids, any excuse I can think of for not seeing him, other than the truth. I want to see him, desperately, but I'm too afraid to do anything other than focus on doing everything right at home.

Evan hasn't said anything about the deleted *Proof* file, but that doesn't mean he hasn't noticed, or that it wasn't backed up somewhere else. I watch him closely while he watches me. I see him take note of the glass of water I bring to dinner each night, the cups of tea I drink while reading in the evening. I watch him examine rooms when he comes home. I answer his questions of interrogation about my day, which he thinks are masked as simple husbandly interest.

Last week I watched him talk to Libby for almost twenty minutes at the end of the driveway while putting out the garbage, ending with a squeeze of her arm before she walked away.

This morning I decide to walk the girls down to the bus stop. Only a few feet away, I immediately wish I hadn't. Libby is there waiting with her own kids. She's dressed, full makeup on, her hair blown dry to pin-straight perfection. I threw my long, puffy winter coat on over my pajamas, no makeup, with a beanie crammed on my head to cover my unwashed hair.

She doesn't notice me at first; she's too busy fussing with the twins, zipping their coats up as high as she can, risking pinching their soft neck skin in the zipper, tugging their matching hats down on their heads. She only looks up when the bus arrives and then guides them both with her hands on their backs to the steps, as though they might lose their way somewhere along the two feet of sidewalk they have to travel. I get a quick side hug from Gracie, a barely discernible nod from Rose, and keep my hands to myself as they make their way onto the bus.

"I don't often see you out in the mornings," Libby says to me as soon as the bus has pulled away from the curb.

"Be sure to let Evan know that I was out here doing my motherly duties, will you?"

She cocks her head to the side, and her bob goes swinging. "Sorry?"

I turn to leave without answering her, but she reaches out and puts a hand on my arm, her nails scratching along the quilted surface of my coat. "You should know, Hannah, that there have been several more sightings of the lurker. We have footage caught on one of the security cameras of him coming out from the side of your house just the other night. I told Evan, but he may not have told you. He said he didn't want to worry you."

I give my arm a slight tug, and her hand easily slips free. "You and Evan keep each other abreast of a lot of things, don't you?"

She gives her head another exaggerated tilt to one side. "I'm not sure exactly what you're getting at, Hannah. We're neighbors and we look out for each other; it's just the neighborly thing to do. We have a serious threat in our community right now with this lurker, and it's imperative that we all stick together and keep one another informed about all the comings and goings. How else will we stay safe?" Her cheeks are starting to flush, and her hands open and close into tiny fists at her sides.

"What's the threat exactly, Libby?" I throw both hands into the air. "This lurker, has he broken into any houses, stolen anything, kidnapped any of our kids?" I've convinced myself that my own sighting of the figure in our backyard was just a drunken hallucination, no real threat at all, so it's easy to dismiss Libby's warnings.

She puts a hand to her chest, her mouth forming a perfect round O of dramatized shock. "Is that what it has to come to for us to do something?"

"You know what I think?" My finger involuntarily rises and points right in her face. "I think the lurker is you, Libby. I think as soon as it's dark outside, you put on some black clothing and a hood and roam the neighborhood, making sure to hit the best camera angles, doing just enough to incite fear in everyone. I think you want us all to believe we're in danger so that you can put up your cameras and make your neighborhood rounds, collecting intel on everyone, which you deliver to a select few like freshly baked apple pies. You're a crazed busybody, and the lurker is your grand master plan to have the ultimate control over this boring-as-hell cul-de-sac. And that's what I think about your lurker." I air quote the last word, loving the look of true shock and disgust on her face.

"That is a not only an insulting theory but also an insane one." She spits the last few words out so aggressively that saliva goes flying, leaving white flecks on the sharp pink of her lipsticked mouth. "You are not a well person, Hannah. You really aren't, and I feel so very sorry for you." She spins around, her feet slipping on an icy patch of sidewalk, but she recovers quickly and is gone before I have a chance to say another thing.

As I stare at her ramrod-straight back marching back toward her house, her words ring through my head like an alarm bell: *You're not a well person.* The high I felt while finally telling Libby what I thought about her is quickly turned to a rapid low that sinks my stomach. She will tell Evan about this, and in her version, I'll most certainly look unhinged, aggressive, and not at all like *a well person.*

I hurry home. I fish the neighborhood contact directory, which she made and laminated for everyone on the street, out of the kitchen junk drawer and dial her number. It goes straight to voicemail. I leave a very calm, composed, ass-kissing but generic apology that she will surely understand, even though I don't mention my offense in any way, should it be used against me. Then I flop down on the couch and wonder how bad it's going to be.

JANUARY 16, 2019

It's one of those hectic mornings, when everything feels as though it might tip you over the edge—mayonnaise on the knife handle, the end of the milk carton, your oblivious husband stepping in front of you to get his coffee, the request for the perfect ponytail. Since my run-in with Libby yesterday morning, I've been on edge, waiting for the hammer to drop, sure she would have run and told Evan about it the first chance she got, but he hasn't said a thing.

I don't fully exhale until he leaves for work with a surprisingly cheery good-bye. Waiting for Rose to come down, I'm standing at the front door combing Gracie's hair into the high ponytail she's demanded when I catch a glimpse of Libby on the sidewalk in front of our house. Evan tosses his briefcase in his car and walks over to her.

It's my third attempt at no bumps on Gracie's scalp, so I don't let go until I've secured it with an elastic, even though I'm panicking on the inside. I feel my phone in my back pocket buzz with a text, but I ignore it, keeping my eyes trained on Evan and Libby. They talk for a minute, then both look up at the house and back at each other. Libby says a few more things, then gives him a friendly wave and walks away.

Only then do I pull out my phone and swipe open the new text. *Do you dare?*

I stare at the words in confusion. What would make Thomas think I suddenly wanted to play the game again?

"Do you dare?" I jump as Rose appears behind me, looking over my shoulder at the text, her fourteen-year-old voice holding its

164

regular hint of disdain, but this time tinged with curiosity. "Do you dare what?"

I quickly slide the phone back into my pocket. "It's just some promotional spam."

"You know you can block that kind of stuff, right?" Now the disdain is coupled with disgust. How easy it is for her to see her mother as a complete idiot.

"Block what?" Evan asks, unexpectedly appearing in the front hallway with a travel mug of coffee.

"Nothing," I snap. "Just everyone mind your own business." Rose huffs; Evan shoots me a nasty glare. "Where did you even come from?" I ask him. "I thought you left."

He holds up his mug. "I forgot my coffee, so I went through the kitchen door to get it, since you were all crowded in here." He stares at me for a few seconds, and I'm sure he's going to say something about Libby, but he just pushes past me and reaches for the front door with his free hand. "Try to have a good day, Hannah," he says before slamming it shut.

I wait until Evan's pulled out of the driveway before ushering the girls toward the door.

"Aren't you going to walk us to the bus like yesterday?" Gracie asks while running her hand over her tightly pulled back ponytail, relishing its perfection.

"Not today, sweetie." I pull her in for a tight hug before she can start protesting and then guide her outside after her older sister, releasing a guilty sigh of relief at the final departure of my family. My phone buzzes with another text. *Today-10am.*

Looking at it closely, I realize that both texts have come from a number I don't recognize. Not Thomas's, but it's his words. His taunt. A call to the Daring Tree no longer produces the swoop of butterflies through my belly or the flutter in my chest that it did in the beginning. It's gotten way too complicated, way too dangerous. I'll meet Thomas at the tree, but it won't be to continue the game; it will be to end things. I don't see any other way.

* * *

He's already at the Daring Tree when I get there, pulling something out of our secret hiding place in the crevice. As soon as he sees me, his face lights up and he moves toward me. "My god, it's so good to see you, Henny." He lifts his arms as though to embrace me, but I hold up a hand and take a step back.

"Not here, Thomas. Someone could be watching."

He freezes, confusion all over his face. "I don't understand. Why did you call me to the Daring Tree if you're afraid someone might be watching? I swear that person at the zoo was just a fluke. You don't have to be so paranoid."

"Wait. What do you mean, why did I call you here? You called me here."

"What?" He gives his head a shake. "No, I didn't."

He pulls his phone from his pocket and holds it up for me to see. The exact same texts that I received sit on his screen, from the same unknown number at the exact same time.

Without a word I pull out my phone and show him what I received this morning. "So, you're telling me you didn't send this?"

He shakes his head, shoves his phone back in his pocket. "No more than you sent the one to me, I'm guessing."

I point at the thing he pulled out of the tree that he seems to have forgotten he's still holding—a red envelope. "And that?" I ask.

He shakes his head. "I didn't put it in there."

I take it from him and roughly rip it open. Inside is a piece of red card stock that matches the envelope perfectly, with the words *Tell the truth* typed across it in black.

"What the hell does that even mean?" I ask, showing him the card.

"I have no fucking clue." The look of concern on his face is deeply unsettling. This is not some practical joke he's playing on me. "What I'm more concerned about than the meaning of that dare is who left it here." He holds up his phone with the text message. "Somebody else obviously knows about the game. About us?"

I turn in circles, scanning the area in every direction, but for what exactly, I don't know. Panic slowly builds as the reality of exposure sets in. If they know about the tree, about the game, about us, they could be watching right now. I want to crouch down low, protect myself, but from what? From who?

"How, Thomas? How could anyone have found out. We've been careful." My voice rises in panic with each word, and I already feel tears coming.

"Is there any way that Evan knows?" he asks. The look on my face must tell it all. "Henny, what's wrong?" Thomas puts his hand on my shoulder and looks into my eyes, as though he can pull the information right out of them.

I tell Thomas about the file I found on Evan's computer, including Libby's accounts of my comings and goings. And I tell him about the fight I got into with Libby and how I'm sure she'll tell Evan and it will go right on my record.

"That's really messed up." He runs a hand through his hair and glances around nervously, as though Evan might jump out from behind a tree at any moment.

"I don't know what to do." The tears can be heard in my voice, even with me holding them back. Thomas goes to put his arms around me, but I take a step back. "Don't. Somebody could be watching. Taking photos, even." We both look around again, but there's no sign of anyone. "We can't see each other anymore, or at least for a little while. I can't risk losing my girls if Evan finds out."

Thomas's eyes widen in surprise. "So that's it, then? You're just going to let Evan bully you into staying in an unhappy marriage."

"If it was just about me, then no, I would walk away and leave everything, but I won't do that when it comes to my girls."

"The courts wouldn't take kids away from their mother," he insists with a shake of his head. "Evan won't be able to do that."

"You don't know Evan. The lengths he'll go to win."

"I think you're giving him way too much credit, Henny. And besides, he's probably the one behind this fake dare and already knows. If anything, we need to get through this together. I'll help you fight him. I'll get you the best divorce lawyer money can buy. Don't just end—"

"Thomas," I say loudly, interrupting him. "Stop. I can't even go there in my head right now. Let's just try to figure out who sent those texts calling us here. I don't think it's Evan." I hold up the envelope. "This is not his style at all. He's not the game-playing type. If he knew about us, he would have already filed the divorce papers and changed the locks on the house."

Thomas snaps his fingers. "What about Libby? Your nosy neighbor. She even got my phone number at your Christmas party, so she could have texted me."

"I don't know. I was watching both her and Evan talking outside our house when the text came in. She wasn't on her phone, and neither was he."

"There are ways around that. You can schedule when to send texts."

I shake my head. "She's a busybody, but there's no reason for her to go to these lengths. What would her motivation even be?" I hold up the envelope. "Besides, she's the type of person who wants everyone to know it's her doing things; she's not the secretive type. And if she knew about the Daring Game, then Evan would know about the Daring Game."

An icy wind blows through the cemetery, finding its way through my coat, around my tensed muscles, and deep into my bones. All I want to do is run from here as fast as I can, all the way back in time.

"It could be a bunch of kids, Henny." Thomas continues to theorize. "They saw us meet here. Figured out about the game and are now fucking with us. It can't be anyone important. Anyone who could do damage, or they would have already."

I put my hand to my forehead to massage away the start of a headache. It feels like metal is lodged there, the pain traveling down to the fillings in my back teeth. His theory is full of holes, but I want to believe it.

I hold the note up. "Okay, but what about the note?"

"They could mean anything. The message is vague and could be talking about a million different things."

"So, then what do we do?"

He grabs the note from me and rips it into tiny little pieces before throwing them up in the air. "Nothing. Absolutely nothing."

I stare at the tall, ancient tree in front of us. I imagine cutting it down. Slicing a chainsaw through its pulpy flesh and watching it fall. Wishing it could take all our sins right down with it.

"Okay." The word is barely a whisper. "We ignore it." There's no relief in making that plan. A heavy lump of cold dread quickly forms in the pit of my stomach. I came here today to end it, to save myself and my family, but deep down is the very real fear that it's already too late for that.

"Henny." Thomas comes as close as he can without touching me. "Everything is going to be okay. I'll make sure of it. I won't let anything bad happen." I look up into his dark-brown eyes, which plead with me to trust him. I wish I could. I wish I could just lean into him, let him shelter me from the wind, the worry. The truth is, though, that if he hadn't come back to town in the first place, there wouldn't be anything to shelter me from.

THEN

As soon as I realized that Scarlett had probably just handed Jefferson a beer laced with acid, I raced across the crowded room to try to stop him from drinking it. By the time I got there, he'd already downed more than half of it in one heroic sip. He gave Thomas a pat on the back and then slipped away to talk to another group of people.

"He's not a bad guy at all," Thomas said when I reached them.

I ignored him completely and turned my full attention to Scarlett. "You did it, didn't you?"

Her green eyes widened at the thrill of what she'd just done. "If you mean did I help Thomas complete the last dare of the season, then yes, I did."

"What are you talking about?" Thomas asked, still not putting it all together.

I grabbed Scarlett roughly by the arm and dragged her out of the building and to the quiet of the front lawns. Thomas followed close behind.

"You gave the quarterback a beer with acid in it?" I hissed the question at her, working hard to keep my voice down.

"Technically"—she drew the word out—"Thomas gave him the beer with acid in it."

"Are you fucking kidding me?" Thomas said, his voice raised in a way I'd never heard before. I put a hand on his arm to quiet him and nodded my head toward a group of people sitting on the lawn not too far away.

"Why, Scarlett? Why would you do that?" I asked.

"I hate the guy."

"But why?" Thomas asked, throwing his hands up.

"He called me a slut," she blurted out. "At a party before Christmas, when you"—she thrust a finger at Thomas—"dared me to get ten condoms by the end of the night. I asked him, and he handed me one and said, 'Here you go slut.' And I've seen him treat people like crap. He's just not a nice guy. Okay?"

I couldn't help but shake my head. "I'm not down with guys slut shaming, trust me, but giving someone drugs without them knowing— that's pretty messed-up stuff, Scarlett."

"What's the worst that could happen?" she asked, tossing her hair over one shoulder. "He'll get a bit paranoid, but he'll probably have one of the best nights of his life."

"You'd better hope that's all that happens, Scarlett," Thomas said, already backing away from her. "And you'd better keep an eye on him." He turned and headed across the lawn.

I went to follow him, but Scarlett grabbed my arm. "Please don't leave too, Hannah?" The vulnerability in her voice kept me there. I watched Thomas disappear back into the party. "Can we just try to enjoy the night? Not get all worked up about Jefferson Smith? I swear, it's not going to end up being a big deal. And people slip drugs into other people's drinks all the time. No one will know it was us."

"You," I said firmly.

"Me what?" she asked.

"Don't say nobody will know it was us; it wasn't us who did it, it was you."

She rolled her eyes in exasperation. "Yes, fine, it was me. I get it. There's no more us. Just you and Thomas and ME." She yelled the last part, and people nearby turned to stare.

"This night was supposed to be about us." I hissed the words so that people couldn't overhear. "One last night together partying before exams and before Thomas leaves for the summer. You're the one who went rogue on us and did something stupid."

Scarlett's whole face tightened, and she leaned in closer to me. "And how about when you two snuck off to go have sex in that cabin and left me wandering around looking for you like an idiot?" She glares at me. "There was no us in that twosome, now, was there?" She suddenly started moaning, and I knew right away she was imitating what I'd sounded like having sex with Thomas. People all around us stopped talking and stood there staring, some of them laughing.

"What the fuck, Scarlett? Were you watching through the window?" I once again hissed the words.

"I didn't have to, Hannah. You made sure the whole camp heard you. Hannah Warren finally has a real boyfriend, and she wants everyone to know it." She said the last part the loudest, and a few of the spectators laughed. She glanced over at them and smiled.

My face went beet red. I imagined reaching out and slapping her hard across her smug, angular face, how satisfying it would be to see her shock, to turn that flawless pale skin pink. The heat of my anger and embarrassment spread from my cheeks down into my neck and into my arms until it pulsed in the palms of my hands. I decided to leave before I did anything I'd regret.

Turning, I was stopped by the sight of Thomas, who was headed our way with a scary look of determination on his face.

"I told him," he blurted out as soon as he'd reached us.

"You did what?" I asked.

"I told Jefferson that I thought somebody might have put something in his beer."

Scarlett put a hand on Thomas's chest and pushed him away from the very crowd she'd just been playing to, causing me to move with them.

"You did what?" she snapped as soon as we were out of earshot of anyone.

"You heard me."

"And why the fuck would you do that, Thomas?"

"So that the guy didn't think he was suddenly losing his mind. So that he can tell his friends and they can watch out for him. You know, try to minimize the damage of your stupid revenge plot. You're welcome." He spat the last two words out, leaning toward her, the anger all over his face and body.

"Very noble of you, Thomas, but the least you could have done is talk to us first before you fessed up like that. I certainly hope you didn't use my name in your moment of truth."

"Don't worry, I kept names out of it, but I can always go back in and let him know." He shifted as though he was about to leave.

"You wouldn't dare." Scarlett grabbed at his shirt, yanking him back.

"Isn't that what it's all about, Scarlett? Daring?"

She let go of him and thrust her middle finger up before spinning away and stomping off.

As soon as she was gone, Thomas turned to me. "I couldn't just let the guy trip out unknowingly. Tell me you understand, Henny."

"Yeah, of course," I said, nodding. And I did understand, but that didn't mean I was happy he'd done it. Now the whole night was ruined. I could possibly have come back from my fight with Scarlett, but there was no way she'd forgive Thomas for telling Jefferson.

The party seemed to ramp up all around us, the music getting louder, more people spilling out into the clear night, but our moods no longer matched it. We found a quiet spot on the lawn overlooking the lake and sat down together to share a bottle of wine that Thomas had stolen from inside.

After a little while I spotted Scarlett tucked into a group not too far away. She was swaying in place, so she'd obviously been speed drinking. I thought about going over to make sure she was okay, but the thought exhausted me. Instead, I moved in closer to Thomas.

We watched as a handful of people stumbled down to the docks, some of them stripping off clothing as they went. The others cheered them on, goading them to get into the icy April waters. A few of them did, jumping off the end of the dock, then frantically scrambling up the ladder to escape the cold lake.

"I had a feeling that was going to happen at some point tonight," Thomas said with a laugh.

Before I could reply with a dare for Thomas to do the same, a wild roar—human, not animal—echoed through the air around us. We looked for where it had come from and saw the quarterback doubled over with *the force of it, his face a deep red. The posse of people around him laughed heartily and clapped him on the back. He laughed with them but then just as quickly stopped and began frantically stripping out of his suit.*

"This doesn't look good," Thomas said, just as Jefferson let out another roar and began running toward the dock in only his underwear, where the skinny-dippers still lingered, though they were now fully dressed.

Thomas got to his feet, and I quickly followed. Glancing over at Scarlett, I saw that she, along with everyone else, was watching the very high football player run for the dock like he was heading for a touchdown.

A lifeguard chair stood against the side of the boathouse, and with superhuman speed and agility, Jefferson scaled the chair and was on the roof of the boathouse in seconds flat. Thomas started moving down toward the docks, murmuring, "No, no, no," under his breath. I followed him, glancing over at Scarlett as we passed her. She looked back at me, fear dulling the electric of her green eyes.

The loudest roar of all pierced the air, and then the quarterback began to lope across the peaked roof, the moonlight illuminating his body, turning it pale, highlighting the tensed muscles in his legs as he moved. He was like some caged animal who had finally been set free. A collective gasp escaped each observer as he launched himself in an unexpectedly graceful dive off the front of the boathouse into water that was nowhere near deep enough to swallow him up safely.

JANUARY 17, 2019

Libby's husband Rob opens their front door, his broad shoulders filling the frame. "Hannah, how are you?"

I'm caught off guard by the warm welcome. "I'm good," I say, the surprise evident in my voice.

"Come on in. The meeting is about to begin." He ushers us toward the living room, and I catch a whiff of his expensive cologne.

The smell makes my already nervous stomach turn over. I did everything in my power to not come to this community meeting, but Evan refused to let me get out of it. I can't tell if it's because he knows about what I said to Libby on the street the other day or because he doesn't. Apparently, she told him it was imperative that everyone be there, which meant there was no way to get out of it.

All I want to do is hide away in my house after receiving the call to the Daring Tree yesterday from the unknown number—wait it out like a bad storm. Being out in public makes me feel too exposed, but could that be why Evan insisted I come? Right now, everyone is a suspect, everyone is an enemy, until I find out who sent that message.

Most of the neighbors are already there, sitting on dining chairs set up in rows, or the couch, or standing up against the wall. Evan moves right into the room and sits down on the arm of the couch, leaning in to talk to someone, leaving me to find my own spot. I find some free space in the corner and tuck myself away. Libby glances over from her place at the front of the room, her eyes narrowing at the sight of me before looking away to address the group.

"Welcome, everyone. Thank you so much for coming on such short notice. I felt the need to call an emergency meeting because we still have a predator in the neighborhood, and we cannot underestimate the danger of this." She looks right at me. "We cannot be complacent when it comes to our children and their safety." She points the remote in her hand at a large TV mounted on the wall. "I'd like to show you just a few clips of the footage we've caught with our security cameras to give you an idea of how deeply he's infiltrated our community."

As soon as the grainy black-and-white video pops up, I look away from the screen to survey my surroundings. I've never been in Libby's house before, just the backyard when she's hosted barbecues, and I rarely stay long at those, excusing myself to go home if I need the bathroom and then never returning.

Over the fireplace is a giant family photo, the kind where everyone appears to be sitting in a white room, forced into casual seated positions but looking as stiff as mannequins. Libby and her husband are both dressed in expensive-looking gray sweaters and dark denim jeans, and the twins are in matching navy-blue gingham dresses. Looking at the rest of the room, the couch, the carpet, the accents, I quickly realize that Libby dressed everyone in the photo to match the living room decor, right down to the navy-blue gingham throw pillows. I have a moment of pity for her at how exhausting it must be to work so hard at perfection but am distracted at the sound of my name.

"Not sure if you caught that last part, Hannah," Libby says, causing the whole room to look over at me. "I saw your eyes wandering." My face is instantly full of heat and I'm sure the deepest shade of crimson. "I was saying," she continues, "that in the last few weeks, there's been more sightings of the lurker in and around Evan and Hannah's house than any other one on the block."

She points the remote at the screen again, and this time I pay attention. The camera is doing a sweep of our section of the street and captures the front of our house exactly at the moment that a hooded figure emerges from alongside the garage and breaks into a slow run as soon as he reaches the sidewalk. It's too dark, and the person is too well covered up, for me to see any distinguishing features, but the height and build look most like those of a grown man.

Libby clicks a button on the remote, and the next clip of video is of the same figure emerging from the bushes of the house across the street from us. The person stands on the sidewalk looking up at our house for a few seconds, then slowly walks away. A chill races up my spine, landing on my neck, then traveling into my shoulders. I shiver, which helps shake it away. Could the lurker have something to do with the *Tell the truth* dare? Is it me bringing this person into the neighborhood?

"Now I'm sure you can all agree that this figure appears to be a man, due to their size and build." Libby once again looks right at me. "Not at all likely to be a woman." She then waves a hand at someone sitting on a nearby chair. "I've invited Joanne from our local police department to lend her thoughts to our dilemma."

A short, stocky woman with a long blond ponytail and pink cheeks rises from her chair, and only then do I notice the badge displayed on the pocket of her khaki pants. She starts by telling the group that she does believe it's a male perpetrator. Given the footage Libby has provided, she says, the police feel he's enough of a threat to start doing regular nightly patrols of the street.

I raise my hand, and the police officer nods her head in my direction. "I'm just wondering how much of a threat you think this person really is. Considering they haven't done anything yet. No vandalism, no break-ins. Would they not have committed a crime by now?" I'm looking for reassurance. I want this woman to tell me it's not that bad, that everything is going to be fine, but I know the question must have come out sounding like a challenge, because Evan turns around and shoots me a look like I have three heads and he wants none of them in the room with him. "Just so we all know what we're really dealing with," I add.

"That's a fair question," the police officer says, and some vindication blooms in my chest. "But a naïve one." The vindication quickly dies. "From what I can tell, this person is taking their time to really stake out this neighborhood. Learn people's routines and habits. Who knows what he's planning? You really can't underestimate the time a person will take in preparation for committing a crime."

The police officer's words of grave warning and the look of satisfaction on Libby's face make the room feel like it's closing in on me. A hot sweat breaks out on the back of my neck, and I'm finding it hard to get full breaths in. I take a few subtle side steps toward the door of the room, and when I'm sure nobody's watching, I duck out of there completely as the police officer continues detailing ways to protect ourselves and our homes.

I debate whether to hide in the quiet of the front foyer or just go home. Glancing up the stairs, I see Libby's twin girls staring down at me from the top, both in matching pajamas, looking like a scene right out of *The Shining*. I smile and wave, but they don't respond, just stand motionless looking down at me, two more neighborhood spies. I have to get out of this house.

Shrugging my coat back on, I pull open the front door and step outside, closing it quietly behind me. The cold night air brushes away the hot sweat on my neck, and I feel like I can breathe again. I'm just about to scurry home when I hear the door open behind me.

"You really are unbelievable." I turn to see Libby framed in the glowing light of her house. The part of her facing me is all in shadow, so I can't tell what her expression is. "I called this meeting for your own safety, and you're too rude to even stay until it's over."

I have no fight left in me for this woman. I hold up both hands. "I'm sorry. Truly. I think I started having a panic attack in there. I just needed to get some fresh air."

She steps out onto the front step, and I'm able to see the skepticism in her expression. "Does that mean, then, that you're finally taking this seriously?" The question is already laced with self-righteousness.

"Was it you?" My question is almost a whisper.

"Me what?" she spits back. "You're not accusing me of being the lurker again, are you? I mean, honestly, Hannah, how much proof—"

"The dare," I say—loudly, to interrupt her. "Was it you who sent me the *Tell the truth* dare?"

She crosses her arms against the cold. "I have no idea what you're talking about, and I've had more than enough of your accusations. I don't know anything about any dares." The last sentence comes out shrill and high-pitched, as though she might be on the verge of crying or hitting me. Evan and Rob choose that exact moment to step out onto the porch with us.

"Hannah!" Evan immediately scolds, even though he has no idea what's going on. "That's enough." I can't tell if I imagine it or not, but I'm sure I see Libby's frown twitch slightly into a smile with Evan's scolding, but she turns and rushes back inside before I can be sure. "It's time to go," Evan orders. "I think you've done enough damage for the night." He stomps off the porch, expecting me to follow behind like a sheepish puppy.

I wait for him to get a safe distance away from me, just enough so that I don't look as pathetic as I feel. "I'm sorry," I say to Rob, who surprisingly didn't go after his wife. "I didn't mean to cause a scene here; it's just a big misunderstanding."

"She does mean well," he says flatly. "But she gets too involved in other people's business. It's been an issue for us before." The criticism of his wife leaves me speechless. "I'm sure it will all blow over in a couple of days." He shrugs as though there's not much more to say on the matter.

"I hope so," I say, actually meaning it. "Have a good night, then."

He nods. "You too. And stay safe out there. You never know what's lurking in the bushes." He turns abruptly and walks back inside, taking the warm glow from the open door with him. His words send a shudder through me.

On my walk home, I wonder if the people still at Libby's meeting are watching me on the cameras as I walk home. Did she switch the feed on to show them what a bad neighbor I am, causing a scene and leaving early? To point out that I'm not a team player and everyone should be as suspicious of me as they are of the lurker? Is she telling them my secrets right now?

There's a rustling sound in the bushes beside me, and I break into a run, glancing back over my shoulder to see a cat emerging. I don't stop running, not sure who I'm running from exactly—Libby, her strange husband, the lurker, the person who sent us the dare. Only days ago it felt as though my secrets were safely hidden. Tonight they feel out in the open, exposed and coming for me.

The relief I feel when I reach my house is short-lived. Evan is there to greet me in the front foyer, a familiar look of disdain and disappointment on his face.

"What the hell happened back there, Hannah? First you stumble out of the meeting, and then you start accusing Libby of things on her own front porch. This is honestly a new low, even for you."

I turn away from him to hang up my coat and grasp at a few seconds to come up with an explanation. "I had a panic attack. That's why I rushed out of there so quickly. Seeing someone lurking around our property—Evan, it scared me." It's not a lie; it's just not the whole truth. Nothing is these days.

His nostrils flare with frustration, but then his face softens. He reluctantly lets go of his annoyance with me. "You don't have to be scared, Hannah. I won't let anything happen to you or the girls."

"What do you think the person even wants?" I'm looking for reassurance anywhere I can get it, even from him.

"I'm not sure. It does seem strange that he's been doing this for months now but hasn't committed a crime. Maybe he's just a creepy peeping tom. I think Libby may be making a bigger deal of it than needed. You're not the only one she's got scared. I overheard Mrs. Simon say she was going to get a gun, which is a terrifying thought."

I'm surprised to hear Evan disparage his favorite neighbor. "Her husband said she gets too involved in other people's business. That it's been a problem for her."

Evan's eyebrows rise in surprise. "Really? Rob said that to you. I can barely get five words out of that guy."

"He said it on the porch after she stormed off and you left."

The mention of my exit from the meeting seems to remind Evan of something. "What were you and Libby arguing about anyway? Something to do with a dare?"

I quickly shake my head. "No. She misunderstood what I was saying. I was having a hard time explaining myself because I was a bit muddled from seeing that video."

He doesn't seem to buy my explanation completely, as his eyes narrow with a look of doubt, but he nods anyway. "Hopefully, the police catch whoever it is, and we can all just go back to normal."

I don't even know what normal looks like anymore, but I agree with him to hold on to the slice of peace we've miraculously found after a debacle of a community meeting.

He yawns. "I'm going to head up to bed. I'm exhausted. Haven't been sleeping well. I'll get the girls sorted for lights out."

"Okay, thanks. I'll be up soon. Just going to have a cup of tea and read for a bit." He starts up the stairs but stops when I say his name and turns back. "Sorry about the scene I caused tonight."

He sighs and gives his head a shake. "Yeah, not so good for neighbor relations. You really should apologize to Libby tomorrow. She's not the kind of person you want to have as an enemy." He continues his way upstairs before I can tell him I think it's already too late.

I'm filling the kettle up at the kitchen sink when I'm sure I see a shadowy figure emerge from the brush at the back of the yard and disappear behind the shed. Grabbing a knife from the block on the counter, I pull open the back door into the darkness. The yard is still and quiet, no sign of anyone, but this time I'm not full of wine and I know what I saw.

"I have a knife, and I'm calling the police." I say loudly.

A form emerges from behind the shed. I'm frozen to the spot, the knife dangling from my hand at my side, as a figure, dressed all in black with a hood pulled up, heads right for me. My instincts finally kick in when it's only a few feet away, and I thrust the knife out in front of me.

"Whoa," a familiar voice calls out in surprise. "Henny, it's me." Hands go up to the hood to pull it down, and Thomas is revealed.

"What the fuck are you doing?" I hiss at him before reaching behind me to quickly close the kitchen door, glancing in at the same time to make sure no one from my family is in there watching.

Sticking the knife in the dirt of the garden beside the door, I grab his arm and start pulling him back toward the shed to get us out of sight. I ignore the wet of the snowy lawn seeping through the fabric of my slippers and the cold night air penetrating the thin cotton of my sweater.

"You should not be here, Thomas," I say, as soon as we're hidden behind the shed. "There are cameras all over my neighborhood and police on patrol."

"What? Why?"

"Someone's been going around the neighborhood at night in and out of yards. Looking exactly like you do right now. It's got the whole community on high alert."

"Shit," he says, and even in the dark I can see his expression of concern. "That's not good. I swear, if I'd known that, I never would have come."

"Why on earth did you?" I ask, swatting his arm gently.

"I was worried about you. After getting those weird text messages, and then I didn't hear from you, and with what's going on between you and Evan and him threatening to take the girls from you—I was afraid to text but wanted to make sure you were all right. I thought if I could just see your face, I'd feel better."

My whole body trembles from the cold and the release of adrenaline. Thomas pulls me up against him, wrapping his arms around me. I know I shouldn't, but I lean in, let him hold me up and keep me warm, because I suddenly feel so tired and cold, and he smells so nice and feels so good.

"I miss you, Henny. When will you come back to me?" He whispers the words in my ear; his voice is soft and pleading. The exact combination to dislodge my better judgment and reserve.

I lead him out from behind the shed to its door, unhooking the dangling padlock to let us inside, ignoring the lights on in my house that mean people are still awake, ignoring the sense that the houses in this neighborhood have eyes, ignoring the fact that we are on my property, only yards away from my family.

The shed houses the lawn mower, our outdoor furniture, and a deflated kiddie pool, all neatly stored away by Evan. Inside smells like summer—gas, cut grass, and plastic that's baked too long in the sun. The winter chill feels very out of place in here, just like we are.

While shuffling Thomas over to a chaise longue pushed up against the wall, I pull at the button of his jeans, frantic, wanting it to happen but wanting it to be over at the same time so we don't get caught.

"Are you sure?" he whispers, and I put a finger to my lips to quiet him. We don't have time for debate or hesitation.

I navigate him to a sitting position on the end of the lounge chair, the tarp covering it crackling under his weight, his underwear and pants around his ankles. I free just one leg so that I can straddle him. Desire makes it all feel so worth it in the moment—the risk, the dirty, awkward setting, the cold eating its way into my flesh.

He leans up to kiss me, taking hold of the back of my head. The pressure of his lips against mine, the surge of his tongue in my mouth, his hot, shallow breath—all give evidence of how urgent his own want is. The time apart works like fans, not water, to the flames.

I guide him inside me and he lies back, gripping my thighs, thrusting his hips up to go as deep as he can while I rock back and forth, the friction building fires in every part of my body. There's a screw that must be loose in the frame of the chair underneath the tarp. As my bare knee rubs against it, I can feel the skin start to rip, but I don't stop. I can see part of my house out the window of the shed and a shadow moves across the light in one of the upstairs windows, but I don't stop. Our combined heavy breathing sounds like a hurricane of wind, but I don't stop.

Only when Thomas moans and bucks his hips even harder and my insides contract, sending volts of electric pleasure through me, do I stop. My body folds forward onto him, my mouth up against his neck, where I kiss the warm flesh, not yet ready to surrender him.

It's the cold that finally pushes me off him. My fingers are numb as they pull my pants back on, my teeth chattering, my knee throbbing.

"Don't go back out onto the street," I whisper. "There are cameras out there, and maybe police. Go through the gate at the back of the yard. There's a trail that leads behind each property and comes out on Scarlett's old street. It will be overgrown. Nobody uses it, but it's safer."

Thomas pulls me into him. "Wow, the surveillance is pretty heavy in this neighborhood. Are you sure it's safe for me to leave you alone here?"

"You're a bigger threat to me than this lurker ever has been, so once you're gone, I should be fine."

"May I remind you that you're the one who pulled me into this stinky shed and seduced me? I was just here to make sure you were okay after we got that weird dare sent to us."

"I asked my neighbor Libby if she was the one who sent it, but she didn't seem to have any idea what I was talking about, and I actually believed her." I pause, almost afraid to say it out loud, to take responsibility for it. "I'm starting to wonder if this neighborhood lurker might be connected somehow."

"The two don't really seem related, in my opinion. What about Scarlett?" he asks. "She's the only one who actually knows about the game, and she's twisted enough to try and fuck with us."

"She's halfway across the world. There's no way she could have."

"Don't underestimate her." His voice is laced with bitterness.

"Trust me, I never have, but it can't be her." My feet feel like blocks of ice. I step away from him to get the blood rushing back. "I'm freezing, and Evan could be looking for me. I have to go inside."

"When can I see you again?" he asks, taking my hand in his. "Really see you, in a warm room with a real bed, not in some smelly toolshed."

I give his hand a squeeze. "Soon. Let's just keep in touch." Based on his deep sigh, I know he doesn't like my answer. "Right now we need to be really careful," I add. Letting go of his hand. I move toward the door of the shed, already regretting the risk I've taken, already wondering if someone was watching us slip inside.

All the windows upstairs are dark by the time I head back inside the house. My whole family has gone to sleep, oblivious to what I was doing out here in the cold. A mixture of relief and guilt moves through me like a sandstorm. I grab the knife from the garden and let myself into the kitchen, kicking off my dirty wet slippers and shoving them out of sight, then hiding the dirty knife in the dishwasher.

Sitting down on a kitchen chair, I pull the leg of my pants up to examine my knee. A thick trickle of blood has dried against my shin, escaping from a gash that sits on my kneecap, surrounded by pink skin rubbed raw. I push a finger into it, sending a twitch of pain through my leg—punishment for the pleasure.

JANUARY 18, 2019

"Hurry up," I yell to the girls as I pass their room on my way downstairs. I hear Evan in the bathroom. He's up later than usual. He normally has a pot of coffee on by now.

The stairs creak as they always do on the way down. The sky outside is gray and the sun isn't fully up yet, so everything is covered in a charcoal blanket of shadow. Something lies under the mail slot at the front door. A package?

I flip the hall light when I reach the bottom of the stairs. The black-and-white cover jumps out at me, slapping away the early-morning fog and injecting my heart with a shot of adrenaline. I reach down and grab it. Pull the front door open and step out onto the porch. The cold of the January morning finds its way into every open bit of my robe, nipping at my bare skin.

The street is silent, no sign of life or movement. No dog barking as somebody passes, no cars revving to life. Whoever left it must have done it before I got downstairs and after I went to bed, because it wasn't here last night. I step back inside and quietly close the door, already thinking of hiding places for the notebook.

"What's that?" Evan's voice startles me. I spin around. He's halfway down the stairs. He reaches the bottom and points at the notebook. "Did someone drop that off?" He yanks his tie into position but has his eyes trained on the notebook.

I hold it up. "This? No, it's mine. For lists and stuff."

He eyes me with suspicion. "Since when do you make lists?"

I hug the notebook to my chest. "I make lists." Somehow, I manage to sound indignant. "And they're none of your business."

He narrows his eyes, looking like he might challenge me, but then nods at the door. "Were you coming or going?"

I glance back over my shoulder. "I thought I heard someone knock."

He gives me a strange look; there's mistrust there. A reminder that we're still on shaky ground despite the protectiveness he showed me last night. He moves past me and disappears down the hall into the kitchen.

I wait until I hear the sounds of busyness and then duck upstairs to shove the notebook into a drawer in my nightstand under some magazines. Coming out of my bedroom, I almost run into Gracie. I swerve out of the way, which causes me to bump my knee on the hall table, the same knee that I injured while having sex with my lover.

Gracie's wearing tights and a sweater, holding up two skirts. "Which one, Mom?"

I shake my head. "It's the middle of winter, Gracie. Use your head— it's not skirt season." She glares at me and stomps back into her room.

Downstairs, Evan and I dance around each other in the kitchen in silence as he makes himself some breakfast and I make the girls' lunches. It takes effort to keep my mind on task.

"Hannah?"

I look up at the sound of my name and realize I've been standing with the fridge door open, staring at nothing for god knows how long. I reach inside for some strawberries and shut the door, ignoring Evan's puzzled look.

Rose comes into the kitchen and performs a fake gag. "You'd better not be putting those in my lunch."

I look up from the cutting board, where I've already prepared a pile of strawberries ready to be put into little Tupperware containers and packed for lunch. "Since when don't you like strawberries?"

She sighs with exasperation. "Since I saw Julia Brown puke them up in gym class right after lunch. Only over two months ago."

"Well, sorry, Rose, I didn't get the memo. Maybe you should start making your own goddamn lunches." Her eyes go wide in shock.

"Hannah," Evan calls out sternly. "What is wrong with you?"

I give my head a little shake. "Sorry. I'm tired, that's all."

"Mom's grumpy," Gracie says upon her arrival in the kitchen—wearing a skirt. "And for the record, it is skirt season, because I went outside and it's perfectly warm out there."

I take a deep breath and go back to the strawberries, filling one container for Gracie and putting the rest back in the fridge. Out of the corner of my eye, I watch Rose sullenly getting some cereal and feel a sharp pang of mother guilt.

I turn to my next task: inserting bread into the toaster. As I stare at the shiny silver appliance, my thoughts drift to the notebook sitting upstairs in my nightstand. It feels like a blob of toxic waste that could leak all over the house at any moment and poison everything.

The pop of the toast makes me jump. I pull it from the slots with shaky hands. Turning to get the jam, I notice Evan watching me from the kitchen table while he sips his coffee. Questions lie behind his eyes. If he gets up the nerve to ask them, I might break like a dam, flooding the room with truth.

"You didn't sleep well?" he asks, rising from his chair to put his cup in the sink.

"Not really," I answer, spreading jam on the toast so meticulously I can't take the time to look at him.

He comes up from behind and puts both hands on my shoulders, causing me to jump again. To my great surprise, he starts to gently massage them. "You're awfully jumpy this morning. Is it because of the meeting last night?"

I force myself to relax and not slide out from under his grip. "Maybe a little bit, but mostly I'm just—"

"Tired. Yeah, you said." He lets go and then leaves the kitchen, and I exhale.

"Gracie! Your toast is ready."

She appears almost immediately and comes right to me, wrapping her arms around my waist. "Do you need a hug, Mom?"

I put my arms around her, holding my sticky jam hands away from her hair. "Thank you, sweet girl. That does help." She gives me an extra-tight squeeze and then lets go to retrieve her toast from the counter.

"You spread it right to the edges." She smiles up at me. "My favorite." So oblivious, so trusting, so unaware of what I've done, who I really am under this thin skin of motherhood.

Evan comes back into the kitchen to grab his suit jacket from the back of a chair and stops short, pointing at my leg. "What happened?"

I look down and see a bright-red stain of blood soaking through the knee of my gray leggings. "I must have done it when I ran into the hall table upstairs."

Evan comes over and bends down to get a closer look. "It looks pretty serious, Hannah."

I brush away his hand and move toward the door. "It doesn't even hurt. I'll clean it up after the girls go." I feel his eyes on me as I leave the room, their scrutinizing glare burning a hole right between my shoulder blades.

As soon as the kids and Evan are gone, I find my phone and text Thomas. *Did you drop the notebook at my house?* I can't imagine why he'd do it, risk everything, but I have to ask.

No is his curt response.

Not through the mail slot? I try again.

I haven't seen the notebook since our last dare. Why? What happened?

I stare at the phone in my hand, the realization slowly sinking in. Someone was at my door last night. Someone who had that notebook and wasn't dropping it off as an act of kindness. What if Evan had been the first one down? Could I have explained my way out of it then, after he'd seen the dares, the details? The thought weakens my knees and brings me down onto a kitchen chair.

The ringing of my phone pierces the quiet of the room, causing me to jump yet again. It's Thomas.

"Henny. It's me. What's this about the notebook?"

I glance over my shoulder, as though somebody might be there listening. "I came downstairs this morning, and it was by the front door. It had been put through the mail slot."

"So you got to it first, not Evan?"

"Yes. I told him it was mine and then ran and hid it upstairs. He didn't get a look at it."

"Well, that's good. Right?"

"Thomas. If it wasn't you, that means somebody else got their hands on the notebook. Somebody else saw our dares and knows what we've been doing. The same person who called us to the Daring Tree the other day. Someone is fucking with us, Thomas, and I'm scared." My voice cracks on the last word, and I put a hand to my mouth to hold back tears.

"I think you're right." His words heighten the fear. I wanted him to say I was crazy, not agree with me. "But I don't think we have to be scared. It's probably just someone who saw us at the tree and then, when we left, went and found the notebook inside and figured out what we were doing, so decided to have some fun with it."

"They came to my house, Thomas."

It sounds like he puts a hand over the phone to talk to somebody else. "Sorry about that," he says, after a few seconds. "I'm at work, and we're going into a meeting. Can we meet for a drink later to talk about this in person?"

"No," I say, without even giving it a thought. He feels too dangerous right now. "I don't think it's a good idea to see each other, especially not in public."

He gives a little huff. "Okay." There's hurt in his voice, and I want to scream at him. Tell him my life could have been blown up by this morning's delivery. "But we can't not see each other, Henny. We have to figure this out. Right?"

"I don't know right now. I need some time to think. I'll be in touch." I hang up before he can say anything else. For a split second I consider calling Libby to ask if I can see the footage from the security camera last night, but that will only pique her interest, cause her to watch it herself if she hasn't already. She'll see that something was dropped into the mail slot and start asking questions, possibly tell Evan. Asking her for that favor would be like shooting myself in the foot. Not to mention that she most likely hates me after that meeting.

I sit there for a few minutes, listening to the tick of the kitchen clock, staring out the window of the back door. A sleet like rain has begun to fall. Gracie must have been right—it is warm out there for this time of year; otherwise, it would be snow. My mind won't stop replaying the scenario of Evan coming down to find the notebook and not me. I can envision the confusion on his face, which would quickly turn to anger once he realized what he was reading: essentially a log of my affair with Thomas.

In need of distraction, I swipe my phone open and tap the Facebook app. There isn't another message from Scarlett, so I decide to go to her page to see what she's up to.

The last post she made was four days ago, and it's of an airplane wing cutting through a sky colored by the pinks and oranges of a sunset. One simple caption: *#homewardbound*. Does that mean home here? I wonder. My mind races, and my heart beats in an attempt to catch up with it. I realize in this moment how much I like knowing Scarlett is at the safe distance of all the way across the world.

I tap on messages. *Just saw your homeward bound post. How exciting! Are you in the neighborhood? Will I get to see you???* I hit send, hoping she won't detect the worry behind my forced enthusiasm. There could not be a worse time for Scarlett to come home, right in the middle of what's going on with me and Thomas. The thought snags on something. Thomas's words from last night—*She's the only one who actually knows about the game, and she's twisted enough to try and fuck with us.*

The list of suspects is growing, but so is my confusion and anxiety. If I don't figure out who it is soon and stop them, Evan is going to find out.

I force myself away from the table and my ominous thoughts and go upstairs, where I take the notebook out of its hiding place. Sitting on the edge of the bed, I examine it closely, looking for some clue as to who had it last. I open it and flip through the pages.

The evidence of our dares is all still there—water tower photo, coaster from the bar that contains Thomas's phone number, receipt from the hotel lounge, ticket stub from the zoo. Even more incriminating than the souvenirs, though, are the notes Thomas insisted on writing. He said he wanted to have them to look back on when we're too old to play the game. But we're already too old to have been playing the game—the stakes too high, too many people to hurt. Why didn't I see that?

I bring the notebook to my nose, desperate enough to be looking for a scent. Who put the note in the Daring Tree? Who dropped this notebook through my mail slot in the middle of the night?

The questions pound through my head, and my vision blurs from staring too long and hard at the black-and-white-speckled notebook cover. I get up from the bed and go downstairs.

In the basement I find a metal bucket and some lighter fluid. Then I bundle up against the rain and take it all out into the backyard.

Tossing the notebook into the bucket, I douse it in lighter fluid. Kneeling down beside it and making a shield with my body, I try several times before I'm able to get a match lit. When I drop it into the bucket, blue flames jump up above the metal rim, defying the wet sleet that's falling faster now.

I watch as the book turns to something unrecognizable, destroying all evidence that there ever was a Daring Game, but it's far too late to be reassuring. Eyes other than Thomas's and mine have seen what's inside. A third player has been added to the game against our will.

The fire lessens, so I squirt more fluid into the bucket and bring it back to life. I take my eyes off it and scan the yard, sure I'll find somebody there looking right back at me.

THEN

Jefferson Smith surfaced facedown in the lake, his arms outstretched out as though he'd been crucified, after his swan dive off the camp boathouse. Some other football players jumped into the cold water to fish him out and drag him up onto the lawn into the light from the buildings. He was unconscious, unmoving, looking as good as dead. Somebody called 911.

People rushed around, somehow knowing what to do, getting blankets to put on him, checking his pulse. Scarlett had migrated back over to me and Thomas, the fight forgotten as we stood locked together in fear.

The ambulance finally arrived, after what felt like more than enough time for him to die five times over. They took his vitals and, thank god, announced to the party that he was still breathing, alive, with steady vitals. But not once did he move or open his eyes. When I heard one paramedic say to the other that there was most likely spinal damage, I turned away from the crowd and buried my head in Thomas's shoulder so that no one would see my tears.

The police arrived shortly after the ambulance. As soon as Jefferson had been rushed to the hospital, they started moving through the party, slowly, like sharks in deep water, asking questions. Scarlett wanted to run and hide in the woods to avoid them, but Thomas talked her out of it, saying it would make her look guilty. No one pointed out that she was.

Thomas made us rehearse our story—we didn't know the guy that well, only enough to say hi. We had noticed that he'd been acting strangely earlier on but hadn't thought much of it. He agreed to do most of the talking and told us to just go along with him. He said it was okay to act scared and upset, because we'd just seen something scary and upsetting. For the first time I can ever remember, Scarlett was speechless.

I watched closely as a police officer talked to a group of Jefferson's good friends. That's why I noticed when one of them turned in our direction and pointed. The officer followed the direction of his finger, and her eyes landed squarely on Thomas. She started in our direction, never taking her eyes off him, never giving me the opportunity to warn him without making us look even more suspicious.

Only a few feet away, her face lit up in a well-rehearsed smile, meant to reassure whatever culprit she was out to catch. "Good evening, guys." Her tone was as practiced as her smile. "I'm Officer Baker." She put a hand on Thomas's shoulder, already taking possession of him. "I was wondering if I might steal you away for a little chat?"

Thomas glanced at us, and it was the first time I'd seen him look scared. "Uh, yeah, of course." His voice didn't betray a thing.

The woman led Thomas away, giving us one last smile, as though there was nothing to worry about. On her way she motioned for two other officers to join her. They took him over to where their patrol cars were parked, a territory of lawn that they'd claimed for themselves.

I kept my eyes on Thomas only, hoping that from his facial expressions I'd be able to tell how well or badly things were going. Scarlett started to say something, but I hushed her, not able to give anyone else my attention in that moment. I was surprised when Thomas suddenly broke free from the huddle of police officers and jogged slowly back to us.

"They heard that I warned the guy that someone may have put something in his drink," Thomas explained breathlessly as soon as he got to us. He must have glimpsed the fear on my face, because he reached out and put a hand on my arm. "It's okay, Henny. I told them I only said that because I'd noticed his pupils were so big and he was acting strangely. I'd meant it as a joke. Got it?" His eyes flitted over to Scarlett. "Just stick to the story."

Then he reached down and grabbed his backpack, which was sitting on the ground with my bag and Scarlett's. "They want to search my bag," he explained, already starting to back away.

"What, why?" I asked.

"Don't worry; they said it's just protocol. They're going to search everyone's. And it's good—when they don't find anything, they'll let me go. Be back soon." He gave us a confident smile and turned to run back to the police.

Thomas handed his backpack to Officer Baker. She put it on the hood of her car and started to rummage through it, holding her flashlight aloft to see better. I held my breath, waiting for her to zip it back up and hand it to him. She paused, moved the light closer, and then pulled out what looked like a white envelope. After looking inside, she passed it to another officer. He looked inside and then passed it to the third police officer, who finally turned to Thomas and said something.

Shock registered all over Thomas's face, and he shook his head. He grabbed for the envelope, but the police officer pulled it away, handing it back to Baker. The largest of the officers put a hand on Thomas's shoulder and leaned in close to say something to him. Thomas nodded, his body going slack. Only then did he look over at us, shock and confusion all over his face. I moved to go to him, but Scarlett grabbed me.

"Don't, Hannah. Whatever's happening over there, you do not want to be implicated."

I spun around to face her. "Implicated in what? He hasn't done anything, and neither have I."

I turned back in time to see Thomas being guided toward a patrol car. Every single person at the party was suddenly out on the lawns, the sound of them a buzz that sawed at my insides. Everyone watched as Officer Baker held the door open for him and he slid into the back seat.

"What's going on? Why are they taking him?" I asked no one in particular. Scarlett stood at my side as stiff as a mannequin, her expression unreadable. The police car with Thomas in it backed up and disappeared down the long dirt road that led away from the camp.

JANUARY 22, 2019

The buzzer signaling the end of the third quarter in the basketball game sounds at the exact same time that my phone vibrates in my pocket. I wait until Rose is off the court to look at it. She always seems to glance over when I'm not paying full attention.

Do you Dare? Tonight 7pm.

My stomach drops; it's another call to the Daring Tree from the unknown number. Seconds later a text comes in from Thomas: *Just got a message to go to the tree at 7pm. You?*

I got the same message.

See you at 7 then?

Okay

I want to say no, tell him to stay away from the tree, to just ignore the texts, but after the notebook was dropped through the mail slot, I'm afraid of what could come next. We need to find out who's sending these dares and why so we can put an end to it.

The rest of the game goes by in a blur. I clap when the other school parents around me clap. Wave at Rose and give her the thumbs-up when she glances over at me. Each time the buzzer sounds, I jump a little, my stomach tightening as the minutes tick away.

On the way home, Rose goes over the game play by play, and I do my best to fake my way through it, feeling like one part of me is hovering somewhere outside my body, thinking about the text, while another part pretends to be a mother.

In my desperation, I offer a stop at McDonald's for dinner. "For the win," I say.

"We lost by one," Rose quickly corrects me. "Were you even paying attention, Mom?" Another failure to add to the list.

It's just after six by the time we get home. Evan has only just walked through the door himself after a late meeting. I toss him a bag containing a cold hamburger and fries and tell him that I'm going to go meet some former library coworkers for a drink. He frowns and looks about to protest, but I ease out of the room, mumbling something about a person retiring, a chance to get caught up, so that he doesn't have time to ask any concrete questions.

The sun is just starting to set when I step outside. I decide to walk, figuring Thomas can drive if we need to go anywhere. It also means I've been able to throw back a couple of shots of vodka to still my nerves.

The unseasonably warm weather has continued. It feels more like March than midwinter; the snow has started to melt, and my hands are actually sweating in the gloves I'm wearing. Being outside clears my head and sharpens my senses. Passing people on the street, I feel envious of them and what I imagine to be their clear-cut lives. No games that could destroy their families or mystery stalkers tormenting them. It's my own fault, I know, which makes me want to stop them on their way, to tell them to appreciate what they have and take good care of it.

Thomas is already at the tree when I arrive. He's holding a piece of red card stock, which he hands to me when I reach him. "You're not going to like this," he says flatly, as though all the fight has already been dared right out of him.

The dare is to drive to a location; the address is listed, but it's not familiar to me. It also says on the card to be prepared to spend the night.

"You've got to be kidding me." I fling the piece of paper at the tree. "I can't spend the night somewhere with you."

Thomas holds up a hand to calm me and picks up the piece of paper. "We'll cross that bridge when we get to it, Henny. First, let's just drive to this place and see if we can find out who's gotten us there in the first place."

"Drive to some unknown location in the dark? That does not seem safe, Thomas." I can feel my heart rate accelerating at the mere thought.

"What choice do we have? We didn't do the last dare, and the notebook ended up through your mail slot. We can at least attempt this one and see how it goes. If there's any sign of danger, we'll get out of there immediately."

I know he's right. Whoever is doing this has all the power, and I can't take another risk like I did only a few days ago. "Okay. Let's go." My voice somehow comes out sounding far braver than I feel on the inside.

Thomas plugs the address into the GPS, and we start to drive, realizing in no time that it's taking us out of town. We talk about who might be sending the dares. Thomas is convinced it's someone who watched us in the cemetery and caught on to what we were doing and is now screwing around with us, maybe setting us up for blackmail. It feels more sinister to me, more personal. I tell him that I still suspect my neighbor Libby, even though her denial seems sincere.

Again he asks me about Evan, and a part of me does wonder. Maybe he knew all along, but I can't imagine him living with me as though nothing has happened. Knowing I've been unfaithful while carrying out his own vengeful version of the game that caused the affair in the first place. It just doesn't seem like his style. But I also didn't think he'd compile a log of my infractions for the purpose of taking my children away from me, so perhaps I don't know him as well as I thought I did.

I purposely don't tell Thomas about Scarlett's homeward-bound post. I'm afraid if I do, he'll fixate on her and only her, blind to any other possibility, and act rashly. I've driven by her house a few times, and there's been no sign of her; no answer to my message and no more posts. I'll tell him only when I have more cause to think it could in fact be her.

About twenty minutes out of town, the GPS announces that we've arrived at our destination. It's a wide driveway leading into thick forest without any signage, but there's a chain across it to prevent people from going in.

"Are we supposed to walk in?" I ask, my voice rising with terror at the thought.

"There's no way we're walking in there blind," Thomas says firmly.

"Let's just go home, then." Now that we're out here in the middle of nowhere, I've lost all courage and resolve to find out who's doing this.

Thomas puts the car in reverse and pulls out into the road, but instead of heading back toward town, he guns it back toward the chain, breaking through and launching us up the driveway.

"We're not giving up that easily," he says, seeing the look of shock on my face.

The road hasn't been plowed all winter and still has a thick surface of snow, despite the melting, which makes navigating tricky even with four-wheel drive. There's no doubt that something used to be out here; it's more of a road than a driveway that we're moving along. And something about it is familiar, but I can't place it. We silently take in our surroundings, both on edge, waiting for the punch line to this dare.

It's only once the trees clear, a frozen lake comes into view, and we pull up to a large log building with dozens of other cabins scattered around it that it hits me. We've been dared to revisit Berkshire Lakeside Camp, the location of our last dare, the place where everything went wrong.

"You know what this place is, right?" I ask Thomas. He nods, his expression dark.

The camp has clearly been abandoned for a while. Moss covers the roofs of the buildings, the windows are boarded over, and everything looks overgrown, even in the dead of winter. I take out my phone to get some up-to-date information on the camp, but there's no reception.

"What are we supposed to do now?" I ask, hoping Thomas says turn around and go home.

"I think our instructions are probably on there." He points to the door of the main building, which is illuminated by the headlights of his car. Tacked to the wood is a piece of red card stock.

We both get out of the car, leaving the lights on to guide our way. Only then do I notice the imprints in the mud and remaining snow. "Thomas, look." I point to the indentations that attest to the fact that someone was here not that long ago.

"They must have come on foot, because there weren't any tire tracks on the drive in." He bends down to get a closer look at one of the footprints. "And they don't look that fresh, maybe a few hours old."

I turn in circles, scanning the trees around us and the buildings for signs of life, but it's dark, with only a small area illuminated by the headlights. "Did I tell you how much I don't like this?" I say, still searching for signs of other people out there. "I feel like a sitting duck."

Thomas takes my hand and starts leading me up to the door. "Let's just get this over with," he says. I don't take my hand from his; what's the point in hiding things now? Whoever lured us here already knows all our secrets.

Up close, we see that the red card stock has only one word on it: *Enter*.

I give the door a nudge with my foot, and it swings open easily. Stepping inside, we're greeted with the overpowering stench of animals who must have made their home in the walls and then died, as well as damp wood and dust. I think back to the night we were here when this place was brightly lit and decorated, full of college students having the time of their lives, none of them knowing how badly it would end.

"So now what?" I whisper to Thomas. "We're supposed to get out our sleeping bags?"

Thomas uses the flashlight on his phone to do a wide sweep of the room. It seems completely empty at first, but then the beam of light shines on a small table in the middle of the room with something on it and another piece of red card stock. Thomas motions me over, and we find a small, clear glass box with the card stock leaning against it, the words *Eat me* written across it. A take on *Alice in Wonderland*, but this feels more horror movie than whimsical children's book.

Thomas picks up the glass box and shines his light into it. On the bottom are two small, perfectly square pieces of paper, each with a smiley face on them. "It's been a while, but those look like tabs of acid to me," he says. We both study them for a few more seconds, and then he lets out a bitter-sounding laugh. "They're daring us to take acid." Without warning, he chucks the box hard against the wall, and it smashes to pieces. "This has Scarlett written all over it. No one else knows about this shit but her."

The volume and force of his words cause me to step back from him. It's not like Thomas to lose his temper, which only heightens the tension of it all.

"I want to go home. Now." Without waiting for his answer, I turn and start for the door. Sliding across the mucky ground, almost falling as I rush to get back to the car, I'm relieved to hear Thomas behind me. I slide into the passenger seat and wait impatiently for him. He moves slower, looking around as he goes, his face still furrowed with anger. He thinks he's looking for Scarlett, and now I think he may be right.

Movement from across the wide lawn catches my eye. Leaning forward, I'm sure I spot a figure crouching down at the edge of the forest. It's so hard to tell, though, because the lights of the car only reach so far. Thomas gets in beside me.

I point in the direction of the figure. "Does that look like a person to you?"

He narrows his eyes to get a better look and then turns on his high beams. That's when we see the figure move, retreating into the woods.

Before I can stop him, Thomas jumps out of the car and begins running across the lawn, as fast as the snow, ice, and mud will allow him. He stumbles a few times and then rights himself before disappearing completely into the woods.

I open the car door and have one foot out, ready to go after him, but then as quickly as he was gone, he reappears. Walking this time, his shoulders slumped, shaking his head.

"I couldn't see a thing," he explains, once he's made it back to the car. "And my phone just died. I think they were long gone anyway, with the whole lawn in between us as a head start."

"Let's just go," I say, louder than I meant to. "You shouldn't have run off into the woods anyway. We honestly don't know who we're dealing with."

Thomas maneuvers back down the road at a much slower place so that we don't go sliding into the ditch on either side. I tell him about Scarlett's post. I don't think it's fair to keep it from him anymore. It's clear we're not dealing with some kids from the cemetery. This is someone who knows not only our present but also our past.

Thomas stops a few blocks from my street to be safe, but even being this close makes me nervous. I promise to message Scarlett again to try to get the truth out of her.

"Do you think it was real acid?" I ask, with one hand on the door handle.

Thomas shrugs and shakes his head. "I really don't know, but I wasn't about to test it."

"You know that means we failed the dare again?"

He reaches out and grabs my hand and gives it a squeeze. "Don't worry, Henny; there's no hard evidence of what we've done, other than that notebook."

"Let's hope so," I say, although there's nowhere inside me for hope to grow. The weeds of fear and dread have taken over.

JANUARY 28, 2019

I order a chamomile tea to settle my stomach, even though I'm pretty sure what's happening inside me is immune to its herbal properties. We were given almost a week's reprieve after the failed Berkshire Camp dare before the punishment arrived.

Now I'm sitting across from Thomas in some tucked-away coffee shop he insisted on meeting at. I've worked in a trip to the bank and some other errands so that I can account for the time out if Evan quizzes me later.

"What exactly happened, Henny?" Thomas asks. "Start from the beginning."

I lean in closer, afraid someone might be listening. "I was in the kitchen, cleaning up after dinner. Evan was in the family room watching TV, and the girls had gone up to their rooms. Evan had left his phone on the counter, which he often does after work." I take a sip of my hot tea, and it burns the tip of my tongue, which I barely even register.

"I was wiping off the counters," I continue, "and went to move Evan's phone out of the way. He has the text preview function turned on—you know, when you can see part of the text even if you have a passcode?" I go to show him on my own phone, but he nods in understanding. "He'd gotten ten texts while we were eating dinner. Most of them were photos. But there was one with a message." I lower my voice even further. "*Do you know what your wife has been up to?*"

Repeating those words to Thomas makes my entire body itch with shame. The game, the affair, Thomas—the things that gave me an escape from my life, made me feel like my own person again, that woke me up inside—look so dirty through that lens, so clichéd and superficial. I'm just a wife who betrayed her husband.

Thomas looks surprised but not much more. He's not the one wearing a Scarlett letter. He's just the single man who started it all and could walk away at any second unscathed. "Who were they from?" he asks. "Did you see a number?"

I shake my head. "It said unknown."

"Were you able to get into his phone and see what the texts were?"

"I used the passcode that he gave me for his computer, and thank god it worked. There were photos." The words catch in my throat as I try not to cry. "Of us, at the zoo, when we were in the tunnel, doing . . . you know."

Thomas's mouth drops open in shock, and he sits in stunned silence. The gravity of this situation is finally sinking in. "That's disgusting" is all he manages to finally get out.

"It must have been that person we saw at the end of the tunnel. There was no one else around, which means this started all the way back then and we didn't even know it." I let the severity of my words sink in. "Whoever is doing this has been following us for who knows how long and planning it, collecting evidence. This is even bigger than we thought."

He lifts his coffee cup to his mouth and drinks mechanically before carefully placing it back down, as though his mind is having trouble taking it all in. He finally nods. "You're right, this *is* bigger than we thought. Not just some random kids. It's someone out for blood."

"But why?" I ask, as though he has some answer I don't. "Why go to all of this trouble? Why not just confront us or blackmail us or tell my husband? What do they want from us?"

He shakes his head, as at a loss as I am. "You deleted the text with the photos, right?" is all he comes up with.

"Of course," I snap back. "Immediately." I take a sip of my flowery tea to help swallow the tears away.

"Right. I'm sorry," he says, reaching out to take my hand as though it might be of some comfort, but I slip it under the table. I don't know who's watching us, who's taking photos, who's ready to jump out of the woodwork and catch us in the act.

"I blocked the number." My words are spoken in a calm, hushed tone. Inside I'm screaming, crying, scared for my life. The trendy little coffee shop Thomas has chosen as our meeting spot is not a venue for this level of emotion. Dozens of Edison bulbs hang from the exposed pipes above us; the tables are made of raw wood; there's a melodic chill mix playing softly and a cluster of loyal twentysomething customers speaking in equally hushed tones.

With one finger he taps his own phone on the table. "Good thinking."

"What if I hadn't been there to intercept the text?" It's the question that keeps charging through my mind, making my whole world feel as though it could implode at any moment. No matter the problems that Evan and I have, I wouldn't want him to find out about my infidelity that way. It would be cruel and devastating.

Thomas spins his coffee cup around, staring into the black liquid. "Maybe you should just come clean. Tell Evan the truth about us and the game. Then that person wouldn't even be a threat anymore. Would they?"

"That's easy for you to say," I hiss back at him. "You have nothing to lose."

He leans forward, his chest knocking his coffee cup so that it rattles in its saucer. "Of course I do. I could lose you."

"Imagine if Evan had gotten those photos. Think how that would feel for a person." The tears are stubborn and finally insist on making an appearance. I put one hand up to cover my face. He reaches for me again, but I pull away even more dramatically than the first time.

Roughly wiping at my tears, I pinch my nose and take a deep breath to compose myself. "We need to find out who it is and stop them, not give them what they want—the unraveling of my family and my girls taken away."

"I told you—I will not let Evan take your girls away from you, Hannah. And I thought we'd already established that it's Scarlett doing all of this." There's venom in his voice when he mentions her name.

I grab my phone from the table and swipe it open to show him the evidence on Facebook that it can't in fact be her. She's not even in the area yet. I show him the post I saw last night of her at a spa in Hawaii, with the location listed on it. Then I show him the message she sent me.

Not in the neighborhood quite yet. Just making a few fun stops along the way. I really hope we can get together. I need to see for myself that Thomas isn't getting you into too much trouble. See you soon, expect a grand entrance! xo

He studies the message for a few seconds, his eyebrows furrowed, his lips pursed. "You know you can fake that kind of thing on Facebook, your location? She's smart enough, Hannah, to be here and pretend not to be at the same time. How do you not see that?"

Thomas glances away from me and out the window to the street. The sunlight hits his face in such a way that the lines there are magnified, the white stubble more apparent, the bags under his eyes looking darker. He runs a hand through his hair, sighs, and turns back to me. "She will do anything to keep us apart. She's already setting it up that way. Saying she's coming to make sure I'm not causing too much trouble for you. She's the one who causes trouble, Henny. She always has." His voice is getting louder with each word, so I shush him harshly, even though not one person in the café is paying any attention to us. They're too busy analyzing the satire in pop culture or discussing the next iPhone upgrade, nothing near as sinister as what we're dealing with.

He leans in closer, his face a storm of intensity. "We cannot let her separate us again," he whispers. "Promise me you won't let her do that."

A server drops a plate behind the counter. The sound of it smashing into pieces makes me half duck under the table. Threat feels so present. Like it's everywhere.

I reach for my purse and coat. "I have to go."

"No, Henny. Please don't go."

"I don't have any more time left. Somehow Evan seems to know how long I'm out every day, so I have a limited window without it raising suspicion."

Thomas leans back in his chair, a scornful look in his eyes. "And this is the man you want to stay married to?"

"I want to keep my children, Thomas. At this point that's all I really care about."

THEN

After Thomas was taken away by the police, the buses came back early. The police and the camp owners wanted the place cleared out after the accident. The ride home was torture, bumping along country roads, the vibration of the bus rattling right up into my jaw until my head pounded. People all around me were talking about "the asshole who drugged the star quarterback of the football team." The story grew with each mile, some saying they'd seen him do it, others saying they'd overheard him tell the quarterback he'd spiked his beer, but only after the entire beer had been drunk. None of the stories were true, but the longer I sat there hearing them, the weightier they became, making me question my own version of events.

When we got back to town, I told Scarlett I was going to go home. I didn't. I went right to Thomas's, foolishly thinking I might walk in to find him there, sitting on the floor, his records spread out all around him, telling me it was all just one big misunderstanding.

The apartment was dark and silent. I stripped out of my borrowed dress and climbed into his bed to wait for him.

* * *

I must have fallen asleep at some point. It was the ringing of Thomas's phone that woke me. I scrambled for it, sure it was him calling from the police station, knowing I would be at his place. The sun was up, which meant I'd slept right into the day.

"Hello?" My voice came out weak and cracked from crying.

"Hannah?" Disappointment flooded me when I heard Scarlett's voice.

I cleared my throat. "Thomas isn't here. He hasn't been home all night."

"I know. He called me from the police station. I called to talk to you. I figured you'd be there."

My brain, cloudy with sleep, wine, and shock, took a few seconds to compute what she was saying. Thomas had called her from the police station, not me. I had not been his first call—she was. My whole understanding of him, us, the world we had created suddenly became lopsided and undependable.

"He called you?" I asked.

Scarlett ignored the question. "Jefferson Smith is paralyzed from the waist down. They think he must have hit his head on the bottom of the lake, probably a rock, when he dove off the boathouse. And they found acid in his blood. It's not good, Hannah, like really bad, as in Thomas could be looking at criminal charges."

"But he didn't do it, Scarlett. You did. How did that acid even get in his bag?"

She sighed heavily on the other end, as though I were some great annoyance to her. "You don't know the whole story, Hannah. Thomas did do it. When I handed him the beer for the quarterback, he slipped it in there and then gave it to him. After only ten minutes talking to the guy, Thomas realized what an asshole he was and wanted to go through with the dare. You just weren't supposed to see us do it, but when you did, I let you think it was me to cover for him so that it wouldn't cause problems between the two of you. And the acid was in his bag because he's the one who bought it."

None of what she was saying made any sense to me. Thomas had gotten so angry at her, had even gone to Jefferson to tell him his drink had been spiked. Had he really been pretending all of that? And why had he called Scarlett from the police station and not me?

"But he never wanted to do the dare in the first place," I said, trying to poke holes in Scarlett's version of the night.

"You know Thomas," she was quick to reply. "He's unpredictable, changes his mind from moment to moment. One minute he was totally into the dare, and then the next he was yelling at me about it and acting like he had nothing to do with it. I wanted to tell you right then, in the moment, but I was trying not to ruin the whole night." She paused, waiting for my response, but words had fully escaped me. "I hate to tell you this, Hannah," she continued, "but you're a bit blinded when it comes to Thomas. He's not exactly the stand-up guy you think he is."

I swung my legs out of bed, needing to have my feet on the floor. "What are you talking about, Scarlett?"

"He tried to be with me, Hannah, after you guys got together, but I said no. He was trying to play us both."

"That's not true." My voice held no conviction; it was caught somewhere down in my heart.

"Then why was he with me at that party? And why did he keep your relationship a secret for so long? So that you and I didn't talk about what was really happening and compare notes. Then there was his professor; he was taking things way further than I dared him to until you stopped it. He's like that, Hannah—a player, unpredictable, only out for himself. You just didn't want to see it because he got in your head."

You're in my head, I thought, but I kept the words to myself. They were both in my head, and I had no idea which one I hated more in that moment. I carefully placed the phone onto the receiver, then pushed myself out of Thomas's bed. The feel of his sheets against my skin suddenly disgusted me, the musty smell of the basement causing me to gag. Stumbling out into the living room, I found where I'd discarded my black dress, and with shaky hands I pulled it back on.

Tears fought hard to fall when I caught a glimpse of Thomas's dog-eared copy of Catch-22 sitting on the coffee table. One of his T-shirts was draped over the arm of the couch. I made the mistake of picking it up and putting it to my nose, breathing in the scent that had become so familiar to me. These details were part of the person I'd thought I'd known so well but had just realized were only one side of the two-sided coin that was Thomas.

FEBRUARY 3, 2019

It's been a week since the photos were sent to Evan, with no new call to the Daring Tree or any other activity from our tormentor. Surprisingly, I haven't cracked. I can rate my anxiety, just like they do pain in the hospital, from one to ten. It fluctuates through the day, usually between a six—on the verge of frowning, eyebrows furrowed—and a nine, the frowning face but without the beads of sweat. It rises whenever there's an unexplained noise in the house, when the mailman steps onto the porch, every time my phone rings if I sit idly for too long.

Right now it's at its lowest, a five—the faintest hint of a smile and no furrowing. That's because we're all safe and sound in the car, traveling back from Evan's parents' place, where we spent the weekend celebrating their wedding anniversary. It did me some good to get away. I had full hours of forgetting. But then I would remember and find ways to sneak Evan's phone away for a few seconds to make sure he hadn't received any texts. I'd go through my own phone, check on the girls. Then stare out at the fields of farmland surrounding us, wondering if someone was out there.

By the time we pull into the driveway, it's dusk, the gray blue of the sky only just starting to get edged out by its aggressive older sibling, navy. Evan goes first to unlock the front door and turn on some lights. I take my time shrugging back into my coat, collecting my purse and overnight bag, scolding the girls for arguing as they gather their things.

When I get to the front door, Evan is there, concern cutting hard lines through his features.

"Somebody's been in the house. Keep the girls out here until I've made sure they're not still here, and call the police."

My anxiety level moves from a five to an eleven—mouth open wide in a scream. I tell the girls to go back to the car and lock the doors. Then I step inside. The house is ablaze with lights. Evan has turned on every single one.

I see it right away, on the hall mirror, where nobody could miss it. In red marker, the words *Don't you Dare* are scrawled across it. I move into the dining room and see it repeated there on the mirror that hangs above the sideboard. Then in the downstairs bathroom—shorter, tighter script to fit inside the small powder room mirror.

"Evan," I call out, suddenly aware that if something happens to him, it will be entirely my fault. "Evan?" I make my way upstairs and see the same words, *Don't you Dare*, written on every mirror in every bedroom. Taunting me, reflecting back to me every crime I've committed in the past seven months.

I race away from the gallery of accusation and back downstairs. "Evan." Panic is laced through my voice.

"Hannah." His voice sneaks up behind me, and I jump. "What are you doing in here? I told you to stay outside."

"I was worried about you."

"Where are the girls?"

"In the car with the doors locked. Did you find anything?"

He shakes his head and frowns, looking like his terror level is at about a seven. "Other than the cryptic writing on the mirrors, no. It looks like the house is empty. Whoever did this is gone. Are the police on their way?"

I look down at the phone clutched in my hand as though just realizing it's there. "No. I didn't call the police." I look up at him. "Do you think we should?"

His eyes go wide in disbelief, and then his familiar exasperation sets in. "Someone was in our house. Writing all over our mirrors. Of course we should call the police." He pulls his phone from his coat pocket and stomps off to another room to call them.

The police get there quickly. I've only just returned from taking the girls to the neighbors. I don't want them in the house until I've had time to clean every mirror. I don't want my sins reflected back on them—words meant for me, tattooing themselves on their innocent minds.

There's a female officer, somewhere in her thirties, attractive and stone-faced. There's also a male officer, somewhere in his fifties, good-looking, but it's fading. The skin around his wedding band is puffy. I imagine him taking it off each night and rubbing the finger back into circulation.

They perch on the edge of the couch, their guns making it difficult for them to get comfortable. Their trained eyes take in everything, their notebooks open and ready to record. I know it's the time to tell the truth.

But I don't. When the male police officer asks if I know who might have done this, I say no, which isn't actually a lie. When he asks if we've had any other intrusions or strange things happen, I say no. So much of me wants to just let it all go, tell them everything, hand it to them like an unpinned grenade. A wall of fear keeps it all dammed up instead.

When it's clear that we have nothing of importance to offer, the male police officer leaves to move around the house in heavy boots, listing each graffitied mirror in his notes. The female police officer checks each door and window.

"No sign of forced entry," she says, when she returns to the living room. "And all the windows are locked. Are you sure you locked both doors when you left for the weekend?" She directs the question at me.

"I'm positive." Evan is the one who replies. It's his job. I make sure the girls have everything they need. He makes sure the house is secure.

"You're positive?" I ask him, even though I know that in fourteen years of marriage he's never left a door unlocked. He gives me an incredulous look that the police officer makes note of.

"Any keys left hidden outside?"

"There's one under the planter on the front porch." I start walking in that direction.

Outside I point to the planter. She huffs slightly as she bends over to lift it. There's a dark shadow of a key stained into the wood of the porch. Beside that is the actual key. She sets the planter to one side and points. "Have you or anyone in the family used this key recently?"

"No. Evan has his own key, and I'm always home for the girls after school."

She nudges the key with the toe of her boot, moving it an inch or so to reveal clean wood underneath. "Looks like your intruder used the key." She points to the dark stain. "It sat there for some time and was moved, but not so long ago that it made another mark in the wood." She looks up at me to make sure I'm following.

I give her a guilty smile. "I guess it's a pretty obvious place for a key."

"True. Or someone knew it was there and used it to get in." She turns so that her whole uniformed body is facing me. "You're sure there's nobody you can think of that might have done this?"

I glance down at the key and its shadow, as though I'm racking my brain in thought. I shake my head, make sure not to look directly into her eyes. "No. I really can't."

She picks the key up off the ground and hands it to me, leaving only the shadow of it there. "You might want to keep that inside from now on."

They give us a card with their number and tell us more than once to get in touch if anything else like this happens. The male officer tells us to talk to the kids; they may have friends who knew we were going away, knew where the key was kept, and wanted to play a practical joke. I pretend to think it's a real possibility and then shut the door on the officers' receding backs.

Evan is staring at the mirror in the front hall. "It just doesn't make any sense. Don't you dare what?" I see it happen, the lightbulb going on in his head. He turns to look at me. "Wait, weren't you and Libby saying something about dares at the last community meeting? She got upset and said she didn't know anything about any dares."

I give a firm shake of my head. "No. Remember? She misunderstood what I was saying. I wasn't talking about any dares."

213

He reaches out and rubs at the word *Dare* with his thumb, then looks from the mirror to me again. "Still, seems strange. All this talk of dares. Don't you think?" He's searching my face. It's not a question—it's a test.

I go to deny it, but the denial gets stuck in my chest. Carrying on the lie suddenly seems so futile with all that's working against me. I just don't know how long I can keep it up without cracking.

"Hannah?" he says, confused by my silence.

I stare back at him, remember the file on his computer: *Proof.* Remind myself of the threats he's made. "I can't imagine how they're connected, to be honest." I somehow sound so sure of myself. "I could call Libby, though. Just to see if she has any idea."

Evan glances back at the mirror and nods his head. "That's a good idea. I think I'll actually get in touch with her now to see if we can get some footage from those cameras."

"Ah, yes, the cameras."

"You won't be so opposed to them when they help us catch whoever did this, will you?"

"I'm going to start cleaning the mirrors," I say, turning to go get some cleaning products. "I don't want the girls to see this."

With nail polish remover and some scrubbing, the marker comes off. I start upstairs. By the time I'm ready to move downstairs, my cloth looks as though I've cleaned up after a dead body. With each mirror, I can feel my seams slowly splitting. What have I brought into my house?

At the top of the stairs, I hear voices. When I reach the bottom, I see Evan in the hallway, pointing out one of the defaced mirrors to Libby. She's studying it with deep confusion.

"How horrifying," she says. "And you have no idea what it means?"

I interrupt them with my arrival. "No. We have no idea what it means." I answer the question firmly, resolutely.

Libby narrows her eyes suspiciously at me. "Really? It just seems like a personal message to one of you. Don't you think? Not random graffiti at all."

I shrug. "Well, it can't be that personal if no one in the house knows what it means." She nods, but I can tell she doesn't buy my cover. She knows I'm lying. She remembers me accusing her of sending that first dare.

"Well, I'll definitely go through the footage and let you know if I see anything." She passes me in the hall on her way out. "I'll also let the other neighbors know so that they're more diligent about locking their doors, that kind of thing."

"Of course you will," I say under my breath while rubbing at the hallway mirror.

"I'll walk you out, Libby," Evan says, reaching for his jacket on a hook by the door. "And then I'll go get the girls and take them for dinner while you finish cleaning the mirrors off. Okay?"

I wait for Libby to disappear through the front door. "Play this down to the girls. I don't want to scare them."

Am I protecting them or myself?

Evan gives me a reassuring look. "I will. Don't worry. Lock the door behind me," he says over his shoulder as he leaves. "Just in case."

*   *   *

I'm on my last mirror in the downstairs powder room. The nail polish remover has run out, and the cloth I'm using is just making wide red streaks across the surface. Frustration, fear, panic that this thing has infiltrated my house, regret—they all bubble up and make me feel as though I'm going to explode. I smash the side of my closed fist into the mirror as a sob breaks free from where I've worked to keep it caged. The mirror splinters but doesn't fully shatter, a sliver of it slicing into my flesh as I lift it free of the damage, but I'm lucky. It could have been much worse.

Blood quickly appears, but tears obscure my ability to see how bad it is, so I just grab a hand towel and wrap my whole hand in it. I want to leave the mess behind and go upstairs to bed, climb in there and let the crying take over. Uncoil from the tightly wound place I've been in since we got that very first dare. I want to fall apart and have someone else put me back together again, but there's no one who can do that, and I can't leave this mess here for the kids to see. I lift the small mirror free from its place on the wall and head down to the basement.

Finding a spot behind a shelf that holds mason jars, vacuum bags for a vacuum we no longer have, flowerpots, and bottles of alcohol that have been gifted to us over the years but neither of us drink, I tuck the mirror away where no one will see it. From the selection on the shelf that includes crème de menthe, sherry, triple sec, and lime sour puss, I grab a bottle of cheap Scotch whisky. I unscrew the cap and stand there in my sock feet on the cold cement floor, taking quick sips, ignoring the way it burns and the rubbing-alcohol taste of it. Waiting for it to numb my nerves, clear my mind, messily stitch the seams back up.

I don't know how long I've been down here or how many times I've knocked the bottle back when I hear the front door upstairs open and close. The girls are chatty, still happy from the surprise of a fast-food meal. Evan's obviously done a good job protecting them from what happened. Their sweet voices bounce through the open door of the basement and down the stairs like a red rubber ball.

I put the whiskey, which alarmingly has started to taste just fine to me, back onto the shelf and bang some things around, as if I'm down here for some other purpose.

"Mom," Gracie calls out to me.

"I'm here," I call right back.

"Are you going to come up? I want to show you something."

I don't want to leave the shadowy depths of the basement. I feel at home here, like a troll under a bridge. It's where I belong.

"I'll be right there," I say, wondering if my words sound as slurred as they feel. I slip the good-mother mask on and start up the stairs, hoping the kids don't detect the ugly truth lying underneath.

FEBRUARY 8, 2019

Putting makeup on is a struggle for me on a good day, so with the slight tremor in my hands that's happening currently, it's near impossible. It started this morning and hasn't let up. Combination of lack of food, sleep, two glasses of wine on an empty stomach, and most definitely anxiety about tonight. I call to Rose for help.

She arrives in the bathroom looking extremely put out but doesn't hesitate in taking the makeup brush that I'm holding out to her and getting right to it, biting her lower lip in concentration.

"So where are you going again?" she asks, as she rubs the brush through some gray eye shadow in my makeup pallet.

"My fifteen-year college reunion."

"Close," she orders. I do as she says, relieved that I don't have to look her in the eye while discussing the most recent dare that arrived only three days after someone broke into our house and wrote on all the mirrors.

"And why do you want to go to it? Doesn't seem like your kind of thing at all. Especially if Dad's not going." She blows gently on my eyelid to remove any excess shadow, and the scent of her sweet, hot breath on my face makes me want to cry. "And especially if he's not forcing you to go."

She's spot-on, and that scares me. A harsh reminder of how much kids observe and understand. Has she noticed anything different in me in the last six months? The dreamy distraction of the early days of the affair, the sharp edges of my longing when I went days without seeing Thomas, my slow unraveling when the anonymous dares started.

"I'm going as a favor to my friend Thomas." Rose is no longer brushing makeup onto my eyelids, but I keep them closed anyway. "He bought two tickets and had a date, but then she backed out last minute, so he asked if I'd go with him."

"Why can't Dad go as well?" She grips my chin with her soft, cool hand. "Open."

"Tickets are sold out." I only open my eyes when the last of the lie is out. The very same lie I sold to Evan when Thomas and I got the dare to attend the reunion.

She swipes some bronzer on places that never would have occurred to me, then pulls back to survey her work. "Yup," she says, with one decisive nod. "You look hot. For someone your age, that is," she's sure to add. She leans forward and plants a quick kiss on my cheek. "Have fun, Mommy." Dropping the brush in the sink, she leaves the bathroom, unaware that she's left me holding my heart and fighting back tears.

"Thank you, my love." The words are barely a whisper, working hard to find their way out around the lump in my throat that even a sip of wine can't dislodge.

*　　*　　*

I wait for Thomas in the shadows, leaning against the oak tree outside the Student Complex, an old redbrick building that's been here since the school started in 1910. It houses a large study hall, library, and student lounge and is where tonight's event will take place. People file into the building, looking excited and happy, looking forward to a night of reuniting and reminiscing. They aren't here by force.

We're still in a warm spell. It's been weeks now of record-breaking highs that have environmentalists and the like in a panic. Almost all the snow is gone, and I only had to wear a light coat for the fifteen-minute walk here. Normally it would have me quite unsettled as well, but with everything else going on, I've barely even paid attention.

Thomas and I were called to the Daring Tree on Wednesday at three in the afternoon, where we found the invitation, a thick piece of rose-colored card stock with gold lettering and two tickets. I'd seen it before, the invitation to our fifteen-year college reunion, which starts tonight with a cocktail party and continues all weekend. The very same invitation I threw in the trash over a month ago when I got it in the mail, along with deleting the email invite. I hadn't gone to my ten-year reunion and certainly didn't plan on going to this one either.

A cab pulls into the parking lot, and after a few seconds Thomas emerges and heads right to the tree, looking very serious, running a hand through his thick hair, giving it one good tug, a habit since I've known him. Even amid everything that's going on, the sight of him electrifies me. Although now it's coupled with too many other things— longing for how it was at the beginning, regret for letting it happen, sorrow for the end that now seems inevitable.

As he makes his way over, the past rushes at me with a velocity too fast to dodge. Every moment Thomas and I shared on this campus flashes through my mind: each time we met in this exact place, each time his appearance lit a fire in my belly, each secret we kept from Scarlett. And here we are, right back where we started, essentially with a secret affair and the Daring Game gone wrong. How did I not see it coming?

I take all of him in the closer he gets. The dark, slim jeans he's wearing with a crisp white shirt and gray herringbone blazer, a trim tan overcoat open to reveal all the stylish layers. It's distracting how good he looks—and smells. The scent of him surrounds me as soon as he gets to the tree.

"Henny," he says, as though he just likes to hear himself say my name. He leans down to kiss me on the cheek, and I tense. "How are you holding up?"

I hold a hand up to show him the tremor. "About that well."

He takes it in his and squeezes tight before letting go. "We're going to end this tonight. Don't worry. I'll make sure of it."

"Should we go in, then?" I ask, sounding braver than I feel. He nods and reaches for my hand, but I slip both into my coat pockets.

"Sorry," he says. "Force of habit."

*   *   *

The Student Complex is exactly as I remember it, dark wood paneling everywhere, with arched doorways and coffered ceilings, the floors covered in the deep-red industrial tiles that all the schools used to have. Even the smell is the same: old books, leather, and aged wood.

"This certainly brings me back," I say to Thomas under my breath as we arrive in a line to hand in our tickets.

"Same," he replies, glancing around. "And not in a good way."

We step up to the table, and I freeze. Libby is the woman collecting tickets.

"Hannah and Thomas," she says with a plastic smile, and there's a tone to her voice, but I can't tell what it is: self- satisfaction, arrogance, or enjoyment. In any case, she doesn't seem surprised to see us at all. "I saw you'd both bought tickets, but I wasn't sure you'd show, Hannah. Being the introvert that you are." She begins to dig around in a box, looking for our name tags.

"What are you doing here?" I ask, not even trying to sound friendly.

"I'm taking tickets and handing out name tags," she answers, as if I'm an idiot. Then she holds out our badges to us.

"I mean," I say, through nearly gritted teeth, "why are you taking tickets and handing out name tags?"

"I'm on the reunion committee. I help organize these events."

Thomas puts a hand on my back and tries to lead me away, but I shift so that he can't. "You mean you went here?"

She nods and looks at me as though it's the most obvious thing in the world. "I know I don't look it, but I was two years ahead of you. We wouldn't have run in the same circles."

"But how did I . . ." I want to ask how I didn't know that, having been her neighbor for the last four years, but I can't phrase the question without making it clear that it's because I go out of my way to not talk to her.

The person behind me tuts their annoyance at me for holding things up, and Thomas gives my coat a gentle tug.

"Coat check is down the corridor," Libby explains, holding out her hand for the next person's ticket. "An open bar is included with the cost of your ticket. You'll find one at each end of the study hall." She looks back up at me with a glint in her eyes. "I'm sure you'll make good use of both."

I want to reach out and yank out a chunk of her perfect black bob, but Thomas pulls me away before I can, leading me to a quiet part of the foyer away from Libby.

"Do you want me to check our coats?" he asks, holding out a hand. I nod and pull mine off, wondering if we look too much like we're on a date together. Then I remind myself that it doesn't matter even if we do, because the person who got us here in the first place already knows all about us.

"Wow," Thomas says, taking a small step back. "You look amazing."

I look down at the dark-green velvet jumpsuit that I bought specially for tonight. The legs of it are loose and draping, while the top is sleeveless and fitted and low-cut enough to show cleavage. I felt a bit ridiculous buying an outfit for an event I was being forced to attend against my will, but when it boiled down to it, I didn't want to show up to my fifteen-year college reunion looking as frumpy as I feel most days.

"Thanks," I say, running my hands along the soft fabric at my hips.

While Thomas checks our coats, I pin the name tag to my chest, up high so that my hair will cover it. A shiver runs down my spine at the thought that someone else, without my knowing, arranged for this. It makes me think it must be Libby. It's far too much of a coincidence that she's on the reunion committee.

When Thomas gets back, I quietly tell him my theory about her, the indisputable evidence. He doesn't disagree, but he doesn't seem entirely convinced either.

"It's not that strange that somebody in your neighborhood went to this college," he explains. "It's within walking distance, and with internships set up by the school which turn into jobs." He shrugs. "Makes sense people would end up near here." He leans in closer. "And how would she know about our dare at Berkshire Camp? Whoever got us here knows what happened. She said herself that she ran in different circles."

I purse my lips, thinking Thomas is underestimating my aggressively nosy neighbor, but then I also wonder if I want it to be her for my own vindication.

"Let's go inside and take a look," Thomas suggests, cupping my bare elbow in his hand, sending little bolts of heat into my arm. "You'll want a drink, won't you?"

"Yeah, whatever," I snap back.

Thomas and I walk into the study hall, both scanning the room for anyone who stands out to us or takes notice of our entrance. They've taken the large tables out of the space and replaced them with several bar-height round ones covered in white tablecloths. Tall helium-balloon bouquets, done in the school colors of black and gold, litter the room, and a banner in the same colors reading *Class of 2004* hangs on the far wall.

We head to the bar in the back corner. I can feel people's eyes on me as I move through the room. Everyone is curious to see if it's someone they might know from years ago—their lab partner, dorm roommate, one-night stand, their enemy that hopefully hasn't aged well, that one-off foray into bisexuality that they still talk about today to sound more adventurous than they really are. I keep my eyes locked on my destination. My only real friends were Thomas and Scarlett. I didn't have any interest in anyone else and still don't to this day.

At the bar, I order a glass of red wine and am dismayed to see them pour it from a box. It tastes of the chemicals that leach from the plastic wineglass that holds it. Thomas orders a soda water, saying he wants to stay sharp. I ordered wine for the exact opposite reason.

On a raised platform off in one corner of the room is a live jazz band, the Earnest Hemingways. Someone must have handed them an early 2000s set list and told them to play jazz covers of each song, as though it would make them more palatable at our age. Waiters move around the room with doughy-looking hors d'oeuvres on trays, which I refuse every time, even though I know I should really eat something with this wine.

"Let's go up there." Thomas points at the shadowy mezzanine above us that runs the entire length of the room. "That way we can see who's coming and going better."

With drinks in hand, we sneak through the door that leads upstairs, despite the NO ENTRY sign taped to it. It's a good vantage point from up there. I notice Libby's husband Rob in a small group of men dressed just as nicely as he is. One of them is clearly telling an engaging story, his hands gesturing, his face flushed. Everyone in the group is either smiling or laughing with their eyes fixed on the storyteller—except Rob. He's stone-faced, staring across the room at Libby, who's already abandoned her badge-distributing job. She's leaning in to whisper in another woman's ear, most likely filling her head with gossip about someone else on the reunion committee. She doesn't seem at all concerned with me or Thomas or a dare she's the mastermind of.

I feel the warmth of Thomas's body suddenly pressing up against mine from behind. He pulls the hair away from my neck and leans down to softly kiss me.

I slide out from under him. "Not the time or the place, Thomas," I scold. "We're not on a date, for heaven's sake."

He moves closer and puts his hand on my lower back, his thumb running across the soft velvet of my outfit. "Couldn't we pretend for just a minute or two? We're all alone up here."

"How can you even propose that, Thomas? It's what got us here in the first place. How do you not see that?"

My rejection causes him to brush his hand across the crotch of his jeans, trying to settle down what was beginning to grow there. "I do see that," he says calmly. "I guess I just have a harder time not being with you than you do. I guess you matter more to me than any of this other bullshit." He turns away from me, putting his hands on the railing, looking down into the crowd.

He's sulking, and it infuriates me. What a luxury it is not to have anything to lose. I have a million responses I could shout at him right here and now, but that won't do any good at all, so I swallow it all down.

"What is the point of this dare?" I ask, after a few seconds of silence, attempting to get us back on track, focused again on why we're here in the first place. "It can't be just to come to this bloody reunion and drink wine and listen to bad music."

Thomas doesn't answer. I think at first it's because he's still sulking, until I look over and see his jaw is set in a hard line, his eyes narrowed in fury.

"Why don't we ask her," he suddenly says, pointing into the crowd. I follow his gaze and quickly understand. The sight of her white-blond hair causes me to gasp out loud.

Scarlett has just entered the study hall, a bright beacon amid the drabness of everyone around her. Tall, tanned skin stands out against a peacock-blue dress that hugs her lean body and makes her eyes glow even from up here. The sight of her causes a surge of excitement akin to the biggest drop on a roller coaster, where you're loving it and petrified at the very same time. Looking over at Thomas, all I see is anger.

"I'm going to end this once and for all," he says before pushing away from the railing and heading toward the stairs.

I grab his arm to stop him. "Let me go first," I command. "We don't know that it's her, and we need to approach cautiously. Just hang back for a few minutes and let me talk to her."

He takes a few seconds to consider my suggestion, then gives a reluctant nod and gestures for me to go ahead.

Scarlett has moved over to the bar for a glass of white wine, but she's still scanning the crowd, most likely for us. Only a few feet away, her sharp green eyes finally find me, and she breaks into a wide grin, moving forward to meet me.

"Surprise," she says, before bending down to give me a tight hug.

"What on earth are you doing here?" I ask, once she's let me loose. "Is this why you came home?"

She scoffs and shakes her head. "God no! I went to your house to surprise you, and your hubby told me you were here. So I went back to my hotel, put on a dress, and convinced them to let me in without a ticket." She throws her head back and laughs, like it's all one big joke. Not like she's orchestrated it all. "I cannot believe you're here, Hannah. You hate this kind of thing." She pulls me in for another hug, as though my antisocial nature is so endearing.

"Is it you, Scarlett? Are you the one leaving the dares?" The band starts back up again, and I have to yell the last part.

She looks confused and bends down closer. "Am I what?"

Before I can answer, Thomas arrives at my side. Scarlett straightens to her full height and surveys him for a few seconds before stepping forward to give him a hug. Thomas pulls away from her and knocks into me, which causes me to collide with a man coming from the bar carrying a fresh drink. His old fashioned, ice and all, slides right down the open front of my jumpsuit.

"Shit," Thomas says, his anger and bravado quickly disappearing. "I'm so sorry." He starts pawing at my chest, as though that will do any good.

I shove his hands away. The ice is beginning to bite at the flesh of my breasts. "I have to go to the bathroom." I hold up a warning finger. "No fighting. I'll be right back."

I drip all the way down the hall to the women's room and make it into a stall, where I pull my jumpsuit and bra down, releasing ice cubes to the ground. Using toilet paper, I soak up as much of the wet as I can, but the velvet is drenched through, soaking up the alcohol like a sponge. Part of me wishes I could stay in the stall all night, avoiding the tension of Thomas and Scarlett, but I have to find out why she's home and prevent him from saying something he may regret. I slip the small purse I brought over my head and arrange it across my body to help detract from the dark stain.

Stepping out of the stall, I find Libby at the sinks, dabbing at her eyes. She sees my reflection in the mirror and starts, probably because I'm the last person in the world she wants to see right now.

"Are you okay?" I ask, matter-of-factly.

She turns away from the mirror and gives me a weak smile. "Just a little tiff with Rob. Nothing serious. He neglected to tell me until five minutes ago that he's leaving on a business trip for a few days right after the cocktail party."

I'm surprised that Libby's letting me see the hairline crack in her family's perfect veneer. "I wish Evan would go on some last-minute business trips," I blurt out, despite myself. "Leave me with some peace and quiet."

She chuckles and gives a conciliatory nod. "I usually do appreciate the peace and quiet. Just not when we're supposed to attend a whole weekend of events together and he's leaving me to fly solo. I even got my parents to take the kids for both nights."

"Is this where you met?" I ask.

"In a roundabout way," she answers. "His brother went here, and we were friends—well, more than friends, actually—but it didn't work out, and I ended up with Rob instead."

"Ended up?"

"No, no, that came out the wrong way," she says, waving both hands in front of herself, looking panicked that she might have given me the wrong idea. "I'm so happy it worked out that way. It was really meant to be."

I nod and smile, although I don't find her entirely convincing. There's a story behind her relationship with the brother, I can feel it, but I know she'd never tell me. Probably some big family scandal where she got drunk one night and fooled around with Rob while his brother was supposedly asleep in the next room, only to wake up and catch them in the act.

She pulls the balled-up Kleenex in her hand open to reveal smears of eye makeup before tossing it into the garbage. "You should get back to the reunion," she says, sounding more like her bossy self. "The night's young." Turning away from me, she opens her purse and takes out some mascara.

I wash my hands beside her, then pull a rough brown paper towel free from the box on the wall to dry them. "If I see you out there, how about I buy you a drink?" I offer.

"It's an open bar, Hannah." She looks at me like I'm a total fool.

"I know, Libby. It was a joke. I just meant we could have a drink maybe, get your mind off Rob's business trip."

She nods and gives me a tight smile, probably because we both know that deep down, we don't really like each other and there's no point in pretending.

I'm almost free of the bathroom when she calls out, "By the way, I took a look at the security camera footage for the night someone broke into your home." She waits for me to turn back. "It was so dark and blurry that it was hard to make anything out at all." She seems almost pleased, as if she's enjoying the fact that my fear will be prolonged.

I shrug, doing my best impression of not caring. "Oh well, thanks for looking." I make a quick exit before she can say anything else.

I don't see Scarlett and Thomas anywhere in the study hall but do a few laps just to be sure before taking out my phone to text Thomas. Only then do I notice the text he sent me almost ten minutes ago while I was in the restroom with Libby.

Just got the text to go to the library. I'll go in first. Don't come unless I text you that it's safe. Wait outside. I'm not letting Scarlett out of my sight so told her to come with me because you're waiting for us there. One way or another we're going to figure out who's doing this.

I read the text over a few times and realize that he thinks I got a message to go to the library as well, but his was the only text I received while in the bathroom. Why is he being called to the library but not me?

Typing as I walk, I send Thomas a message that I'm on my way. That I didn't get the same text and to take it easy on Scarlett.

Just outside the study hall, I spot Libby and her husband over by the coat check. He's got his coat on and seems ready to leave, but they look like they're in the thick of a very serious disagreement. Libby's eyes are like hot laser beams burning into his face. Rob glances over and catches me staring, so I turn quickly and flee.

The library is on the second floor of the building. The stairwell leading up to it sits in darkness, and there's a rope across it with a sign that reads *Do not Cross*. I assume Thomas and Scarlett haven't let that stop them, so neither do I. Stepping right over it, I continue on my way.

The entrance is at the very top of the stairs. I pause there to check my phone to see if there's a text from Thomas telling me it's safe to come in. Still nothing.

Leaning against the door, I'm sure I can hear voices coming from within. I decide to disregard Thomas's warning. He shouldn't be in there alone either, especially with Scarlett.

The library sits in darkness as well, except for the dull orange glow of the streetlights filtering in through the tall windows. Inside I'm able to make out that the voices belong to Thomas and Scarlett. It sounds like they're arguing.

"Thomas," I call out. They don't hear me over their quickly escalating back-and-forth. Taking my phone out of my purse for the flashlight,

I move slowly, following the sound of their voices deeper into the library. I'm thinking they must be in the study area around the circulation desk.

Relying on memory alone, I do my best to find my way over there. It's an old-style library made up of cramped aisles and short hallways, not like the newer kinds that are all open concept. I get turned around a few times but then spot a sign on the wall that says *Circulation Desk* with an arrow. Starting toward it, I hear a quiet shuffling behind me.

Before I have a chance to turn to see what it might be, pain explodes across the back of my head. There are bright white flashes, and I feel myself stumbling forward, but before I hit the ground, everything goes black.

THEN

Thomas wasn't arrested right away for putting acid in Jefferson Smith's beer that night. There was an investigation and things came out, including suspicion about our Daring Game. The professor Thomas had been dared to seduce came forward when she heard what Thomas was being accused of. She thought it was part of our Daring Game, and she was right. Her version of how she'd found out about the game was very different from what had really happened, making her out to be the victim of an attempted setup. Of course, the three of us were in no position to argue details.

Scarlett and I were brought into the dean's office and questioned, not only about the existence of the game but also about the acid-in-the-drink incident. There was nothing for me to worry about, though; Scarlett was so adept at denying it all and lying that she convinced even me of our innocence, making our close friendship with Thomas, the Daring Game, and our threesome seem like some made-up fantasy.

At that point I was moving through the world like a zombie, confused, my whole life turned upside down, not sure who to believe, who to trust, who to hate, who to love. Thomas had gone home with his uncle; he was suspended and not allowed on school property while the investigation was being conducted. The college wanted the story to go away, and removing Thomas was a big part of that.

He called my house a few times, but because my dad worked at the college, he knew what had happened and forbid me to talk to him. I could *have found a way around my dad, but at the time it felt as though I were being protected from something. If I spoke to him, I'd have to try and wade through what was truth, what were lies, search for the Thomas I thought I knew among the wreckage of the Thomas who had taken his place, and I didn't know how to do that.*

In the end, Thomas wasn't arrested for putting acid in the quarterback's beer that night. Jefferson confirmed Thomas's story of warning him, and there was no known bad blood between them; they were virtually strangers, so there was no motive and not one person had actually seen him do it. The family of the quarterback wanted Jefferson to be left in peace to recover and the college wanted to bury the whole thing, so Thomas signed an agreement, promising he would never step foot on school property again. And then he disappeared without a trace.

*   *   *

My recovery was slow and of Shakespearean proportions. I spent most of the summer after Thomas left in my room, asleep or lying on my bed, staring at the wall. To her credit, Scarlett spent a lot of it right there with me, her tall, thin body curved around mine, her steady heartbeat against my back, beating for the both of us because I was sure my own had shattered into a million pieces. She stroked my hair, read to me, put on movies for us to watch, brought me popsicles, and eventually found ways to make me laugh.

When school started back up, I was healed enough to leave my room, still cautious and holding my heart in a sling but ready to return to the girl I used to be pre-Thomas—studious, safe, predictable, no drugs, no threesomes, no dares. Scarlett and I had at some point made an unspoken rule not to talk about the Daring Game or Thomas, which meant we essentially never spoke about our entire second year of college. It was easier that way.

We went back to being as we always had been, entirely focused on each other, the skin of our friendship slowly growing over the wound that was Thomas. Even when we went to parties, I avoided meeting any new people, scared that they would infiltrate the friendship again and destroy me the way Thomas had. Scarlett and I would drink alone together in a corner, making catty remarks about the people around us and then, if we were brave enough, claiming a spot on the dance floor but ignoring the boys who pushed in and the girls who thought we were like them and threw us conspiratorial smiles. It was safer that way.

Some nights, if we were drunk enough, we climbed into Scarlett's bed in her dorm room in just our underwear to sloppily kiss, pet, and rub up against each other like we used to with Thomas. I didn't really enjoy it. It wasn't the same without Thomas, but I didn't want to hurt Scarlett's feelings, and she was always the instigator. And sometimes I was so desperate to be touched, so sick of my own hands touching my own body, that any hands or body would do, even hers with her long, cold fingers, her sharp angles and bones that jutted into my soft flesh.

FEBRUARY 9, 2019

I come to in total darkness. A pounding radiates from deep within my skull. I can feel hard floor beneath me and smell the harsh scent of industrial cleaner. I lie there for a few seconds, trying to piece things together. I was looking for Thomas and Scarlett in the library, and then everything went black. I remember the flash of intense pain and then nothingness. Someone must have hit me from behind.

Very slowly I push myself into a seated position. The pounding in my head intensifies, and a wave of nausea rolls through me. I reach around and find a nasty bump on the back of my head, making me think I may have a concussion. When I extend both arms out in front of me, my hands connect with something hard, a wall or a door. Reaching out in other directions, I feel things around me—jugs of something, the bristles of a broom, a bucket, some boxes, and walls that are close to me. I figure I must be in a janitorial closet.

Slowly shifting myself into a standing position, I feel around until I find a doorknob. It turns fully in my hand, but when I push to free myself, I can feel something pushing back on the other side. Someone has put something against the door.

My purse is still slung across my body, but reaching inside to find my phone, I remember I was using the flashlight on it and would have dropped it when I was hit. Pressing my ear against the door, I listen for Thomas's and Scarlett's voices, but it's silent.

I start pounding and yelling, ignoring the thunder of pain it sends through my head. I keep at it until my throat is hoarse and my skull feels swollen two sizes bigger.

When I stop, there is nothing in response but silence. The sounds of the reunion don't even reach me. I slide back down to the floor, overwhelmed with nausea from the hit on the head and the realization that nobody is coming to save me. Where have Thomas and Scarlett gone? Have they left without me, or has the person who hit me hurt them?

My mind races through every scenario, each more gruesome than the first. My anxiety builds to a fever pitch until the nausea finally wins and I vomit into the darkness around me. I can't see where it landed, but I can smell it. Every time I shift position, I feel more of it dampen parts of my body, seep through my clothing.

Hours pass. Somehow I drift in and out of sleep, propped up in the corner leaning against what feels like a tall box; it's the only way to escape the pain in my head. Slowly a line of light begins to appear underneath the door, and I know it must be morning.

At some point I hear the heavy library door open and close. Using the doorknob, I pull myself up on legs stiff from a night in cramped captivity.

Pounding on the door, I do my best to call out, but my voice is strained from the yelling I did last night, my throat dry and feeling as if a hand is gripping it tightly. So I pound harder, ignoring the throb in the palm of my hand. I hear footsteps approaching and then someone say, "What the hell?"

"I'm locked in here," I yell, my voice cracking on each word. I hear some rustling on the other side of the door, and then it finally swings open to reveal an old man in gray coveralls.

He takes a step back and frowns, probably due to the bitter scent of vomit that has been released along with me. He knits his unkempt white eyebrows together. "You the victim of some kind of prank?" He points to a heavy chair that sits only a few feet away. "That was pushed right up under the doorknob."

"Thank you so much," I say, not bothering to explain. Where would I even start?

"This yours?" he asks, holding up a phone. "Found it just here on the floor." I nod, and he hands it over to me. "Should I be callin' the police?"

Of course he should, I think to myself. *Someone knocked me out and locked me in the closet for the night.* But I don't say that, because then I'd have to start from the very beginning and reveal all my secrets. I just push past him and race out the door.

On my way downstairs, I look at my phone. It reads five thirty AM. I calculate that I was in that closet for about seven hours. Evan must not have noticed that I didn't come home, because there aren't any missed calls or messages from him. The only message is one from Thomas, sent at 10:47 last night.

Hey Hannah, looked everywhere but couldn't find you. I'm heading home. I have to go away for work tomorrow and have an early morning. Will get in touch when I'm back.

Several things seem strange about that text. First, that he calls me Hannah and not Henny. Second, that he left without me, which he would never do, considering all that's going on. Third, no mention at all of Scarlett, and fourth, that he was going away for work but hadn't said anything about it to me last night.

I press on his number to call him. It goes straight to voicemail. I take a quick look at Facebook to see if Scarlett has sent me a message, but there's nothing from her. Also strange, since we got separated at the reunion and didn't say good-bye to each other.

Downstairs it's empty, but the place has been cleaned of the cocktail party debris and looks ready for the next reunion event. I go to the coat check, hoping my coat is still there. It is, and hanging right beside it is Thomas's, meaning he either forgot he checked it or never got the chance to claim it.

*   *   *

The sun has only just started coming up, coloring the horizon deep orange. I've finally made it to my front door, the fifteen-minute walk from the college having taken over twenty, as I'm on shaky legs with a pounding head. I've tried Thomas again, but it went straight to voicemail.

It takes me three attempts before I'm able to fit the key into the lock. My hands are clumsy and untrustworthy. I slip inside and lock the door behind me, standing there for a minute formulating a plan. I need to get upstairs, then get out of my clothes and into the guest room before Evan notices.

I very carefully put my purse down and am just slipping out of my coat when a dark shadow appears at the top of the stairs.

"Are you just getting home now?" he asks, coming down the stairs.

"It's not what you think."

At the bottom of the stairs, I can tell from his look of repulsion that he's caught a whiff of me, hard alcohol from the man spilling his drink down the front of my jumpsuit and vomit from the closet.

"Must have been some reunion, Hannah. I can still smell it on you." His voice is taut with anger. "Nice of you to leave your boyfriend Thomas and actually come home to your family."

"I know it looks bad, but I wasn't with Thomas all night, and the smell of alcohol is from someone spilling a drink on me. I actually got hit on the back of the head and passed out, and when I came to, I threw up because of the pain. I think I may have a concussion." I turn my head slightly to show him the bump, but he just stands there staring at me, cold mistrust in his eyes, not even bothering to look at my head.

"And all of that took you until after five AM in the morning?"

"I got locked in the library. The janitor said it looked like someone had played a prank on me." I'm throwing every scrap of truth I can at him to tape together some version of events that will explain things without revealing the bigger truth that he can never know, and I can tell it's not working.

"The janitor?"

"He's the one who let me out of the library this morning."

"And while locked in the library, you didn't think to text or call me—or anyone, for that matter—to get you out?" He crosses his arms and narrows his eyes, which are still puffy from sleep.

"I dropped my phone when I got hit on the head—"

He holds up a hand to stop me. "I've heard enough. We can talk about this later. Go clean yourself up. You have puke in your hair, and you stink." He moves away from the stairs and heads into the kitchen, ending the conversation.

His dismissal scares me. It means he's too angry to even talk about it. It means he doesn't believe a word I've said.

I lock myself in the bathroom, put the plug in the tub, and start running the water. While I wait for it to fill, I make the mistake of looking at myself in the mirror. The back of my hair is a beehive of tangle rising over my head, and there are bits of vomit in the strands around my face. The makeup Rose helped me put on before going out has worn away, leaving me looking pale and splotchy with dark circles under my eyes and crusted black mascara smudged into my crow's-feet.

I peel the green velvet jumpsuit from my body and step into the hot water, slipping right down below its surface, pulling myself up only when my lungs beg for air. Reaching for the soap, I rub it over every inch of myself, scrubbing hard, as though there's still a chance of ever becoming fully clean again.

* * *

I wake to late-afternoon sun and am confused. Grabbing my phone, which is charging on the bedside table, I see that it's two thirty PM on Saturday afternoon, and it all comes rushing back. I got in bed after my bath and must have fallen fast asleep. I assume Evan told the girls I wasn't feeling well, because nobody has bothered me for hours.

My stomach sinks when I see there still aren't any calls or texts from Thomas. I was sure I'd hear from him by now but tell myself it might simply be that he's being extra cautious. My stomach growls, deep, low and long, and I realize I haven't eaten anything in over twenty-four hours.

I'm surprised to find the kitchen empty and spotless. Usually when Evan's left to his own devices with the girls, he leaves it looking like a war zone, as though he's forgotten how to clean up after himself, as though he has a maid on the ready to clean up after him.

"I guess he does know how to load the dishwasher," I say, even though no one's there to hear me.

I don't notice the note on the kitchen table until I sit down there with a cup of tea and a piece of toast. It's a folded piece of paper with my name on it in Evan's handwriting.

I've taken the girls to my parents.

The first line causes me to choke on my bite of toast. I have to swallow hard to make it go down. He explains that he called to ask about tickets for the reunion and found out that it wasn't sold out at all—I'd lied. He says he doesn't know who I am anymore and doesn't feel like he can trust anything I say. That all of these strange things have started happening—our break-in, my outbursts at the neighbors, the crazy story I told about the reunion. He believes there's something much bigger happening that I'm not telling him, and until I do, he feels the need to protect the girls.

Protect the girls. The line turns the one bite of toast I've had into a rocklike pit in the bottom of my stomach. Protect them from me. Evan has done it again, placed me on an island all by myself and disappeared with the girls, once again claiming I'm not fit to be around them.

But this time I did it to myself. The harsh thought breaks through the self-pity. What he said in that note is not wrong.

That's why I have to fix it. I can't tell Evan and the girls to come back before I've put an end to the Daring Game—in all its twisted forms. I need Thomas. He might have learned something in the library last night, and even if he didn't, I still need his help.

I Google the contact information for the company he works for. I remember it from the FOR SALE sign at the house with the lake that he took me to see.

I get an answering service, because it's Saturday. Thinking Thomas probably has a work phone that he may be checking more frequently, I give his name and ask to leave a message. The operator returns after a few seconds, saying that nobody by the name of Thomas Sutton works there. I tell her to try Thomas Beverley, remembering that he took his uncle's name, but her answer is the same: nobody with that name works there.

I want to tell her to check again, to explain to her the texts he got from work, the meetings he had to rush off to, the transfer he took to come back here. Even as my brain moves through the catalog of the many times he referenced his job, I think of the many times he was free during the day, the meetings he said he canceled to spend time with me. I'm confused but also sure that Thomas has a reasonable explanation.

I hang up the phone and quickly find the number for the Somersby. Giving his name and room number to the man at the front desk, I'm told that he checked out two weeks ago. Why didn't he tell me that? And where has he been living? Desperate, I try his cell number again, but just like before, it goes straight to messages.

I go back to the website of the real estate company that he claimed to work for and scroll through the list of agents, looking for Thomas, but also looking for the one who was listed on the sign for the lake house. The one he was supposedly helping out. Thomas is not listed there, but I find a name that seems familiar, and there's a cell number listed below it.

He picks up after only a couple of rings. I tell him I'm calling in regard to Thomas Beverley, asking if he remembers the name.

"Ah, yes, Thomas. I sold him the house off Country Road 7."

"You mean the glass one with the forest and the lake?" I ask.

"That's the one. Gorgeous place. Hope he's enjoying it."

"So you never worked with Thomas professionally, then?"

The Realtor pauses, clearing his throat as though suddenly not comfortable talking to a stranger about one of his clients. "I just sold him the house, that's all. And what's this call regarding?"

I hang up. I have enough information.

Thomas is not away for work. He is not a commercial property real estate agent with the company he said he was, and apparently he bought a multi-million-dollar property for himself. None of it makes any sense, and I can't understand why he'd pretend to work somewhere that he didn't. I remember Scarlett's message from months ago: *Where has Thomas been all these years? There isn't a trace of him anywhere and then he suddenly just shows up on your doorstep. Something doesn't seem right!*

I've lost my appetite. I drink half the tea and pour it down the sink and take one more bite of toast before tossing it as well. Standing at the front window looking out at the street, I try to figure out what to do next. I'm getting further away from unraveling the truth. Now the mystery of Thomas's lies have been added to the pile.

Libby jogs by the window in black tights, black running shoes, a black hat, and a black windbreaker. She's obviously just coming back from a run, but she could rob a bank on the way in that getup, I think to myself. And the thought triggers that suspicion again. I just know in my gut that she's connected to all of this in some way.

I call Thomas again, and this time when it goes to voicemail, I leave a message. Telling him I know about his lies, but I'm willing to listen to his explanation. I tell him I don't know who to trust anymore and I'm scared. That if he truly cares about me, he'll call me. He'll help me solve things so that I can get my girls back.

Next, I message Scarlett on Facebook. Tell her she needs to get in touch with me right away. That I'm in trouble and need her help. Thomas's voice rings through my head, saying she's the one behind it all, she always is. Maybe I'm pleading with the enemy, but at this point I have nothing more to lose.

I need to start eliminating suspects so that I can zero in on who's doing all of this. I race upstairs to brush my teeth and wrangle my tangled hair up in a bun. I consider changing out of my tracksuit, but there are more important things to focus on right now. I throw on a coat and head out into the neighborhood, feeling as exposed as ever.

I knock several times, but there's no answer. I know Libby is home, though; I just saw her return from her run. I try the door, and it's unlocked.

"Hello?" I call out into the quiet.

I hear a door open upstairs and the sound of running water. "Come in." Libby's voice rises above it all to reach me. "Just in the shower. Be out in a minute."

I'm surprised that Libby has left her front door unlocked while in the shower. She's the safety patrol of the neighborhood but doesn't seem to feel the same level of risk as the one she's promoting. I'm also surprised that she's invited me right on into her house. I welcome the opportunity.

I do a walk-through of the living room first, but there's nothing in there out of the ordinary or of any interest at all. The room looks like it's been lifted right out of a furniture showroom.

I move on to the kitchen. The white quartz counters are spotless; nothing out of place in here either. I remember then that her daughters and husband are away for the weekend. Just like mine, but for very different reasons.

Libby's purse sits open on the island. There's a black notebook poking out of the top, the kind that looks important. I listen for footsteps on the stairs and, hearing none, ease the notebook from the purse. There's writing on the inside cover: *LogBook#15, Start Date: September 1ˢᵗ, 2018.*

I can't tell what it is at first, but as I move further into the notebook, it becomes shockingly clear. Libby has kept a log of neighborhood activity. My name comes up several times for several different offenses: leaving my garbage bins out too long, missing community meetings, not waving hello when passing her. Other people's offenses are just as mundane but in Libby's view warrant a submission: not picking up their dog's poop, leaving Halloween decorations up five days past the thirty-first, curtains left open after dark and what she observed. She is literally the neighborhood Big Brother, no cameras needed.

The day of my first dare is logged in there, of course, with the date and time and a short description—*Hannah dropped off by handsome man she said is old college friend, his name Thomas Sutton. Does Evan know?* Every other encounter I had with her is in there as well, with notes: each time she spoke to me about the lurker, when I came home from that one dare drunk on Manhattans and spoke to her in my driveway, running into her at the Somersby. The last entry about me and Thomas is from the Christmas party. She notes his attendance there and says there's palpable sexual tension between us—*Affair?*

There's a full account of my outburst at the bus stop and then at the community meeting. I'm not the only one who's activity is cataloged, but mine is the most damning. There are also many entries for Evan, but it's only his coming and going, when he leaves for work, when he gets home, when he shovels the driveway or cuts the grass, when he and Libby speak to each other.

I stare down at the notebook in disbelief, lost fully down the rabbit hole of her twisted community surveillance, feeling a little bit light-headed by the discovery of it. I don't even notice her walk into the room.

"Oh." It's an exclamation of surprise. "I thought you were . . ." She gives her head a shake and then notices what I'm holding in my hand, swiftly stepping forward to grab it from me. But it's too late. I've seen it all.

Her hair is still wet from the shower, slicked back, her face glowing with bronzer. She's dressed in tight black jeans and a loose-fitting white button-down that somehow still accentuates how fit she is. I must look like a hot mess to her in my worn-out tracksuit, no makeup, tangled mess of hair.

"What the fuck is that?" I ask, for once feeling as though I have the upper hand with her.

"It's none of your business." She pulls it tight to her chest with both hands, as though I might try to snatch it away.

"It's actually all my business and all of the other neighbors' business. That's the problem."

"It's just a very thorough neighborhood watch. I started it when the lurker first came around."

"Except it says it's number fifteen," I'm quick to remind her. She doesn't say anything, just stares back at me, knowing her little secret has been revealed. It feels like the perfect time to get the confession I came for. "Libby," I say, working hard to soften my voice and expression. "Please be honest with me. Did you send me and Thomas those texts to go to the Daring Tree? Are you the one behind all of that?"

"I've never sent you or your friend a text in my life," she says emphatically. "And I have no idea what a Daring Tree even is. I've done some bad things, but what you're accusing me of now is not one of them." She pleads with her eyes for me to believe her. "I swear."

The adrenaline induced from thinking I found my culprit drains away, and my body is left heavy with disappointment. "But that weird log." I point at the notebook still clutched to her chest. "That's just for fun?"

Her phone sitting on the counter buzzes with a text. She grabs it, glancing at the screen before sliding it into her back pocket. "It's very complicated, Hannah. I'll have to explain another time. Right now, you have to go. I have something really important that I have to do and I'm late." She takes my arm and starts moving me toward the front door.

I push back, holding my ground. "I want to see the security camera footage," I demand. I expect resistance from her, reluctance to hand over her precious surveillance, especially with me knowing what I know now. Instead, she grabs a pad and pen from a drawer and scribbles something down on it.

Ripping it from the pad, she shoves it at me. "Here's the website and password. Just log in and you can choose whatever day and time you want footage for."

"Oh," I say, unsettled by her cooperation and her urgency. "Thanks. I'll just see myself out then." She nods and gives me a gentle push toward the front door.

As I pull open the front door to leave, I hear the back door open and then a familiar-sounding voice. "Sorry I'm late. Traffic was horrible." I shut the front door loudly to make them think I've gone but remain standing still in the front foyer, barely breathing.

"It's good you were late," Libby replies. "Hannah was just here, and I had to rush her out. She came in while I was in the shower, and I thought it was you."

"She was here? Why?"

"I don't know. She was rambling on about something crazy, as she always does, and then wanted to see the security camera footage."

"Well, that's a bit of a close call. Good thing I came around back. I also parked six blocks away."

With my shoes still on, I walk back into the house and stand in the kitchen doorway. "Where are our children, Evan?" I ask, enjoying the look of shock on his face. "The ones you wanted to protect from me."

He composes himself quickly. "They're at my parents, just like I said."

"Then why are you here?"

He gestures at me. "To find out what the hell is going on with you."

"Then why did you sneak into this kitchen and not ours? And why are you parked six blocks away?" I point a finger at him and then her.

"Is this a thing between you two? An affair?" I air quote the last two words.

For once Libby is speechless, her mouth dropped open slightly in shock. She glances over at Evan, looking to him to explain, which in itself tells me all I need to know.

"Libby and I have grown close over the last little while," Evan explains. "It's nothing more than friendship. God knows I could use some support dealing with what you've been putting the family through." And there's the Evan I know so well. Making it my fault that he's been caught sneaking into the neighbor's kitchen.

I hold up a hand to stop him there. "Save the blame, Evan. I'll leave you both to do your thing." I turn and leave the kitchen. Neither of them says a word to stop me, so I carry on right out the front door and down the street, back to my house.

Only once I'm inside my own house, leaning against the front door, do I realize that I'm shaking. Confrontations with Evan will do that to me. At the same time, I feel oddly numb inside. There's no anger, no rage or jealousy. My own husband appears to be having an affair with the neighbor, and I feel nothing but dead inside. I search harder within myself, looking for any kind of emotion around my discovery, but the only things I come up with are vindication and relief. I'm not the only one lying or sneaking around. I now have an offense I can use against him.

I consider driving to Evan's parents and getting the girls and bringing them home with me, but that would just confuse them even more. And what would I be bringing them home to: more break-ins, more dares, their father spending the night at the neighbors'? They're better off safe and sound at the farm, away from the mess of their parents' lives.

THEN

It wasn't until almost a year after Thomas left that I met Evan. It was by accident, in the library. I didn't even see it coming, and that's the only reason it happened. I was entering and he was exiting, surrounded by a group of friends, all of them a blur of sameness. I would never have noticed him if he hadn't clipped my elbow in such a way, while we were passing each other, to make me drop the armload of books I had, including a binder that, when its spine hit the floor, shot my papers out into a fan all over the tiles.

He looked mortified. Told his friends to go on without him and bent down to help me pick it all up. He was stammering apologies, taking all the blame, so straightforward about it, not once trying to pin the offense on me. I took in his light-brown hair, appreciating how precise the part was down the left side of his head. He wore a plain gray sweatshirt and faded blue jeans, worn for comfort, not statement. The dark-green backpack he carried didn't contain even one pin on it. He would have blended into any crowd, good-looking but in a quiet way, in an up-close way.

Only when we stood up, all the papers put back in my binder and the books back in my arms, did I notice his eyes. A soft hazel, almost the same color as his hair. They were warm, still holding a hint of apology in them. Everything about him felt safe and straightforward. He was the complete opposite of Thomas.

"I'm Evan, by the way," he said, holding out a hand. I took it and felt nothing but skin, no electric currents pulsing up my arm, just a firm handshake.

"Hannah," I answered.

"Again, I'm really sorry about knocking into you. Can I buy you a coffee or something to make up for it?" It was a sly maneuver, turning his offense into a pickup strategy, but somehow coming from him, it didn't feel sleazy.

I shrugged my shoulders. "Yeah, sure. I could use some caffeine before studying." I gave him a fake glare. "And you do owe me."

Falling into a relationship with Evan was easy. I'm not even sure when or how it happened. We just seamlessly, and without any drama at all, went from platonic coffee dates and studying in the library together to sleepovers at the apartment he shared with two other guys and me stealing his soft, well-worn sweatshirts that always smelled of fresh laundry detergent. There weren't any hasty escapes to the woods, or dares or threesomes, or police or lies. There also wasn't the kind of passion that ate at your insides until you satisfied it, and that was fine with me, or so I convinced myself in the moment.

Evan liked CDs, not records. Politically, he was a conservative with left leanings; he didn't drink too much; he never took drugs; he put school above everything else. He had lots of friends, all of them as safe and practical and as academically driven as he was. He came from a family with two parents who had been married for twenty-five years and had one younger sister whom he adored. I was the most wounded thing about him, but he didn't seem to mind that at all. In fact, I think it was what he liked about me, in the beginning.

Evan's being the picture postcard of a college boyfriend meant Scarlett had very little time for him. He was nowhere near exciting enough for her, and because of that she never thought it would last, which meant she kept her jealousy in check. It also helped that I was still able to give her more attention than him. He was a year ahead of me, and by the time we were in a serious relationship, he was about to graduate. In my final year of school, I saw him only every other weekend because he was interning at a company located two hours away.

I never saw Evan as my forever person. He worked to insert himself into my life, and I let him without much thought. He was safe, comforting, confident, pulled together—everything I was not—and I found that appealing, but with an end date. Scarlett and I had planned to go to Australia as soon as we finished college, so I always saw that as a natural end to the relationship.

And then my father got sick with prostate cancer, and everything changed. I was a student by day, nurse by night and on the weekends. I finished college in a blur, eclipsed by the slow dying of my father. Evan and Scarlett revolved through my life, with me barely even aware of their presence. I was losing the only parent I had left in the world. My father had been the one constant in my life. I couldn't imagine him not in it.

Scarlett waited patiently for me and our trip to Australia, which was uncharacteristically kind of her. My father died at the end of August, leaving me parentless and alone in the world at twenty.

It was while helping me put leftover food from the funeral reception into Tupperware that Scarlett brought up the prospect of the trip, saying it would do me good to get away. That nothing was keeping me here anymore.

She was wrong; something was keeping me here, something that would never let me leave again. I was pregnant. It must have happened on one of the weekends Evan came to visit. I'd been so distracted by my father dying I hadn't paid attention to birth control, missing my pill for days in a row.

When Scarlett heard this, she actually recoiled in disgust, then immediately told me to get rid of it. She asked me what the hell I was thinking, said I would ruin my life if I went ahead and had it.

When I didn't say anything in response, she folded her arms and raised both eyebrows. "And are you going to have it?"

I nodded, not even able to verbalize that it was too late to do anything about it even if I'd wanted to. Her eyes narrowed into slits, disdain all over her face. "Well, good luck ruining your life. I won't be around to see it, because I'm getting on the earliest flight to Australia to have the once-in-a-lifetime trip we were supposed to be going on together."

"Scarlett, I'm sorry," was all I could think to say.

"Yeah, well, not as sorry as you'll be once you've had that baby and are trapped here forever." She said those cutting words and then strode out of the kitchen, and we didn't speak again for over two years. That was the first time I'd ever said no to her, and she made sure to punish me for it.

I was too tired to chase Scarlett, too sad to try to convince her not to hate me for fucking up the Australia trip. I finished cleaning up and was just turning off the lights to go to bed when the phone rang. It was Thomas. He'd somehow heard about my father dying.

He sounded so far away, like a dream, his voice shoving me right back in time, bringing my love for him gurgling up from the depths where I'd sunk it. He said he was sorry to hear about my father and hoped I was doing okay. That he was also sorry about the way things had ended with us. Then he started talking about how, after leaving school and being away from me, he'd realized what real love looked like—you might meet people along the way that you thought you loved, but there was really only that one person for you.

I thought it was his way of telling me he had found someone he loved, that he'd realized he hadn't really loved me. I know now that he was talking about me, but my response was to tell him that I was pregnant and that I was going to marry the father, because of course Evan had proposed as soon as he found out. That I was happy and that things had turned out exactly as they were meant to be.

His stunned silence satisfied something in me. But when he finally found words to tell me he was happy for me, I could feel my heart break along all the fault lines he'd created the first time he'd left. He told me he was sorry again for the loss of my dad, and I hung up on his kind words. Then folded in on myself with sobs that shook my entire body.

Evan found me on the kitchen floor, a ball of grief and pain. He helped me up, his body scaffolding me so that I could stand. He was the only person I had left, so I clung for dear life. In that moment, whether consciously or not, I let go of Thomas and Scarlett and gave myself over to Evan. He'd won by default—he was the only one who'd stayed.

I didn't know back then that I deserved more than tenacity. That we all do.

FEBRUARY 9, 2019

I'm still clutching the piece of paper that Libby gave me for the security camera access. Her easy compliance in handing it over makes more sense now that I know why she was in such a rush to get me out of there. I can't shake the feeling that Libby wasn't entirely honest with me about the footage of our break-in a couple of weeks ago, and I'm sure there's a key to who it was in there.

I pour myself a glass of wine and grab my iPad. Before logging in to the security camera website, I check my phone. No messages from Thomas or Scarlett. It's now four PM. In a matter of hours it will be a full twenty-four hours since the reunion. Since they both disappeared from me without explanation.

It's surprisingly easy to watch footage from the cameras, and from almost every angle. Libby neglected to explain quite how invasive these cameras would be into our quiet cul-de-sac. They fall just short of catching people inside their own homes.

I fast-forward through hours of footage until I come to a part with the lurker. Slowing it down, I study everything about him: his clothes, his height, the way he moves. I make notes and take photos with my phone. Then I fast-forward to the night before we came home to find that someone had been in our house and our mirrors had been vandalized.

At 12:57 AM a figure approaches our door. Libby was right; it's dark and hard to see because our porch light wasn't left on. The figure moves the planter and retrieves the key, letting themselves inside. About two hours later the figure emerges, locks the door, puts the key under the planter, and leaves. As the person passes under a streetlight at the end of our driveway, it's obvious—to someone studying the footage for similarities—that the lurker and our intruder are the same person. Same walk, same dark clothing, same height, same casual movements, as though they're just on a stroll through the neighborhood.

Next, I go to the night I discovered Thomas in our backyard, the night we ended up in the shed together. I'm relieved to see that the range on the cameras only goes to the side of our house. Fast-forwarding to just before the time he stepped out of the shadows, I look for when he arrived at our house. There's no sign of anyone, so I go back even further, before Evan and I had even come home from the meeting. Still no sign of him.

It's around dinnertime, just as the sky is getting dark, that I see a figure stroll right down the driveway and into our backyard, which would mean he was in our backyard for hours. I slow the footage down. There it is again, that casual way of moving. The white wine turns to cold metal in my veins, and the lump on the back of my head begins to throb. The lurker, the intruder, and Thomas could all very well be the same person.

* * *

It's just getting dark when I set out. I took time to call the girls, make sure they were okay and not aware at all of what's really going on with their fucked-up parents. Gracie rambled on about helping her Nana make an apple pie, Rose said she got some good Instagram shots in the barn. Apparently, Evan told them he was visiting a friend who needed some help, that he'd back for them in the morning. I resisted the urge to just drive to them, leave all of this behind, but I know there's no such thing. What I've gotten myself into will travel with me, taint everything, until I've put a stop to it.

I don't have a plan, because I'm not even sure what I'm walking into. I just know the first step is finding Thomas. It's a good thing the Realtor mentioned that the property is off Country Road 7. I'm not sure I would have remembered that on my own. It's still unseasonably warm for February, and my headlights cut through a fog that rises from the wet road. A soft rain has begun to fall, making visibility even worse.

I slow right down as soon as I turn onto Country Road 7. I remember turning left into a long driveway, so I keep my eyes on that side for anything I recognize. About five minutes along, I spot the FOR SALE sign, this time with SOLD plastered across it. I'm lucky the Realtor hasn't been out here to take it down. I really don't think I would have found it otherwise.

The driveway is a mess, the fast-melting snow turning it into a muddy lake. I push on, hoping I don't get stuck. I forgot how amazing the house is, and seeing it lit up at night is even more impressive.

Thomas's car is in the driveway. Just as I'm pulling up beside it, my phone rings. It's Evan. I send it right to voicemail.

Walking up the path to the front door, I have no idea what to think or feel. Should I be scared, angry, vengeful? All I feel is confused and hopeful. I want Thomas to explain all of it away—the lies about his job, this house, the uncanny similarity to the figure on the security footage.

The door's unlocked. "Thomas?" I call out, stepping into the front hallway. There's no answer. The house is quiet, museum quiet, with its concrete floors and thick glass windows. "Thomas," I call out again, self-conscious at how it echoes through the vast space.

I move farther into the house and come out into the open-concept kitchen and living room, which I saw through the window the last time I was here.

There isn't any furniture, just a mattress on the floor with a pile of bedding on it and a coffee table that's littered with takeout containers and beer bottles. Every wall is bare except for one that holds a messy collage of photos, tacked up with packing tape. I have to move right up to them to make out what they are, and when I do, my hand jerks to my mouth to catch my gasp.

It's a gallery of photos of me and Thomas. At the Somersby hotel, his arm wrapped around my waist as we wait for the elevator. Our faces are only visible from the side, but you can tell it's us. Me lying back on the rock by the lake on this very property, Thomas's head between my legs. Thomas pressed up against me in the tunnel at the zoo. Me on my knees in front of Thomas in the same tunnel. The very photos that were texted to Evan that I thankfully intercepted, here taped to a wall in Thomas's house.

There are pictures of Thomas holding the side door of the Somersby open for me as I exit after an afternoon together, and of him dropping me off at my house. All are time stamped, a visual history of our affair. My heart is beating so fast it feels like it's trying to separate from my body, free itself of my rib cage.

On the floor under the photos is a manila envelope. I pick it up and look inside, sure I'm going to find more graphic proof of my adultery. There's a folded piece of white paper. I pull it out and open it. It's an invoice, made out to Thomas Beverley from Morris Investigative Services. The description of the service is *collection of photographic evidence of extramarital activities*. Thomas paid to have our affair documented—the lover, not the scorned husband, as it should be.

I tear each photo from the wall, ripping them into pieces, the details of them blurring behind my tears. I risked everything for him, betrayed my own family, and then he betrayed me.

The bang of the back door rings through the space, startling me out of my rage. I expect to see Thomas stepping through it, but nobody's there. It was just the wind. The door must not have been closed properly. I go over to shut it, and that's when I notice the muddy footprints. Three sets leading across the deck and out into the forest.

Stepping into the night air, I listen. I'm not sure if I'm imagining it, but it sounds like voices coming from the direction of the lake. The light from the house guides me to a path that leads me into the forest, but then, once again, I have to rely on my phone flashlight. There's also a full moon that sits heavy in the sky, making the trees glow gray and illuminating what lies ahead so I can shine my flashlight to the ground to follow the footsteps.

As I crest the ridge, before the land opens up to reveal the lake, there's no longer any doubt that I heard voices. I can make out a woman's voice, sounding as though she's crying between her words, and a man's voice, not shouting but low and loud.

Crouching down, I use tree cover to sneak in and get a better look, turning my flashlight off and putting my phone safely in my pocket. I can make out three figures on the point that leads out into the lake. Moving closer, I see that it's Scarlett sitting on the large gray rock, her hands in her lap. A man, tall and broad, has his back to her and stands right on the point, looking out at the lake.

There's a tension in the air, an aura of fear that surrounds them, that stops me from charging in there to find out what's really happening. Scarlett seems to be pleading with the man, but he's ignoring her. I continue to creep forward. Scarlett must sense my approach, because she looks in my direction. Seeing me, she frantically begins to shake her head, and I'm able to see that her hands are not just placed in her lap; they're tied together in front of her.

Just beyond the man, standing on the ice of the lake, is Thomas, both his hands tied behind his back as he carefully shuffles forward, away from the shore. The man in front of Scarlett seems to sense my presence as well, because he suddenly turns, scanning the landscape. I've dropped to the ground, though, and his sight line is high, so he misses me.

I see him clearly. The gun in his hand, the angry, determined look on his familiar face. Rob—Libby's husband, my aloof neighbor—is holding my two best friends hostage, and I have no idea why. He swings back to face Thomas, who's standing motionless on the ice.

"Keep moving," Rob yells at him. "After all this warm weather, it's only a matter of time before you go in."

I have to do something. I consider trying to reason with him, but why would he listen to me, the neighbor who's always fighting with his wife? I could pop up and tell him about catching Libby and Evan together, distract him from this mission, but that could just make him angrier.

I spot a thick branch not far from me and think it may be the only way.

Looking up at Scarlett, I point to the branch. She shakes her head, mouths *911*. They'll never get here in time, though. If Thomas falls in, he'll drown or freeze to death.

"I think it's only fair you suffer the same fate, don't you, Thomas?" Rob calls out into the night air. He then starts rambling on about karma and comeuppance, and I know this is my chance; he won't hear as well when he's talking. I crawl forward and get myself into a crouched position, grabbing the log with both hands. Staying low, I hide behind the rock Scarlett is sitting on. It's only ten feet away from Rob.

Standing slowly, hefting the branch up onto my shoulder, I run, swinging the branch back behind my head and bringing it forward with all my strength to connect with the back of Rob's head.

He doesn't even have time to turn around and see me coming. He stumbles forward with the impact, then falls hard onto the wet ground.

The rest is a blur. Somehow, despite my shaking hands, I get Scarlett's hands untied. Thomas makes his way off the ice safely, and I untie him as well. Scarlett grabs Rob's gun, which he dropped when I hit him, and we race back to the house.

I try calling 911, but there's no service. It isn't until we're in sight of the house that I'm able to get through.

Then I call Evan. I'm not even sure why. It goes to voicemail. I leave a message telling him where I am, that Libby's husband is here too but there's something wrong with him; he's trying to hurt people.

Scarlett goes around the house, locking the doors, and then we huddle in the living room, waiting for the police to get there. I wrap Thomas in a blanket from the mattress on the floor. He's shivering and looks shell-shocked.

"He's Jefferson Smith's younger brother," Thomas explains, through chattering teeth.

"Rob?"

Thomas nods. "He was the one sending us dares," he explains. "It was all part of a revenge plot for what he thought I did to his brother in college." His shivering slows, and the chattering of his teeth stops as he warms up. "He's the one who texted me to go to the library at the reunion. When he found me and Scarlett there waiting for him, he got really mad. Said he'd only wanted me and now he'd have to bring Scarlett too. He had a gun. Told us if we didn't come with him, someone would get hurt. Then he drove us out here. Tied us up and left for hours."

"It was awful, Hannah," Scarlett adds, tears still falling, the trauma sitting right there in her eyes, on her skin. "We just lay here on this mattress for hours, not knowing what he was going to do with us. Thank god you came. He was going to kill us both. I know it."

"How did I not realize that?" I say, as the truth sinks in, as I remember what Jefferson Smith looked like in college and then mentally place him next to Rob. "So it was him all along?"

"Yes," Thomas says firmly. "He confessed to all of it. Actually seemed proud of his creativity in using the Daring Game to fuck with us."

"But wait," I say with a shake of my head, remembering what brought me here in the first place. I point at the wall where the photos were. "You had the incriminating photos of us at the zoo." I point at Thomas. "You paid someone to take them."

The indignation that was all over Thomas's face when he talked about Rob suddenly drops away and is replaced by guilt—a confession without him saying anything.

"And you're the one who broke into my house," I continue, "and wrote on all the mirrors. Not Rob." The guilt stays stuck on his face, and he doesn't say anything—his silence yet another admission. I push up off the mattress and get to my feet, remembering that Thomas is an enemy too.

He drops the blanket and stands up to face me. There are tears in his eyes, and the guilt has been replaced by a sadness I've never seen in him before. "I'm sorry," he says, breaking my heart just a little. I had hoped he'd deny it all, explain everything away as only he can.

"Did you send those photos to Evan?" I ask.

He nods. "I did it all. Dropped the notebook in your mailbox, texted the photos to Evan, broke into your house."

"But why?" My question comes out soft like a whisper.

"To end your marriage. I knew you were never going to do it, so I'd do it for you. I paid someone to follow us and compile proof. Then when Rob sent that first dare, I realized it was perfect timing to start using what I had and make it look like it was all the same person." He reaches out to take my hand, but I recoil, for the first time ever disgusted at the thought of his touch.

"I did it for us," he continues. "Everything I've done is for us. It's all that matters to me."

Thomas's explanation is making things worse, not better. I feel disgusted by his pleading, by his justification of what he's done. "And you were the one lurking around the neighborhood, weren't you?"

"Lurking sounds so sinister, don't you think?" He laughs nervously. "When I first got back, I went by just to see if you even still lived there. Then when I saw that you did, I went by a few more times to see what your life was like." He shrugs as though it's all no big deal. "Out of curiosity, nothing more. After we reconnected, I'd go walking in your neighborhood, just to be near you, on nights I couldn't sleep. I wasn't hurting anyone. It was only you I was there for."

"And your job?" I ask. "Why did you lie to me about it? You're not a commercial real estate agent. How did you have money to pay for months living at the Somersby and to buy this house?" I gesture to the walls around us.

Thomas puts a hand through his hair and gives it a tug. It's normally an endearing habit, but in this moment, it just makes him look guilty. "My uncle died. He left me a lot of money. But I thought you'd respect me more if I had a good job, a career. If I'd made something of myself."

Scarlett slowly stands up from the mattress, and I can feel the tension in her body. "Thomas, that is some really fucked-up shit."

Thomas's face suddenly hardens, and anger burns through the sadness. He points at Scarlett. "You don't get to have an opinion on this, Scarlett. It was all your fault in the first place. The dare that got me kicked out of college. It ruined my life. It followed me everywhere. No college would take me, which meant I couldn't get a decent job. I spent years waiting tables, moving from place to place doing shitty jobs, having shitty relationships."

He turns away from Scarlett to face me, the hardness in his expression gone. "And all I ever wanted was to come back to you, Hannah, but I couldn't, not like that. Not until I had something to offer you. A way to make a life together." He clutches his hands at his chest, pleading with me. "Please tell me you understand."

I turn away from him and face the wall of windows that look out into the night to collect my thoughts. I see a shadow out of the corner of my eye, but when I look closer, there's nothing there. I tell myself it's just clouds passing over the full moon.

"Scarlett," I say, turning away from the window. "Where's that gun?"

She smacks her forehead. "Shit! I left it on the deck. The door was stuck when we got back and I had to use both hands to push it open. I put it down and forgot to pick it back up. I was in such a rush to get inside."

I don't even bother to reprimand her for such a stupid move. I have to pull hard to open the door, it does stick, and head outside to look for the gun, frantically scanning the entire deck for it. I can't find it. Turning back to go inside and ask Scarlett exactly where she put it, I come face-to-face with Rob.

"I really didn't want to involve you in this, Hannah," he says, sounding like he's regretful for littering on my lawn and nothing more. He got to the gun before I did. He's holding it at his side, not quite threatening me but making certain I know it's there.

"I mean, sure, I wanted to scare you a little," he continues. "Make you pay for having an affair on your husband, which is pretty shitty. Although I've never really been a fan of Evan's—too buttoned-up and better than everyone for my liking." He waves the comment away, as though it's not important.

"How did you even find out about us and the Daring Game?" I think if I can keep him talking, the police will arrive and nobody will get hurt.

"Libby's neighborhood log," he explains, matter-of-factly. "She keeps detailed notes on everyone. I read it from time to time to make sure she hasn't crossed any serious boundaries. She has a bit of a problem." He points to his head, implying that she's the crazy one and not him, the person standing here with a gun.

"That's where I saw his name," he continues. "Thomas Sutton. I knew right away who he was. I remembered. So I started following you, and you led me right to him."

"But why do you want to hurt him so badly? Wasn't tormenting us enough? Don't you think he's learned his lesson?"

Rob shakes his head definitively. "It's not just learning a lesson. It's retribution. After my brother's accident, he was never the same. He got into drugs, and on his twenty-fifth birthday, he overdosed. Did you know that, Hannah? My brother is dead because of what Thomas did." He lifts the gun up and waves me inside, my questions having reminded him of why he's here.

"Rob, I'm so sorry about your brother," I say, standing firm, wanting to keep him outside as long as I can. "I really am, but this will not make anything better." I see Thomas and Scarlett inside, deep in discussion, most likely an argument, having no idea what's going on out here.

Rob takes my arm and pulls me toward the door, gently pushing me through it. Only then do Thomas and Scarlett look up and see what's going on. Thomas moves toward me, but Rob points the gun at him, and he stops.

"Do you know why I'm going to kill you, Thomas?" he asks, and my knees go weak. I put a hand against the wall to support myself.

"Not only did you ruin my brother's life, but you also ruined mine." He pauses to let this fact settle in. "Jefferson was the favorite. Smart, good-looking, a superstar quarterback. After the accident, every time my parents looked at me, every time Libby looked at me, I knew what they were thinking: *Why couldn't it have been Rob?*" He throws his hands in the air. "I was a nobody, bad at sports, average at school. Sure, I got girls, but not the way Jefferson did. He had Libby, you know, but after the accident he shut everyone out, and she came to me for comfort." He laughs, a sharp, bitter laugh. "My own wife I got by default."

He starts pacing around the room, kicking through the ripped-up photos on the floor. Thomas, Scarlett, and I watch him like hawks, our faces drained of color, our eyes wild with fear.

"It was at Hannah's Christmas party"—he stops walking so that he's standing in front of Thomas and Scarlett, while I'm still over by the doorway—"that I decided I was going to kill you. You were full of yourself. Bragging about buying this place, about how much money you had, how successful you were. And it got me thinking. Why should you have everything when my brother had everything good in his life ripped away?" He taps on his chest. "When I had to suffer because of it? It just didn't seem fair." He shakes his head and huffs loudly. "And to find out you're playing that fucking game again." He points at me. "With Hannah, who has a husband and children. Well, that was just too much for me. I knew I had to do something."

Rob lifts the gun and points it at Thomas. I'm sure I hear sirens in the far-off distance. "Rob," I quickly jump in, keeping my voice as calm as the terror inside me will allow. "Don't do anything you'll regret. Right now we can all walk away from this, forget about it. Move on. Do anything drastic and there'll be no going back."

I pause to see if my words have had any effect. He remains quiet, his eyes full of anger, the gun still pointed. "Think about your beautiful girls and Libby." I try a new tactic. "You don't want to do anything to hurt them, do you?"

He looks down at the ground, and I think that last part may have done the trick.

"I hurt them every day," he says, sounding like he may be on the verge of crying. "They'd be better off without me." He lifts his head, and his eyes lock on Thomas again. "Just like the world would be a better place without people like you."

"It was me," Scarlett suddenly yells. "I put the acid in Jefferson's beer. Not Thomas. And then I put the acid in his bag to make it look like it was him, and I went to the police and lied about it all." She pounds on her chest. "But it was all me. The whole thing." She pauses, tilting her chin up with an air of challenge in her eyes. "Your brother was not the hero you think he was. He raped me. At a party one night when I'd had too much to drink and made the mistake of flirting with him." She lets the words settle over all of us before continuing. "I wanted to punish him, and I used Thomas to do it so I could get rid of him at the same time. So I could have Hannah all to myself again." She wipes at the tears on her cheeks, working hard to keep her composure. "I was not in a good place back then, and I made some terrible mistakes. Don't punish Thomas for it. Please."

Rob frowns and shakes his head again. "No. That doesn't make any sense. Jefferson would never do something like that. You're lying to protect him." He thrusts the gun in Thomas's direction.

"I'm not lying," Scarlett yells, the pain of what she's just told us coming to the surface. The anger of not being believed added to it.

With her confession, that whole horrible night in college is suddenly making so much more sense. Her intense urgency to have the dare completed and her insistence on what a bad guy Jefferson was. Then the lies she told me—that Thomas had called her from the police station, that he had wanted to do the dare and had come onto her even when we were together. She used one last dare to bring down Jefferson and Thomas at the same time.

The sirens are more distinguishable now. Rob cocks his head, listening to them.

"Give me the gun and go," I yell at Rob, holding out a hopeful hand. "We won't tell anyone about what you've done."

He shakes his head. "I'm not a coward, Hannah. And I'm finally making things right. I'm finally being the strong one, the brave one. My brother would be proud." He smiles at me, and for the first time that I've ever seen, it reaches his eyes. Then he looks away from me and back at Thomas.

I've never heard a gunshot before. It's far more deafening and shocking than anyone can describe it. Especially back-to-back. One aimed at Thomas's chest. The other aimed at Rob's temple. In a matter of seconds, it's all over. Rob has shot Thomas and then himself.

It feels as though I'm flying. I can't feel any part of my body touch the floor as I move. And everything has suddenly gone quiet, as though I'm underwater. Scarlett's screams and sobs are muffled. The sirens sound like they're farther away now instead of closer.

Thomas's eyes are open, darting around frantically, his body rocking with small convulsions. I put my hand over his heart, as though I can stop the flow of blood pouring from the small hole there. As though it's not too late.

"Thomas, look at me," I scream, causing the whole world to become loud again.

He does what I say. His eyes stop roaming about wildly and settle on me. I keep mine locked on his, even though the fear in them scares me, even though I know I'm watching life literally slip away from him.

"I'm sorry." His words are choked but discernible.

I push down harder on the hole in his heart. "It's okay. It's okay. Please, it's okay." If I say it enough, it will be true in every sense. I'm forgiving Thomas for what's he done and willing everything to be okay again.

"Love you," his words are softer now, just a choked whisper. I hear loud voices, feel the pounding of feet on the ground, but I don't look up.

Orders are being shouted, and someone is gently taking my hands away from Thomas's heart. I hear a woman start screaming, who I'll later learn is Libby when she sees Rob, but I still don't look up.

"I love you." The words aren't even sound, just mouthed through the breathlessness of my tears. "I love you," I try again. Thomas's eyes are still on me. He sees my message, nods. More hands are pulling me away from his body, and then he's swallowed up by blue uniforms working to save him.

Arms suddenly wrap around me from behind, lifting me up from the ground. Even without seeing them, I know it's Evan. His smell, the feel of him against me, our years together have taught him to me sight unseen. I turn into him, unleashing my full grief as I hear them call time of death.

AUGUST 13, 2019

Sometimes the trees are more of a distraction than anything else. I find myself losing time as I stare at the leaves blowing in the wind. Like today, I've only written two pages of my novel and now find myself just staring out into the thick forest that surrounds me. My therapist said it's okay to go slowly, to have time for reflection and meditation. I wish I'd gotten her prescription for this when I was still married to Evan.

My phone buzzes with a text. *Dare you to have a drink with me and Lucy tonight?* It's from Scarlett, of course. She's the only one who would still dare me to do anything and think it's funny.

She didn't end up going back to Australia, choosing instead to stay here with her family and with me. She admitted that it had been lonely for her over there without anyone, despite what her Facebook posts advertised. She'd had a handful of relationships that hadn't worked out, and although her business was successful, it just wasn't enough for her. She's put someone else in charge of the Australia offices and has opened a branch here—still driven and the boss, but doing it closer to home. She's also met someone, my old work colleague Lucy, who I finally got around to having coffee with. Lucy is the only person who seems capable of bossing Scarlett instead of the other way around.

I text back. *Can't tonight. I have the kids.* Rose and Gracie appear on the crest of the hill as though my text has summoned them into being. Their hair is still wet from swimming in the lake, towels wrapped around their shoulders. Gracie is talking away about something, pointing things out as she goes. Rose is listening quietly, her expression pensive, as it so often is these days.

Gracie has adjusted to the separation pretty well, working hard to find the positives. Rose has been trickier. Some days she seems to hate me with a fury that will never be tamed. Other days she's loving and accepting and seems almost happier now that she's out from under the cloud of her parents' unhappy marriage. She's not always thrilled to spend half her time out here in the glass house away from her friends, in the middle of nowhere, but the lake and the beauty of the place are growing on her.

Thomas was right: it's a wonderful place for the girls to be, and for me. That must be why he put my name on the deed alongside his own. He also made me his sole beneficiary in death. I inherited a great deal of money. At first, I didn't even want to take it. The whole thing felt wrong and sleazy. Then Scarlett convinced me to, saying that even if we hadn't had an affair, even if he'd never come back to town, Thomas would have left me everything. Apparently, during one of their arguments after her return, he told her that he'd never loved anyone else but me, that nobody had ever accepted him the way I had. That I was the only person in the world he had felt truly loved by.

I gave Evan the house, the one I'd grown up in. It was time to leave there anyway. The bad memories had begun to overshadow the good ones, and I needed a fresh start. A place to reinvent myself without the influence or pressure of my father, or Evan, or the neighbors, or anyone else who had been in my landscape while living in that house. It was time to stop following other people, letting them tell me what I should be doing, and figure it all out on my own.

Libby moved away from the neighborhood as well. Left New York completely to go back to where her parents lived so she would have support while healing from Rob's death. We became close in the days after Thomas and Rob died, me forgiving her for what was really only the hint of an affair with my husband, her forgiving me for my accusations and overall rudeness toward her.

I found out from her that Rob had struggled with mental health all his life. That he'd never been right after his brother's death but just wouldn't get the help he needed. All along I'd viewed them as the Barbie and Ken of the neighborhood, the perfect power couple, when underneath there was dysfunction, darkness, and something brewing that would change all our lives. Libby's fixation on what her neighbors were doing, her working so hard at perfection, was her way of coping. She worked to control what she could since things with Rob always felt so out of control.

I gave her some of my inheritance to set up a trust fund for her girls. It made the money feel better. And with Rob gone, things had become unpredictable for her, and I knew it would make a big difference for her to know that her girls would be taken care of no matter what. Like she was always saying to me, *We need to keep our children safe; we need to work together to take care of our families.* I finally came to understand the true meaning of her words.

In the end, Evan didn't try to take the girls away. The *Proof* file was never even mentioned. He knew Thomas and I had been having an affair, but not because anyone had told him. He'd had his suspicions, of course, but the hard evidence didn't come until he saw me bent over Thomas's dying body. He said it was the way I was looking at Thomas, with a kind of love I'd never shown for him.

He admitted he'd been planning on having an affair with Libby, that they'd shared rushed kisses in her garage and at the side of our house, quick feels when they passed each other. She was unhappy in her marriage; he was unhappy in his. The day I caught him at her house was the first time they'd ever met up like that secretly. After I caught them, they spent the day talking, and he realized that divorce isn't losing and staying in a dysfunctional marriage winning. That being happy is.

The girls come through the back door, and I get up to greet them. I can smell the lake and the trees on them and inhale deeply, feeling grateful, as I so often do, to be living out here. It may be the scene of one of the greatest tragedies I've ever endured, but it's also been my place to heal, to find a way to forgive Thomas for his betrayal while at the same time grieving the loss of a man I truly loved.

"Good swim?" I ask, taking their towels from them to hang up.

"Gracie dared me to kiss a toad," Rose says with disgust.

"Yeah, well, you dared me to eat a piece of the weeds growing on the bottom of the lake," Gracie shoots back.

"Please don't dare each other to do things," I say, my words holding much more weight than they'll ever know.

"Why not?" Gracie asks.

"Because dares are just things to get you to do something you shouldn't. And there's never just one dare; you're always one-upping the other person until it ends in disaster."

Rose raises an eyebrow at me. "Whoa, no need to get so fatalistic on us. They were just some harmless dares, Mom."

"Here's a lesson I've come to know well in my old age," I say, with utmost seriousness. "There's no such thing as a harmless dare. If you're not careful, you could lose everything."

They both give me a quizzical look, and Rose just shakes her head before they move toward their rooms to change.

Going back to my computer to work on a few more pages of my novel, I pass by the wall that once held the visual proof of my own dares with Thomas, now decorated with photos of the girls. Testament to the fact that good people can do bad things and still be good people, but also an important reminder that in doing so, you dare to lose everything.